Earthcam

A Novel

✻✻

Jenni Rose

Published by Dolman Scott in 2022

ISBN 978-1-915351-06-7

Published by

DolmanScott

www.dolmanscott.com

PROLOGUE

His body suddenly felt disturbingly heavy. Beads of sweat started running down his face. His heartbeat could be felt in his ears and acid rose in his throat. What did he just watch? Was this a joke? Where was the climatic, humorous twist? He wanted the credits to start rolling. He wanted the room to come to light again, like when you slowly rise from your seat at the cinema after watching an absorbing film. Yet, there he was, led in the total absence of light. In his small box of a bedroom within his dingy flat. Having slammed his laptop screen shut, the realisation hit him. He just witnessed a murder live on screen...

JANUARY 2019
TWO WEEKS EARLIER......

ONE

It was Monday morning and January had carried itself into Safe Travel Holidays. Living by the coast in winter could be brutal; the wind whipped from Southsea common and through the streets into the office, 9am approached, each colleague came in, shaking umbrellas, wiping rain-streaked cheeks. A small puddle began to gather below the coats slung over a groaning rack. The kettle in the kitchen area at the back of the building began hissing as they poured coffees, took stale biscuits from the tin and gossiped about what had gone down at the weekend, shopping at Gunwharf Quays, Portsmouth FC's chances in the league, the return of the University students from Christmas break. It was a far cry from the surroundings: posters of couples with pearly white teeth and golden tans grinned from the Seychelles, a red-faced beaming family stood atop a Swiss mountain clutching skis. The last of the colleagues came through the door in his usual attire of a university navy hoodie. There was a chorus of 'Tom-Tom! You're late!' Thomas Walker shuffled to his desk, carefully tucking his hoodie around his chair. His desk was primed for a Monday: 5 pens lay in a perfect row, he had re-filled his stapler Friday afternoon, turned his calendar to the correct day and he had a prewritten checklist for his tasks to do today. His colleagues laughed at his meticulousness, but Thomas didn't care. All that mattered is that Jack O'Neil thought well of him...

'Hey babes'

He jumped. Shania Simmons was leaning on his desk, tombstone teeth and talons of glittering hot pink fingernails. ` How was your weekend?'

'Fine, Shania, fine thank you' Thomas said distractedly. His search engine was taking a long time to boot up and he wanted to have a look at something before the first customer came in.

'You and Emily get up too much?' she pressed.

'No not really...oh why does this thing take so damn long to load?'

'Oh hun, you really need to loosen up, life's too short.' She shook the hot pink envelope.

`We are doing a collection for Gerry babes, it's his birthday next week' she purred.

'Oh right, sure' Thomas fumbled in his wallet for change. He had £2.95 he knew he had to leave £2.80 for bus fare but that only left him 15p. Damn it, he would have to go to the ATM on his lunch break. 'There you go' he reluctantly dropped the £2 into the envelope.

'Cheers doll!'

Shania then went to speak to Ben Grey at the desk next to him. Thomas and Ben had never really gotten along from the day Thomas joined STH. Ben could not have been more different from himself. Looking across at his desk, Thomas could see towers of empty stained plastic cups from the hot drinks machine that was reserved for the customers-Ben could never be assed to even boil the kettle. Crumpled post it notes sat like shells around the screen. A half-eaten bowl of Coco Pops was festering that Thomas swore had been there since Thursday last week.

It wasn't just his personal hygiene...it was his...person. Ben thought he was the 'Big I Am', expecting a room to thank him for the privilege of breathing in it. He was bent over his phone, no doubt looking for the 20th meme that morning to ping to the team WhatsApp group. Thomas watched as Shania approached him and his demeanor immediately changed; he stood up straighter and began tousling his dark blonde hair and grinning toothily at her. Thomas knew that Ben had had a crush on Shania for a while; Thomas was sure that Shania was tied up with a dozen other guys queuing for her so always took private savage pleasure that Shania never took up the bait. Shania was OK enough, so was Gerry Hobbes. Thomas never really socialised with his colleagues, he preferred to keep to himself or with Oliver. Or Emily...

'Hey there Tom!' Thomas was jerked out of his thoughts by his boss, Jack O'Neill. Jack was indeed a 'jack-the-lad'. Suave, a flirt, he was forever chasing women, despite being married. Tenacious, he had established STH from the ground up and had taken pains to hand pick his workers.

'Morning Jack.'

'Listen, we could really do with some meaty sales this week'.

'Well, we had a pretty successful December.' Thomas said. 'Our Scandi Christmas Cruise to Lapland was very...'

Jack cut him off with a wave of the hand.

'I know and you did a cracking job, Tom, my man but now you have our work cut out. It's January, people are broke, fat, yadda yadda yadda but play on that. Give them the whole they could be having their ass kissed by the hot sun on a cruise in 6 months - obviously in your own words kid haha! We are the best on the high street for prices. Hey, we've got that Marshall couple popping in Wednesday, don't forget because they are big spenders! I want you to drive a sale hard, you get me kid?'

'No probs, Jack, I'll add it to my calendar and I have their number from last time. I could give them a call and tell them to ask for me when they arrive?'

'Now that, my lad, is why I hired you. GET IN!' Jack thumped the air.

While you are at it, can you find a snazzy getaway, somewhere UK based? I need to take the Missus away and get myself out of the doghouse.' Jack grinned,

'Which missus?' Thomas wanted to say but didn't dare. Jack was fifty-three years old but still acted like a typical 'lad'. A bit of a pain to work for but he meant well, Jack was always having to make things up to his wife, Caroline. Thomas liked Caroline; she occasionally popped in when she was in town, she attended Portuguese classes at the language school and always took time for a quick chat with Gerry, Ben, or him. She never seemed to engage much with Shania but Thomas privately thought she just thought Shania was 'a bit much'.

'Yeah sure, Jack.' Thomas forced a grin again. Ever the pleaser. I'll take a look this morning.'

'Fabulous. Now, who do I need to screw around here to get a decent coffee? No, not the junk you plebs drink. real coffee and decent biscuits. Oi, Ben-Ben.'

Jack flourished a £50 note from his wallet and gave it to Ben. 'Go down to the Starbucks and get everyone whatever they want'. He turned to face the team and clapped his hands together. 'Kids...and Gerry!' He winked and pointed his finger theatrically at Gerry, the last colleague and the 'dad' of the office. Gerry smiled amiably. 'It's Monday-it's Funday it's January so it's gonna be a tough one. People are still stuffing themselves with Turkey sandwiches...but we don't want them to eat Turkey..we want them to GO TO Turkey..or Crete, or Azerbaijan ... wherever they damn well please. What we want is the MOOLAH!' He rubbed his fingers together. So, I'm treating you all in the hope you will repay the favour... alright! Now, get those doors unlocked and let the people in!'

Thomas smiled to himself. He knew Jack well enough to know that his grand gestures were less to do with generosity and more to do with flaunting his wealth.

However, Jack was a good bloke overall and Thomas was grateful for something to do. Google had finally loaded and he brought up 'EarthCam' on his computer. It was his favourite programme to use when looking up holiday destinations. He had not been sleeping well recently, so would often log on in the middle of the night to EarthCam and look at places all over the globe. The cam was fantastic as it let him explore places in great detail which worked perfectly for his job. He started by turning the camera to Rio de Janeiro, one of the places on his dream list. He watched the Brazilians scurrying like ants around Copacabana Beach dreamily for 5 minutes then thought he's better search more locally.

He looked up Devon and quickly found a good deal for Finlake Holiday Park. A wooden cabin, a hot tub, not too far from the beach. Yes, this would get Jack back into Caroline's good books. Thomas booked it up. Jack's office was still in the main office space was separated from the team by a glass door and wall. Normally Jack would draw the blinds if he wanted privacy. But this time he appeared to have forgotten. Approaching the office, Thomas could see he was in a very heated discussion with Shania. He could tell by their hand gestures that something was going on. Hopefully it wasn't something that affected the team. Jack looked impatient and exasperated. Thomas decided he would let Jack know later and tiptoed away. Gerry had taken the first customer- an elderly gentleman and was talking him through a city break in Madrid. There was another customer waiting, a young man. Thomas felt impatient; he still had some paperwork to complete-this should be Ben's customer, but Ben was still not back from the coffee shop...*slacker*. Thomas smiled at the man and beckoned him to his desk.

Luckily the sale was quick; the man was after suggestions for a stag do. Thomas brought up Earth Cam and relayed as if from a book the Eastern European getaways for people aged under 26. The customer left happy with tickets booked for a weekend in Prague, a city beer tour and an evening booze cruise down the Danube.

'My mate will love this, cheers mate! He said as he left.

'Can you write us up a positive review on Google?' asked Thomas.

'Will do mate and I'll mention you personally. Cracking service.'

Just at this moment, Ben staggered in with the coffees and pastries, a Sainsburys bag, a HMV bag were also on his elbow and a packet of fags in his fist. He looked at the back of the customer, looked at Thomas and snorted. Gerry's customer departed and once again the office was customer free.

'Big queue at Starbucks, Ben?' Thomas asked.

'Huge.' Ben didn't even look at him and threw Thomas's croissant on his desk and his black coffee which sloshed over the sides of the cup. 'Here you go-G-man'' he handed Gerry's cappuccino and bacon roll to Gerry more gently.

'Thanks, sonny.' Gerry smiled. 'Better get this in my belly before the next customer.'

'It's OK, it looks like pet Tom-Tom held the fort down fine.' Ben gave him a sarcastic smile.

Shania and Jack had come out of the office and seized their coffees and pastries. Neither of them showed any proof on their faces of their confrontation.

'Now now boys' Jack said. 'Can't have my two work -sons fighting.'

'Thomas clearly did a fine job with that customer.' Gerry said warmly to him and then fixed his eyes on Ben.

'Atta boy Thomas. Teamwork makes the dream work!' Jack sipped his coffee. 'Any success with that old boy, Gerry?'

'Yes, booked him and his wife on a weekend break to Madrid. It's their Ruby anniversary.'

'Good man! That poor sod, tethered to one bint all these years!' Jack roared with laughter. 'Anyway, break time, Tom, you first, 15 minutes and then Shania, Gerry and Ben and please my lovely ladies and gentlemen, coffee on the office floor is fine but please keep your chamming faces at the back. Anyway, I've got some work to do. I'll be in my office if anyone wants me.'

Thomas quickly ate his croissant but decided to use his 15 minutes to do a bit of office tidying; there was rarely any time to keep the office clean and tidy, Jack refused to pay for a cleaner so it was up to him, Ben (yeah right), Shania (yeah right), Gerry (sometimes) and him to keep things up. He emptied the bin, dusted the central table and laid out a fan of brochures for customers to look through. There was a large bookshelf behind Shania's desk about 10 feet high and the brochures and books were so...uneven. He began re arranging them. He was always in his own head, re arranging, cleaning, tidying, checking, checking again. It felt like sometimes there was a devil on his shoulder whispering compulsions in his ear. Everything about is life was detailed, organized, he HATED feeling out of control. He stepped back from the bookcase and cursed himself. He had been so absorbed in his thoughts he hadn't been paying full attention, he quickly skimmed the books again to make sure they were all in the right order. His heart rate was increasing, his thoughts began racing. *Oh God, not again.*

He had been told to deal with intrusive thoughts by keeping himself busy. He took himself back to his desk, ignoring his colleagues' looks of amusement. He pulled out a piece of paper and began writing a list of his positive qualities. *'Yes, you do deserve to work here...'...'You are a good salesperson....'Your customers love you...'*

'Meticulous and detail orientated, eh?'

Thomas almost jumped out his chair when he realised that Ben was behind him and rudely reading over his shoulder.

'Do you mind?' he snapped. 'This is private.'

'Actually, if this was MY list, it would say: a meticulous planner, hmmm, an excellent researcher, oh and possesses extreme attention to detail' Ben smirked. 'Remember when that Chapman couple came in? You see Tom, it's all very well looking up bloody EarthCam putting two people in a beautiful room, but it is going one step further, isn't it? Remember they were going to Crete for their anniversary and I rang the hotel ahead of time and arranged for their favourite champagne to be beside the bed. I also asked for a copy of their wedding photo and e-mailed it to the hotel so it was framed by their bedside. I got such a lovely review for that.' Jack was singing my praises for a week.'

'Yeah' Thomas muttered. 'In case you have forgotten Ben, I'm the one who came up with that idea.'

'Yes, but I executed it. Rather brilliantly I daresay, my point is Tom, that you aren't the only golden boy in this room, even though it's so painfully obvious you like to think you are.'

From the first day I got here, Ben has taken a massive dislike to me. He always wants one up on me and I do not understand why. Thomas, try and not go down to his level. Be polite. BE polite!

'Why do you always wear that same damn sweater?' Ben gestured to Thomas's University of Portsmouth hoodie. The University's name was emblazoned on the front and on the back...'Eat, Sleep, Art History. Repeat'.

'What's it to you if I do?' Thomas snapped. *It was one of the rare times in my life I was happy.*

'Just saying you ought to wash it sometime.' Ben smirked. 'Too busy looking at EarthCam I suppose.'

'I keep my clothes perfectly washed thank you. You know I work damn hard at this job. I get to really get the feel of a place visually, show it to the customers. You spend half your time looking at your damn phone. If an Eskimo walked in asking for a change of scene, you send him to Antarctica!' You-

'Oh, jog on Tom, stop being a pretentious pillock!'

Ben glimpsed around to check they weren't being overheard and leaned forwards-his fingers stained with coffee splayed themselves on Thomas' pristine desk, making Thomas flinch inside.

'You think you are better than me, Tommy-boy' he murmured, smirking. 'We all know who Jack's loyalties lay with' he pointed his thumb at his chest. 'You and your piss poor history degree, you could wipe your ass with it in this modern world.' Ben gave him a wink, a look of disdain and straightened up again. 'Anyway, another hour, another meme ...' he flicked Thomas' pencil across the desk. 'Catch you later Tom-Tom'.

He walked away and Thomas looked at him with loathing, feeling like he'd been stabbed with a double-edged sword. There was no way to win when it came to twats like Ben.

Things didn't pick up until after lunch and then the agency had a steady trickle all afternoon which helped Thomas keep his mind off of things...his anxiety, the argument between Jack and Shania. He knew what would make him feel better; an evening with his partner Emily. He sent her a text asking if she was free later for dinner at his. She worked as an accountant in a local firm and her hours were all over the place. He was pleased when he snuck a look at his phone and a 'sounds good! And a 😊 greeted him from her. He also sent a text message to his room-mate Oliver, asking if he could make himself scarce this evening, maybe go to the Vue and catch a movie. Oliver hadn't responded which was nothing new. Oh well.

As the clock approached 6, he was once again so pre occupied with EarthCam that he did not see Shania come back to her desk after a long time in the toilet, mascara tears streaking her face....

TWO

Thomas felt exhausted that evening as he left the agency at 6pm.

The rain had been relentless all afternoon and water slopped against his trousers as he beat his way down the high street to the bus stop. He made a detour to the ATM and into M&S and spent an agonising 10 minutes thinking what best to cook tonight for Emily. He settled on two chicken pies. His fingers hovered over the expensive red wine on the rack...January was a long month; payday was still 3 weeks away...sod it, he wanted to treat Emily. He'd skimp on a few meals later that week to make up for it. He topped off the meal plan with a cheesecake and ten minutes later left the store weighed down with a carrier bag and his heart a little lighter at the prospect of the evening ahead. He texted Emily with a swift message 'Looking forward to seeing you tonight! 😊' and was heartened when a quick reply came back saying 'Me too! Love you!'

He stood shivering at the bus stop, longing for it to pull up so he could lean his head against the glass, watch his breath fog up the glass and get lost in thought for half an hour. His heart leapt as the bus drew up. It was comforting, sitting cocooned around strangers, watching the streets go by. Portsmouth was always congested at rush hour and the bus crawled through Fratton, up towards Hillsea and Hayling Island.

Eventually, he made it home to his flat. He fiddled with the keys and almost didn't notice when his front door swung open before he turned the lock. *'Shit, was this open all day?'* Thomas panicked and ran inside.

Thankfully a quick scout of the lounge and kitchen area showed nothing was missing. The TV was still in the corner with the DVD player perched on top, the kitchen had all of its appliances and when Thomas checked the drawer with the emergency cash stash, it was all accounted for. His heart began returning to normal and relief soon gave way to frustration.

'Damn, Oliver, you need to be more careful.'

The bathroom was the last room down the narrow corridor and the two bedrooms were next to the bathroom on either side, facing opposite each other. Thomas's was on the left, Oliver's on the right.

'Oliver? Oli?'

Thomas rapped sharply on the door. No answer.

Oliver could be so private at times. Thomas hesitated and then tentatively tried the door handle. Locked. Oh well. He must have followed up on the favour and made himself scarce tonight. It was only through scouring the flat that Thomas registered what a mess it had become. Cups and bowls had been left on the lounge table, toothpaste stains were all over the sink and clothes lay carelessly by the window. He began cleaning and tidying up, might as well go the whole hog. Oliver had come into his life about 4 months ago; the landlord had wanted to maximise the rent he could get and as Thomas was only occupying one bedroom, he remembered the landlord had interviewed for a roommate for him. Oliver was quite good company; he was exactly Thomas's age, 28, and they had even been born on the same day. Sometimes when they were both alone in the flat, Thomas enjoyed quite extensive conversations with Oliver. He envied Oliver.

They could not be more different.

Oliver was outgoing, energetic; he was too busy out living his life to preoccupy himself with little details such as housework or ironing his shirts; too busy out down Albert Road trying to hit on all the students or taking the ferry to the Isle of Wight for a weekend partying. If he was honest with himself, Thomas envied Oliver and his self-assured personality. But who was he kidding? Who could be instilled with self-confidence when your own mother thought you were a waste of space?...

No, he wasn't going down that rabbit hole tonight. He scrubbed the tables and sink with a brillo pad so vigorously that when he withdrew his hand, there were imprints of the pad on his palm...

Thomas then busied himself in the kitchen; he put Spotify on- he didn't like silence when he was alone in the flat- put the pies on the oven and prepared the instant mash in a bowl ready. He ironed the deep red tablecloth Emily had bought for him as a flat warming present and draped it over the kitchen table. Inspired, he found two old candles in the drawer and lit them. He spent a minute deciding where best to place the wine on the table, deciding facing the entrance so Emily would see it. He was in the middle of polishing the wine glasses when his phone pinged. Emily.

'Hi lovely, I'm gonna be a little late, stuck at work. Problem with a client lol. Will be at yours as soon as I can. Mwah.'

Thomas's heart sank. The pies only had 15 minutes to go, the perfect evening was going to be ruined.

No matter Tom, no matter. You can fix this.

He turned the oven right down so the pies would slow cook. He hoped Emily wasn't blowing him off because she was pissed at him over something. Perhaps he had said something in the week and it had got to her.

Oh God.

Thomas corked open the bottle, poured himself a glass and chugged it, feeling the wine course down his throat, he caught a glimpse of his reflection in the window. A drop of wine was dribbling down his chin, looking like a ribbon of blood…. he slowly wiped it away with his wrist….

It was gone 10pm when he finally heard the door turn.

'Tom, Tom, where are you? I am so so sorry!'

Emily let down her umbrella and came rushing into the lounge. 'Tonight, was a bloody nightmare, honestly! A client has forgotten to submit half of her receipts, the platform we use crashed and I was on the phone to I.T support for an hour… oh what a bloody nightmare.'

Her eyes looked past him into the kitchen. The wine bottle was half empty and the pies which Thomas had had to release from the oven had charred around the edges. The mash was now a lumpy mess.

'It was meant to be a surprise.' Thomas muttered. The wine had gone to his head, without food, red wine made him very woozy. He gestured with his glass. it.it took me 2 hours of wages to pay for this. He gave her a smile that was half genuine, half grimace.

'Oh look, I'm sure we can still salvage it.' She put her bag down. 'The pies are OK, they are warmish. I guess the mash is a lost cause. Do you have beans?'

He gestured towards the cupboard.

'Perfect! Tom, I will make this up to you, I promise.'

She heated some beans on the hob and they tackled the pies, Emily insisted they sit at the table that Thomas laid. After a full belly, Thomas was sobering up a little. He was frustrated that the evening hadn't been perfect but at least was beginning to feel like his old self. Emily looked so tired. There were dark circles under her bright blue eyes, her nail polish was chipped, and her chestnut hair lay limp around her shoulders. Despite this, she still looked beautiful to him and he felt a pang of guilt at not being more sympathetic.

'Sorry, you had such a difficult evening, Em.'

'Yeah. Not what you'd expect from a Monday is it.' She took another sip. 'Mmm, so this is not just wine..it's M and S wine.' She grinned. 'It's lovely and I really appreciate the gesture, Tom.'

'Well, I figured we haven't spent a lot of time together recently...I feel I've been a bit of a lousy boyfriend.'

'Well, I haven't been much better. How was work for you?'

He shrugged and began clearing the plates. 'Same old Monday. As Bob Geldof said...

'I don't like Mondays.' They said this in unison and grinned at each other. A shared love of 80's music had been one of the many things that had brought them together.

'I made some good sales.' He continued. 'Jack is pleased with me. It's just Ben Grey pissing me off as usual.'

'What's he done this time?'

'Taking the mick out of my jumper and the fact I'm always on EarthCam and when I try and explain, he calls me a pretentious prick.'

'I don't know why you are so sensitive to him, Tom. Some people just enjoy being pricks. Let's get real, you wouldn't want to be friends with the guy, so just ignore him.'

'The office isn't really big enough for the both of us.'

'Well, I was Googling on my way here and I just happened to chance upon Totaljobs…'

Oh, not this crap again.

'And…there are a couple of museum jobs that popped up…that I think you would be great for…' Her voice rose up at the end and she kept her eyes fixed on him…

'Em-we've talked about this. It's not the right time.'

'Well, we haven't *really* talked about it…and quite frankly I think it's about time. Tom, I was reading the job descriptions- hear me out… and you would mop the floor with the competition!'

'And where are these amazing jobs exactly?' the rush of irritation had returned and was coursing through Thomas's veins. He began filling up the sink with soapy water to distract himself.

'OK, well one is in Southampton...which come on, isn't too far! The other one is in Guildford; you could get the train and ...'

'Do you know how expensive train tickets are now? These jobs will be at apprentice level, Em, the train ticket will swallow half my wages. I have to pay rent, eat, what do you expect me to live on? Bread and Water and Dreams?'

'Don't be sarky! My point is...well you are 30 in 2 years' Tom. You're the one who is Mr. Planner. You can map out your entire work desk but can't seem to apply the same rules to yourself! OK, you'd have to take a pay cut but at least you'd finally be on the right path. I'd support you. Us...'

'You're an accountant Em, but you're not George Osbourne!'

She bristled. 'That's not fair! I've been damn patient. I work bloody hard at my job and at least I do it with some damn dignity...' She took a large swig of wine.

'Jack's good to me. I think I could get a promotion to supervisor.'

'Yeah. Right. Get real Tom. Everything you tell me about that bloke. Jack O'Neill is a sleaze. I cringe every time I see that cheesy poster of him in the window. Let's face it Tom, it's a small back-end travel company, it's a dead-end job and you are at that dead end. It's time to back up and choose another route!'

'How about if I like my job?'

'Correction. You are *comfortable* at your job. You know, I'd like a time...when... well maybe one day we live together...you are working in the art world, I am working in oh I don't know, somewhere where I am happy. Tom..' she got up then. His back was still to her and he stiffened as he felt her arms around his waist. 'I just don't want you giving your life to a job that has no prospects.'

'OK. OK. Tell you what. I'll read the job descriptions tomorrow and I'll send my CV. Fair enough?'

She brightened. 'Well, that's a start.' She began drying up while he washed up. Her hand pulled out the long sharp knife he had used to cut the pies with. She looked at it for a second, lost in thought, then slowly wiped the knife's blade and put it in the drawer.

'I'd do anything for you.' She whispered. 'Including getting you out of that craphole. Although, if you insist in trying to get the manager's role. I guess I had better sort out Jack O'Neill for you!'

He looked at her in alarm.

'Jokes! silly!'

'Oh. Ha-ha. Sure. '

They put on a favourite playlist from Spotify and both of them kept the conversation away from work. Emily left around midnight. She couldn't stay so Thomas rang a taxi for her, waved her off and waited anxiously in bed until he got the text and a photo to say she was home safe at her flat in Fratton.

Oliver was certainly burning the midnight oil. Probably headed to *Time and Envy* on the seafront. There was no need to wait up for him. Thomas would leave a note for him in the morning to remind him to lock the door. It was another hour before he dropped off and he didn't notice that the front door didn't open all night and the bedroom next to his lay vacant....

THREE

Thomas had grown up in Portsmouth, raised by a single mother, Dolores (her name means misery and sorrow-appropriate!) Walker.

He had never known his father; he had been the product of an illicit fling with a married man. When his mum had gone crawling to his dad for help, begging for cash, he had grabbed her by the scruff of the neck, saying if she ever came round to his place again where his wife could find out, he would beat the stuffing out of her and their unborn child. In short, he told her, he wanted nothing more to do with her.

Thomas was born on a cold February morning (the 3rd) in 1991. Dolores had explained to him when he was only 10, he had been placed in a plastic cot next to her bed and when she looked at him, all she could do was weep. Weep from pity or regret, Thomas never knew.

They moved to the Charles Dickens and Nelson district. Their relationship was a lonely and volatile one; Dolores took two cleaning jobs to support them; one of Thomas's earliest memories was laying shivering in bed as her alarm rang at 5am and she got up muttering and swearing. Even at the age of 6, it was up to him to find his own way to school. After eating a bowl of the cardboard like cereal she would leave out for him, he would shuffle out of the flat and hope to bump into parents walking classmates to school so it would look like he was supervised. If the parents of his friends noticed anything, nobody acted on it. He never had many friends, no one liked to sit next to the scruffy boy with trousers to inches too short.

Things didn't improve with Dolores either; she began coming home smelling of drink; her moods became unpredictable, one minute she was the life and soul of the room, grabbing Thomas and squeezing him breathless, the other she was crying in the corner or screaming at Thomas to get dinner on.

His teen years was a blur. But he knew one thing he was good at. Art. He loved Art. The history of Art. A lack of friends in his childhood meant that he lacked the social skills needed to form lasting friendships, so he spent a lot of time on his own. He began going to the library after school to avoid sitting in their draughty flat and would pore over the books on the Tate Modern and the Museum of Modern Art in New York. The librarian gave him a pad and some pencils; she must have been feeling sorry for him. He would spend a glorious hour looking at pictures and drawing.

He was a little bit older before he started getting into Cubism, the Renaissance, Abstract movement. He loved it all. Devoured it. With art, he could be real in a world where he struggled to feel. He came out of high school with only average grades but enrolled at the local college and took a Diploma in Art and Design.

His relationship with his mum had now almost totally broken down. She was now not working at all and was completely dependent on benefits and a chunk of what Thomas earned at his Saturday job working at a Sports Store in Gunwharf Quays. Their conversations would start with her barking at him from the lounge to bring her dinner or cigarettes or a glass of vodka. In the end, frustrated and angry he would shout at her as teenagers do, telling her to get her life together.

It resented him that one parent had already cleared off and he had been left with the other one totally unfit for purpose. She screamed back, telling him the gamble she had taken in going ahead with her pregnancy had backfired; she would have been better off aborting him; he drove her mad with his little habits, he had never been like normal children, he was strange...he'd never amount to anything.

Despite all of this, in a strange way, he still really craved her approval and when he was 17 and beginning to think about the next step in his life, he began to think if University would be the ticket to a happier life. Not only for emotional reasons; Thomas was pragmatic, and he could see an economic advantage; getting a degree could mean a good job and raising his mum and him out of the shit pit that was keeping her down.

Raising the issue with his mum was a laugh. She had laughed hoarsely through a cloud of smoke when he proposed the idea of university, saying it was the biggest fucking waste of time there was and she had a coughing fit when he said he wanted to study art.

'Anyway, you can't wait to fuck off and leave me. You are gonna leave me.' She croaked before passing out with a glass of vodka in her hand.

So, studying out of city was out of the question; in the end exasperated he had applied to the University of Portsmouth and was surprised but thrilled when he was accepted. Probably a charity case poor student but what the hell. It was a new start, kind of. He wouldn't be leaving the city but ...well...maybe it was better that way. He spent hours in his room, making lists of the types of careers he could go for, reading the syllabus the University sent over. Living in the city, he had busted his ass doing overtime for a month to afford the reading material. Blackwell's, the University bookshop was damn expensive. Luckily, he had found some second-hand books online. He had popped into the student union after the bookshop. He had a bit of spare money left over and decided he was going to splurge on a purple hoodie. To anyone else coming to study in the city, it was a frivolous fashion accessory, but to him, it meant something. It was an emblem of a promise of a better future, he finally belonged somewhere.

It didn't make sense to spend the university loan on accommodation fees in halls as he was already living in the city. Besides, he'd be fairly low down the list. As a result, whilst he genuinely enjoyed the course itself and revelled in the work load, it was hard to connect to his classmates; most had come from quite privileged backgrounds. Not sharing accommodation had made it difficult to engage in the student nights, the banter over who stole whose cheese, the parting at the halls of residence. There was no one who he really connected with.

It wasn't until in his third and final year that he met Emily It was at The One-Eyed Dog Pub. He went in on a Monday night; his third year and his lecturers were really piling the pressure on; he was predicted to get a 1st and he wanted to make sure he achieved it. He hadn't left the studio until 9pm and exhausted though he was, a surprising urge overtook him. He wanted a drink. Just this one night, he wanted to be a typical 21-year-old goddamn student out for a drink after a day's studying. He headed towards Albert Road and the theatre and decided the One-Eyed Dog looked like it had enough of an atmosphere to be student without being over whelming. Crowds overwhelmed him. Walking in, the bartender immediately caught his eye. Long chestnut hair to her waist, eyes a bright green and loads of fabric friendship bracelets adorned her skinny wrists as she buzzed up and down tidying the shelves and emptying the beer trays.

'Can I get you anything?' she grinned.

'Er…pint of Snakebite cheers' he mumbled. He's heard his classmates talking about that drink and thought it sounded 'student'.

'You got it! She gave him two thumbs up, grinned and began preparing the drink.

'Burning the midnight oil?' she enquired.

'What. Oh…yeah. I was in the library.'

'Oooh a DEDICATED student in here, that makes a change'.

'Yeah, I'm studying Art History.' He liked her humour.

'Nice'. Two small pink spots appeared on her cheeks as she looked at him. Was she attracted to him?

'In my 3rd year now' he continued.

'Hoping to get your own show on the History Channel.'

'Well, that certainly would be hard to turn down! I'm a bit camera shy though. I'm thinking something a bit more behind the scenes.'

She set the pint down on the bar and took his money. She didn't ask why he was alone.

'My name's Emily.' She smiled.

'Thomas. Tom'

'Well, nice to meet you Thomas-Tom…oh…'

Their conversation was interrupted by a customer waiting. But she seemed keen to keep coming back to him, dusting and tidying unnecessarily in order to make conversation,

He wanted to stay talking with her. He wanted to tell her about Michelangelo, Dali...The strength of his feelings scared him a bit. He had never like anyone this much at first sight. When he finished his Snakebite, which he had liked more than he thought he would, he ordered another one from her and sat propped up on the bar, reading his books but every now and then, glimpsing up to watch her. She looked about his age and she hadn't yet mentioned a boyfriend. Oh, who was he kidding, like someone like that would be interested in him...'

It was midnight when the last of the customers got up. Thomas swayed a bit as he got up. Damn, he really was out of practice. He stood outside, waiting for Emily, feeling foolish, like a teenage groupie waiting for a boyband member. She came out, a sequinned large crescent moon bag over her shoulder. Being nearer to her now, he could take her in in more detail, her nails were painted a different colour on each one, little silver star earrings in her lobes. Pink lip balm which she re applied. The brown hair, green eyes and pink gloss were a great combination. He couldn't deny it any longer, he was attracted to her. But not only looks wise-she seemed...cool. She seemed surprised and pleased to see him still waiting for her.

'How are you getting home?' he asked.

'Oh, I live just off of Albert Road.' She gestured towards the hill.

'I can walk you.' The words were out of his mouth before he could stop them.

'Oh, that's nice of you. Cheers! It's not too out of your way though, is it? Are you up at James Watson? Rees Hall?

He smiled. 'No. not quite. I actually live in Portsmouth so I didn't bother applying for halls, I live with my mum. 'God, *I sound like such a twat.*

She frowned. 'Most kids our age is dying to 'get out this crappy town!' she said this in an American accent which made him laugh. 'What's the deal with you not heading to London? You've got the bloody Royal College of Art there.'

He hesitated. 'Reasons.'

She nodded. 'Sorry I'm being nosy.'

'No don't worry'.

She lit a cigarette. It was strawberry flavoured and it gave a fruity smell as they began walking towards the hill. 'You want one?'

He shook his head. 'I don't smoke.'

'Health conscious huh?'

'No, not really. Just an unlived soul.'

She laughed. 'You're funny, Tom. I like you.'

The words rang in his ear like a symphony. The Snakebites had made him courageous.

'Say, I don't know how tired you are after your shift, but do you feel like grabbing a drink?'

She looked mock serious. 'Sure, in my job, alcohol is sure hard to come by.'

He laughed yet again; he liked her humour.

'It sure is nippy' she muttered.

'Do you want my hoodie?' Thomas offered.

'Oh cheers, if you don't mind.'

Obligingly he took it off, feeling the sting of the cold on his torso. She threw it over her head and shoulders and put the hood up so only her grinning mouth showed.

'Perfect fit' he grinned.

She linked her arm through his. 'I'm in.'

They found a bar up the hill and spent hours dancing until 4am and the sun was streaming through the window. He had never known a night like this...he felt intoxicated on his own feelings; the night was a blur of them chatting, joking, dancing, he kept replaying the feel of her arms draped over his shoulders or round his waist, her hair tickling his chin. The number of times he swore they had come close to kissing on the lips, he had wanted to so badly but however bold the alcohol made him, his insecurities still stood on the other shoulder. They had ended the morning by getting a kebab and kissing briefly goodbye on the cheek. She did ask for his number and he gave it not really expecting her to text. He paid the price for his wild night; his mum had fallen asleep on the couch and had followed through. He spent the next hour with her in the bathroom cleaning her up while she came too and raged at him for not coming home....

He was amazed when she texted the next day, asking to see him again. He suggested a trip up the Spinnaker tower.

'I'm scared of heights Tom. Can we do something else?'

His name on her lips sounded nice. At that moment he felt like he could do anything for her.

'Sure' he said.

They went to the Vue to see the big comedy film out that season. His choice. It was a hilarious film and they took a walk to the beach afterwards...

They were inseparable from there on out and 7 years later they still were.

'I was in a children's home' she told him, 3 months' into their relationship. They were having breakfast in a greasy spoon and she was pouring ketchup on her sausages. She seemed to be avoiding his eyes. He looked up from his hash browns,

'Yeah, the state raised me, she said ruefully. 'Kids kicked me about. Stole my stuff. It really was a hard knock life for me. But I was certainly no Little Orphan Annie. No one was rushing to adopt me.

'What happened to your parents?'

'Died in a car crash when I was two. They were both only children so I had no other living relatives. No grandparents. So, I was shunted into the system. I was in the care system for years, ten miserable sodding years. She chewed thoughtfully.

'Things had a happier ending. I was adopted when I was 12. I was damn lucky to find a couple to take me on when I was on the brink of being a teenager.'

'And the people who adopted you...they are the parents you have now?'

'Yeah. They are good people. Life got a bit better after that. They enrolled me in a good high school, I started making friends...one thing I always liked was Maths. I.'

'I know you do.' He smiled.

I always had Maths to console me though. I was good at it, you know?'

'We are like Yin and Yan you and me. I ran to Art; you ran to Maths!'

I know right?' She reached for his arm. 'Yin and Yang. The Fish to my Chips.'

...'Sorry, it took me so long to tell you. I was scared you'd judge me.'

'I'd have no reason to judge you. Em- my childhood wasn't exactly Little House on the Prairie.'

She smiled sadly.

'Look, I'm not excusing myself but my childhood made me a little...wild. I shoplifted, bunked off school.' She looked anxiously at him. You- you are such a – a good guy – I didn't think you'd want to get involved with a – well someone like me. You made good decisions Tom. You are on your way to getting a 1st and you'll no doubt be heading to exciting new places...'

'You can too! You can do tons with Maths.'

'I'd really like to become an accountant she mused. 'I like...what's the word...I like fixing things, sorting things, Maths is predictable. I need that in my life.'

'Well do it. You can't work at The Dog all your life. Take an evening course at the college. I've got some money saved...I'll help you.'

She hugged herself. 'Accounting. Real exciting huh?'

'Well. He struggled.' 'OK so it's not to me but...'

He had clearly touched her though by his offering to help her. She had gone pink in the cheeks and looked like she was trying to hide it.'

'Come on, Mr. Walker, I'll show you how Maths can be fun.'

She was always pointing out Maths in everyday life, calculating the circumference of a pizza to make him laugh, explaining Pythagoras's Theorem when helping him pick furniture for his flat...

Thomas graduated with a 1st and did start applying for jobs. However, it was 2012, the world was still reeling from the crash of 2008, jobs were hard to come by. However, he did take on a series of routine admin jobs. His mum had never even attended his graduation at The Guildhall. It depressed him to see his classmates' arms around their parents; he felt cheated. Emily was still there to congratulate him and he went to lunch at one of the local pubs and socialised with the other graduates. He and his mum barely spoke anymore and he finally accepted that he couldn't fix their situation because she didn't want it fixed. He moved out and found his flat in Hillsea. Emily was still living with her parents as it was cheaper. The good news is with Thomas's encouragement she had enrolled at the local college and was doing an accounting course. Working full time, Thomas was able to support with costs.

'I love you, Tom.'

One day she just said it. She said it so simply, so casually.

'I love you too'.

They were standing on the beach by the pier. She had come screaming and jumping into his arms when she got her accountancy qualification. Maybe it was the result of their two damaged souls but it had actually taken them 2 years to tell each other they loved each other. That night they made love and it was something that was...transcendent; each of them had given a bit of their soul verbally to each other. They had gotten each other to where they were and they would carry on together. They were one and the same. Two damaged, cracked people that when together, provided a kind of super glue.

She still kept her faith in him that he would use his degree. However, as time went on, Thomas began to get more lethargic; the rejection letters kept coming; the monotony of bills kept him from saying 'fuck it I'm going backpacking.' Slowly but surely, he felt it. He didn't need her to vocalise it. The way her face lit up when he told her he had found another job and the very, very slight flatlining of her smile when he told her it was *Safe Travel Holidays*. He caught her on a search engine searching '*how to motivate my boyfriend*.' When she eventually moved out of her parents' after securing her first accountancy job, he took her out to dinner but every glass raised seemed a wait of expectation on him. She had risen. He had fallen. She was pursuing her dream. He was in a crappy job and his mind and talents were washing away on a polluted beach. He had once been her hope. Her inspiration life could be better. Now he had proven that he was just as boring and uninspired as the rest. He had disappointed her. And for that, sometimes he hated. No, he didn't hate her...he hated himself.

FOUR

The next morning, another dull, grey Tuesday, Thomas dragged his feet to the bus stop. He had had a restless night tossing and turning. He had woken up to complete silence. Oliver's bedroom door remained closed. However, when Thomas shuffled into the kitchen, he found Oliver sat having breakfast.

'Tom!' He beamed. 'How's it going matey?'

'Not bad' Thomas muttered, running a hand through his beard and pulling out a bowl and a box of Coco Pops. 'Thanks for making yourself scarce last night.'

'No worries, bud, no worries.'

'Mind you, you didn't need to stay out quite so late.' Thomas smiled wryly. 'What time did you get in. Four?'

'Five ha-ha. You know me. I like a quiet life.' He winked.

'Oli, we need to be careful with the door, mate. I came home last night and it wasn't locked.'

'Chill my man, chill.' Oliver spread his arms and smiled, looking utterly relaxed. 'What are they gonna steal, a bread board?'

'Much I like your genial attitude, I'm serious.' Thomas gulped his cereal down, wiped his sleeve.

'I get Cha Tom. I'll make sure the flat is like Fort Knox.'

'Thanks Oli. Right, I'd better dash, crap. He looked at the time. 'Got to get the bus.'

'See you later, man.'

His thoughts roamed to Emily as he jogged to the stop. He hated feeling so disconnected from her; he knew he was starting to feel withdrawn and anxious. He hated it when his thoughts took over and decided to write another positive list, but this time on the note section of his phone away from the prying eyes of Ben.

Thomas sat down at the back of the bus rubbing his eyes which were stinging from tiredness as he looked out to the outside world. He hoped to be left alone. There was always a man in a trilby hat that would join the bus a few stops away and would insist on sitting near him and making small talk. Thomas didn't always mind but today in particular, he was exhausted and wanted to be alone with his thoughts. The man was always friendly enough and would talk to Thomas just like he knew him. *Why did he always want to sit near me? Why does he want to talk to me? Is he after something?* Thomas's thoughts swam in his head staring at the greasy, cracked and rustic iron rod that passed throughout the middle of the bus. *'I wonder how many germs are on that thing'.* He distracted himself with the list: 'Thoughtful', 'A Hard Worker, 'Tidy.' As they arrived near to his work, Thomas was feeling anxious. He did not see the man in the hat but he could not believe just how many people were allowed on the bus at once. Some were clinging on for dear life and hanging from pole to pole on like Tarzan on trees and the smell was just stifling. It was a mix of smoke, body odour, grease, dust and if you were lucky enough, you got a faint smell of perfume. The bus drew to a stop near NatWest. Thomas could not get off the bus quickly enough, gasping for breath as he finally made it to his desk.

Ben was already at his own desk drinking a coffee when Thomas placed his navy hoodie on the back of his chair and parked himself down.

'Good morning, Tom' said Ben with a smirk. 'How are we today?'

'A bit tired but okay thanks and yourself?' Thomas said wearily. Dammit, what was wrong with him. He needed coffee. He picked up his mug. Anything to get away for a few minutes.

Ben always seemed like he was desperate to crack a joke or be sarcastic in some way.

'I am fine thanks' he replied tapping his pen on the desk. He did this to annoy Thomas. He knew Thomas found the tap-tap-tap so frustrating and look up giving Thomas a sarcastic grin.

He made himself a coffee and took some biscuits from the tin. It was Tuesday and Jack always gave a 15-minute pep talk. 'You wazzocks are always too hungover Mondays' he had joked.

It was the chance to catch up on anything going on in the team and how the business was going. Shania and Gerry had already pulled their seats to the middle of the room and were chatting. Ben was at the printer. Thomas frowned.

Ben, working at this time? Surely not.

He made a detour past Ben's desk and looked at what Ben had been printing. This was odd. It looked like Ben was printing a load of...newspaper articles. Was this something Jack had asked him to do? Thomas didn't have time to look closer. Ben came back to his desk.

'Jog on Tom.' He snapped, swiping up the printed papers and shoving them into his drawer.

Jack came out of his office, beaming.

'Lads and lady! Good morning! What did you all watch on telly last night? JOKES! I DON'T GIVE A DAMN. WE ARE HERE TO TALK WORK! Do NOT forget we have the Marshalls coming in today to discuss their requirements and accommodation for Iceland. Remember! they are paying us a lot of money so try and make sure we already have the details of luggage allowance, some form of an itinerary, and tour dates listed. It makes us look prepared'!

'Yes, boss' said Ben straightaway as if wanting to acknowledge that he wanted to take the job over. 'I'll sort this Tom, as you say, you are tired' said Ben with a grin.

'Well, if you need any HELP, I'm here!' Thomas shot back, irritated.

'Sounds like Tom needs a nap!' Ben laughed.

'Ben, just like, put a sock in it, will you?' Shania moaned. 'Are you feeling well, Tom?'

'Quite well' Thomas glowered.

Typical. Ben just wanted to get back at him for obviously snooping earlier. What had Ben been printing...his thoughts began wandering again as Jack droned on. Why was everyone so keen to wind him up all the time. Sometimes, he wanted to hit something...and hit it hard. He'd get on EarthCam in a bit before any customers came in. Do some research....

Mid-morning, the door opened swiftly and the Marshalls, regular customers stepped in.

'We were hoping to speak to Thomas, if possible, please' sad Mr Marshall politely. 'Thomas booked an exquisite trip to Paris for my sister last year and she said he did a splendid job. I was hoping to get some ideas from him if I may?' Mr Marshall stood at the front desk, well dressed in a full suit and tie as if he was heading to an important interview. His wife stood with her arm interlinked in his, her blonde curls sitting perfectly on her shoulders. She wore bright red lipstick, which complimented her trousers suit perfectly. She clutched onto her handbag and smiled at both of them with confidence. Ben, who had leapt up from hid desk grinning looked flustered and self-conscious. 'Oh, um, okay, yyyyes you want T. T. Thomas?' he spluttered, turning to face him who looked equally surprised and a little uncomfortable.

Jack looked out from his office too which made Ben even more flustered. He walked off sheepishly but not before giving Thomas a look of pure hatred. Despite his annoyance with Ben, Thomas felt a pang of guilt but politely acknowledged the Marshalls.

'Mr and Mrs Marshall, can I offer you both a drink? A tea? Or coffee? 'That would be wonderful dear, but it is Louise and Matthias please 'answered Mrs Marshall.

He walked them to his desk where she gracefully sat down, careful not to cause any creases in her suit.

'Excuse me, can you give me one minute?'

Thomas hurried through the back to the kitchen where Ben was standing quietly staring into the fridge.

'I am sorry' whispered Thomas. 'I really did not know they would ask after me but listen we could…'

'You're not sorry but it's okay' Ben muttered, slamming the fridge shut and walking back to his desk.

Thomas couldn't keep the Marshalls waiting. He took a handful of brochures from the shelf to do with Iceland and returned back to the main office. It was an enjoyable sale and Thomas quickly got into his stride.

'Imagine marvelling at frozen landscapes during the day and hunting the Northern lights at night? There are also plenty of tours available which are either privately guided or self-drive so you can take your time that way?' Thomas smiled at Louise and then to Matthias. 'Listen we can go on to EarthCam and have a look now if you like at some of the sites? It will get you both in the mood'. Thomas logged on eagerly wanting to share the excitement with them and his favourite site. He swung his monitor around to face them. 'I use this all the time; I feel like I can see anywhere in the world whenever I want' he grinned.

'That sounds a bit scary if you ask me' Ben suddenly spoke up and Thomas threw him a look.

'Scary how? It's perfect for planning a trip and seeing what to expect when you go, don't you think? Said Thomas enthusiastically. The Marshall's smiled in agreement.

'That's the problem with society these days' Ben argued, 'Everyone, everywhere is watching you. Did you know our own phones can listen to what we are saying now, like every conversation? Have you noticed when you are having a conversation with someone, then you log onto social media and that exact subject that you spoke about is being advertised? It's shocking really.'

Thomas started to feel hot and uncomfortable.

Why is he saying these things now? Cannot we have this conversation after the Marshalls have gone? Is he trying to embarrass me?' Now is not the time for Ben's stupid comments, even if they are true or not. Why did I even have sympathy for him? Prick.

He forced his attention back to the couple. All three sat around the computer and observed EarthCam, each one in awe of the terrific sights on screen.

'Anyway dear, please tell us more about the glacial lagoon Thomas?' Louise started to shift uncomfortably in her seat. Thomas took a deep breath and thought to himself: *ignore Ben, STH needs this sale, come on Thomas! Sell this*!

'I hear the south is truly spectacular during the winter. You can explore the natural sights along the famous Golden Circle route and South Coast as these are beautiful in their winter coats, with the unique light and potential snow. This 6-day tour includes highlights like the Glacier Lagoon where you can see massive floating icebergs, epic cascading waterfalls Gullfoss and Seljalandsfoss and haunting black sand beaches. If you are lucky, the northern lights might make an appearance during your stay and you can enjoy the tranquillity of the winter season, said Thomas brightly.

'Oh, my goodness, you have definitely sold this to us Thomas' cried Louise. 'Let's get this booked please and right away at that' Mattias said quickly, clearly keen to please his wife. Either that or to potentially get away from Ben and his demeanour.

Thomas went to the printer to print the final itinerary. He saw a stray piece of paper already in the tray and discreetly picked it up.

'Here is a full list of your itinerary, now remember on arrival at Keflavik International Airport, you will be greeted by a driver and transferred to your accommodation in Reykjavík. After settling in, take the opportunity to explore the vibrant city centre at your own pace. The main downtown area offers a variety of shops, museums and galleries and these are all within walking distance' smiled Thomas.

Ben could not hide his bad mood and rolled his eyes.

'I trust our Thomas sorted out a good deal for you both Mr and Mrs Marshall' smiled Jack.

'Oh yes, we are very pleased, it was a pleasure doing business with Safe Travel Holidays' said Mr Marshall triumphantly. 'Excellent news, truly excellent beamed Jack and shook both their hands. The office smiled and waved out the Marshalls who left hand in hand.

'Thomas. Walker. That was unbelievable!!' Shrieked Shania, giving him a hug around the waist. Thomas returned it very briefly.

'Well done, Thomas. You were like an encyclopaedia! Gerry grinned.

'Nice one Thomas, drink on me tonight down the pub?' smiled Jack.

'Thanks boss but I really want to take Emily out tonight to our old hang out' replied Thomas. He was feeling good. He's clinched the sale. He WAS good at this job. He would make Emily see that.

'I just want to be alone with Emily tonight - no interruptions'

Thomas returned to his desk, lighter and happier. It wasn't until lunch that he remembered the stray bit of paper that Ben had forgotten about. Waiting until Ben had gone to lunch, Thomas quietly took a look. He frowned. It was a newspaper article, taken from Google so obviously from an archive site. It showed an older teenager, graduating from Uni...it was Jack. He was stood arm in arm with a beaming young woman who must be his girlfriend at the time (she didn't look like Caroline).

The article said Jack O'Neill had graduated with an honour's degree in Travel and Tourism. He had his arm around another young man. The photograph didn't capture the name but was that...Gerry?

Why the hell was Ben printing off stories of Jack. Was this a brown nose portfolio or was he looking to take Jack down? Thomas tried to bring his mind back to

Emily but he didn't like it. He didn't know what Ben was capable of. He didn't like this at all.

FIVE

Ben sat at his desk, the heat of ~~his~~ anger rising in his face and neck.

Thomas selling the Iceland holiday to the Marshalls. *This was meant to be MY gig,* he thought. Ben knew Thomas was in his charming-and-keep-smiling phase which Jack had taught him when he had joined the company. Rule number one - your customer is always right. Rule number two - smile, smile, smile. Without even listening to his words, Ben knew because Thomas' face was lit up brighter than some twat in a toothpaste advert. Dick. He was so transparent.

As he listened to Thomas Ben looked down at his desk; he tried to preoccupy himself. If another customer came through the door, he could sell the shit out of some destination and put Thomas in his place.

He could see Thomas' desk out of the corner of his eye, so pristine, precise. When he looked at his own desk, there were piles of paperwork, used post-it notes, and a thick layer of dust on top of the computer the computer. *This mess is glorious evidence that I work hard and my brain is always thinking of different concepts and ideas*, Ben said to himself. 'Thomas may be a complete anal freak but that's because he has no life aside from sitting in front of a screen looking at EarthCam and all those things other geeks look at. At least I am less organised because I don't have TIME to be...because I have a DAMN LIFE!' Does he do better work than me? Absolutely not' Ben thought.

He looked up again and winced as he saw the smile that Mrs Marshall just gave Thomas. Yep. She was suckered in. They would take the trip; Jack would be happy and probably would give Thomas the big bonus especially if they went for all the extras.

'I will be left once again in the goddamn shadows.'

Ben looked across to Jack's office, the blinds were closed and the door was firmly shut. Coincidentally, Shania's desk was vacant. God, didn't anyone in this place do any work?

He would bet a good amount of money she was in the office with Jack and he felt an annoying pang in his chest that he was sure was jealousy. But he was pissed off that that emotion had attached itself in him where Shania was concerned. They had worked together for a year now. He had thought she was a sound chick but had never thought about her beyond as a colleague. He used to cringe when she laughed her hyena laugh at Jack's shit jokes. He wondered what he was up to in there. Ben could not understand what Shania saw in Jack either. Of course, they tried to keep things under wraps but it was as clear as day to everyone what was going on.

Did she not have any self-respect? She gazed at him with her overly made-up eyes, just waiting for him to tell the next shit joke so she could laugh like a hyena.

'I can tell a joke too' Ben thought bitterly. Jack is married to a poor skivvy wife that probably has no idea how many women he's involved with. He was old enough to be her dad as well but maybe that is what she liked? The older man with all the money. She was just a number on a list of his conquests. When I joined the business, I was the golden boy and Jack took me under his wing almost like his possession. I used to be vivacious and high-spirited Ben thought to himself but almost like when a vampire sucks your blood, Jack almost gives himself youth at your expense. He does not care about anything or anyone but himself.

SIX

That evening Thomas sent a text to Emily on his way home on the bus 'Hey, drinks tonight at the Registry bar? We need to celebrate :) T x' . He sat back on the seat and closed his eyes. Finally, something positive to happen he thought.

His phone vibrated with a response from Emily: "Can do. I will meet you there later as it's month end at work. I may be a bit late. E x'

Thomas got home to the flat and threw his bag down. Once again, no sign of Oliver. He headed straight for the shower letting the heat of the running water rinse his body of the stress of the day. As he opened the door, he was assailed by a cloud of steam and he spent several minutes just staring into the mirror when he caught sight of the translucent shower curtain behind him. Was that a shadow? Don't be so silly Thomas. Where has this paranoia come from recently. 'Too much of the horror channel before bed' he laughed to himself. He grabbed the bath towel and went into the bedroom to find a smart shirt.

As he reached for the rusty brown entrance, he rested his hand on the rough paintwork that coated the door and shards of dark paint crumble to the floor. As Thomas entered, the hinges squealed as if in warning but they were silenced by the laughter and music inside. Memories started to flood his mind, he smiled and went straight to the bar, ordered his Guinness and took a seat. The pub was surprisingly busy for a school night.

There was a darts team in the middle of a serious looking game in the corner of the pub.

Next to them were three men in high end attire drinking whiskey. The smell had definitely changed over the years, once it was cigarette smoke and beer were now a stagnant smell of perfume, different flavour gins and body odour. On another table, were a group of ladies, with heavily made-up eyes and dresses that hugged their figures.

Thomas thought to himself 'no one matches up to Emily', even if they had drifted slightly, he wanted to get back on track.

Finally, she turned up and joined his table, she looked quite flustered.

'Sorry I'm late' she said breathlessly. 'You know what month end is like for us, so many clients, so many figures to get through'.

'It's not a problem Em, honestly. I was just hoping we could talk. I feel so disconnected from you recently. I know you have been busy with work but you have been coming home late for what feels like weeks, we have not had any 'us' time?' Thomas said calmly.

'I know I have been preoccupied' she said. 'We are here to celebrate anyway and what a place to come to' she smiled. 'A lot of memories here. I can't help but feel like we are at a standstill though? I want to feel like we are moving forward? Listen I was looking on Rightmove and...' she added sadly.

'There are indeed great memories here,' interrupted Thomas. 'I know we have been in a bit of a rut recently. I was hoping we could save up a bit of money and go on a nice holiday?'

Thomas noted her disappointment but did not want to get into an argument on their first date in ages.

Why are you avoiding the house talk? What would be so wrong with it, Thomas? She is messy yes but that is no reason to not live with the girl you love...

'Speaking of holidays, I managed to complete on that sale I told you about for the Marshalls. They have booked their trip to Iceland and seemed really happy with what I had to offer them' Thomas said, lifting his pint ready to clink her glass. 'Tom that's amazing news! And a good pay out I bet?' she seemed slightly irritated at the way Thomas scooted around the 'moving forward' comment, clearly hoping for a different response. Regardless she lifted her glass of wine to clink back on his. '

Yes, it's going to be a good commission for me and Jack was happy' Thomas beamed.

'Fantastic news! So, what's the latest drama at work? She added. 'Well actually, you know Jack asked me to get him a quick holiday sorted for him and his wife? I have a feeling there is something going on with Shania at work' Thomas said.

'When is he NOT having an affair is what I want to know Tom. If you aren't happy in a marriage or relationship, you just end it. I have never known a man get involved with so many women. 'What makes you think he's involved with Shania anyway. Isn't she young enough to be his daughter?'

'I know and Ben hasn't been happy about it either, maybe he has a crush on her? But he did not look happy on lunch the other day when Jack and Shania came out of the office looking shall we sat. Red faced.' said Thomas.

'Urgh classy' replied Emily looking up at the door. Thomas turned around to people watch.

He did this a lot when it's quiet at work. As he turned around, he noticed Ben walking in.

'Ben! What brings you here' Thomas asked with a smile. He knew they do not seem to gel well at work but maybe Ben will be calmer away from the four walls. Emily smiled but looked slightly hesitant Thomas couldn't help but notice.

'Tom! I am here for the bar much like yourself' Ben smirked and looked over at Emily with a nod. Ben was by himself and seemed edgy.

'Ben this is my girlfriend Emily, Emily this is my colleague Ben'

Thomas said politely breaking the awkward moment. Ben smiled at Emily but did not seem keen to hang about. 'Nice to meet you' he said and held her gaze. 'You too' Emily replied. 'Anyway, I'll leave you to it,' Ben said and walked off with his head down and went to the bar.

'That was weird,' Thomas said. Emily looked uncomfortable 'it was. I swear I've seen him before. Maybe it where you talk so much about people at work, I feel like I already know them'

It felt nice spending the evening together and reminiscing about their first night of meeting Thomas thought to himself. As they walked home, Thomas wrapped his arm around Emily comfortingly enjoying the peace when suddenly he heard voices. He turned around falling silent expecting someone to be behind them. 'What is it, Tom?' Emily asks, copying him now and turning around.

The brisk wind of the night air washed over his body waking him up slightly. Stars coloured the dark sky and the moon with shining its bright light on the dark road ahead. 'Did you hear that' he said. 'Hear what Tom? There's no one there' Emily uttered 'Are you okay? Do you mind if put your hoodie on, I feel so chilly?'

Someone is definitely following us. What was that? Was that a black cat seriously just walking across a driveway? Isn't that bad luck? Or does it have to be your own driveway? I swear you are going fucking mad Thomas! Get a hold of yourself'

Thomas could hear sirens in the distance as he pulled the hoodie down over the small of her back 'Emily do you think those sirens are for us?'

Emily did not answer and put her head down quietly. 'Sorry, I must be overtired' he muttered. He just wanted to get home as quickly as possible. It's times like this, he wished he and Emily lived together properly. He kept dragging his feet saying instead of spending 'dead' money on rent, he wanted them both to travel and then come home and look at mortgages. The truth is, he knew he was comfortable and sometimes it was hard to face the reality of something new.

After taking Emily home, he jogged the rest of the way to his, the adrenaline kicking in from all the excitement of the evening. His heart was hammering as he opened the door to his flat. Thomas felt incredibly vulnerable even though he locked the door behind him, he felt a significant presence behind him. As he walked down the narrow hallway, he heard Oliver speaking on the phone in the lounge and Thomas breathed a sigh of relief. A little noise of chatter and laughing was comforting and Thomas grabbed a water from the fridge then went to his bedroom trying not to disturb Oliver. He led on his bed, trying to get comfortable. His body was not letting him relax so he decided to look at Earth cam and escape to a new world. He searched for Central Park New York, somewhere he always dreamed of seeing, from the impressive architecture to the peaceful gardens. His computer was in the corner of his bedroom, next to the window. As he took his eyes off the screen, he noticed the light rain starting to patter on the glass and it was almost like a gift of meditation. Instantly relaxing.

SEVEN

Caroline O'Neill sat at her dressing table brushing her hair and feeling optimistic 'it's great that you are coming tonight, Jack, you are actually making an effort' she stared into the mirror, past her reflection, straight at him but he was too busy looking at his phone.

'Hello?'

'Am I talking to myself?' she raised her voice, her frustration growing.

'Sorry I was tweeting a picture of the....'

'Of WHAT?' snapped Caroline. 'Why do you share every little detail of your life Jack ... no! our life! Let's be honest, who really cares what anyone has had for dinner? Or what film they are watching or the fact you have had your precious car cleaned for the THIRD time this week.... '

'Caroline, it's for my peers! My following! My...fans' Jack laughed which just irritated Caroline even more. 'Come on Caz, I mean it's how I define myself, how I build my relationships with my customers – 75% of them are young's with socials, you have to keep yourself in the limelight...'

'By showing people you have your precious Range Rover washed three times a week! How does that...'

'Caz, keeping up appearances is so important in my job'

Caroline was fed up already of this conversation 'are you almost ready? It would be nice to talk to our friends about actual important topics going on in this world' she rose up from her chair. Her bedroom is normally her sacred cocoon where she likes to practice being calm. Unfortunately, whenever Jack was around, that calm was vanquished and she was sick of it.

***

'Denny! Hi! Gerry thanks for coming'

Denise and Gerry walked to the table of the busy restaurant. Denise could sense the tension as soon as she greeted Caroline and Jack. He had a tight jaw as if to be on tender hooks. 'I don't think we have tried this place before have we darling?' Denise smiled at Gerry trying to break the tight atmosphere. They proceeded to sit down; Denise looked around at the artistic pictures hanging from the walls. Laughter filled the room whilst couples and families enjoyed conversations.

It was not long before Jack was smiling down at his phone again

'So, Jack, business going well? Any arousing deals in the pipeline?' Gerry enquired.

'Oh, I'm aroused alright Ger'

Caroline went a lovely shade of red, gritted her teeth and shouted 'Excuse me waitress! A large drink order waiting here when you have a second!'

'Tell me Gerry, do you think social media is taking over all of our lives? Apparently, my husband cannot seem to stay off it' Caroline raised her voice but Jack did not even react or seem to hear.

'Well Caz, I actually think social media can be incredibly useful' smirked Gerry. 'A friend of mine found his long-lost family on one of those ancestry websites – truly amazing really, what you can find out on the internet' Gerry continued. Caroline shot him an evil look but he had chosen to ignore it.

'Lord knows how many seeds you have scattered out there. You may get a knock on the door when your illegitimate kids turn eighteen.'

'Caroline took another large swig. 'We decided not to have kids years ago. I'd rather invest my legacy in some holiday homes – at least you don't have to fork out university fees or wipe asses.

'Well, don't worry babe, one day Safe Travel Holidays will be a dynasty.' Jack grinned. 'Me and you will be reaping the rewards in a villa in Hawaii. 'Aaaand, not forgetting'…he gestured at Gerry 'My ORIGINAL business partner will get a slice of the pie. Maybe not enough for a villa but I daresay enough for a caravan in Skegness.' Jack slapped his knee and roared with laughter.

'My, how generous you are.' Gerry said coolly, sipping his beer. He and Caroline exchanged looks.

'Don't be arrogant, Jack' snapped Caroline. 'We are out with our friends after all.'

'Babe. I'm playing. I've got the Midas touch though. Look how many social media campaigns I've ran- 'Their starters arrived and Jack took a huge bite out of his bread.

'That Twitter hashtag, employing a hot, young team. I headhunted Thomas and Shania. Ben – well he came to me actually but, the point being, they are the team that will attract a millennial and Gen Z customer base. So….to answer my lovely wife's question, Jack swallowed his bread with difficulty. 'Social media may be taking over all our lives and I'm glad! Media means business and business means I can treat you. Caroline …to this!' Jack brandished an envelope at her. It was clear he had been trying to find a way to shoehorn this moment in.

'Caroline opened the envelope.'

'A mini break to Finlake in Devon. Two weeks' time.' Jack rubbed his hands.

A strange, thoughtful look came over Caroline's face. She stared at the confirmation e-mail for a couple of moments.

'A mini break? We go in 2 weeks?'

'Two weeks' babe.'

Gerry was looking over the table, his hands clenching his beer very tightly. Denise was looking at him, a little nervously.

'G-Gerry, are you OK she trembled.'

'Oh. Oh yes, fine.' Gerry seemed to recover and smiled.

Caroline had also regained her composure. 'Well, this is a surprise but...well... thank you...' she leaned over and kissed Jack quickly on the cheek.

'Oh, how romantic.' Denise squealed. 'Wish you would book in a romantic getaway for us Gerry.'

'I will my darling. Gerry smiled across at her and patted her hand. 'As soon as I retire and get my settlement from Jack from what I poured into the Safe Travel ...I will pour it into a trip anywhere you want!'

'Oooh how about a Mediterranean cruise? I've always loved to see The Parthenon.'

'If that is your wish, my dear.' Gerry smiled.

'In a way, I wish I was retiring' said Denise, picking nervously at her salad. 'The hospital can get so stressful.'

'You still in record keeping Denise?' asked Caroline.

Denise nodded. 'It's so -urgh. I'm so behind the times. They've introduced this new database and I cannot get my head around it. Every day they give me boxes and boxes of records to scan and put on the system. It's horrendous. I spent ten hours a day in a dingy basement on the lower ground floor. Feels more like a mausoleum than a hospital.'

'Well, anytime you can get a few days off, you are welcome to come to me to Lisbon.' Caroline smiled. 'A girls holiday maybe? If you ask me, Portugal is simply the most beautiful country on Earth, nothing can rival it. With the most beautiful men too.' She smiled slyly at Jack.

'Oi! He said.'

'Well, it's true. Cristiano Ronaldo is gorgeous.'

'Gorgeous? He's not a real man!'

'Well, let's just say you have had your fun Jack, so I can have my pick of the menu from time to time.' Caroline smirked.

Jack didn't seem to know what to do with that information. There was a brief awkward silence before he downed his beer.

'Waiter, waiter! Another round please!!!'

There were small beads of sweat on his face.

The rest of the meal passed without much incident, the conversation turned to small talk and chatter but underneath the clink of cutlery and the drizzle of wine into glasses, four people sat at that one table, eating, drinking and each filled with a head of so many things unsaid...so many secrets...it was enough to make anyone want to explode.......

EIGHT

Ben was sat at the bar, the alcohol seeping through his veins as he played with a placemat and ripped the sides. 'A clear sign of frustration' he laughed to himself. He spent all day staring at that face at work and then just wanted to come to the bar for a much-needed drink and there he was again. Thomas sat smug with his girlfriend opposite him. It just reminded Ben of everything he did not have. Ben was lonely.

He decided to fly solo many moons ago. He could not deal with rejection anymore. Rejection from just about everyone in his life. Family members, women in bars, ex-girlfriends, friends that were always 'too busy' to spend time with him. Although recently, he felt more emotionally starved for real companionship. Sometimes he felt incredibly disconnected and really uncomfortable in his own skin. Why did he feel so uncomfortable around Thomas? They actually have more in common than Ben would like to admit. Both had dads that did not want to know them or even want to admit they exist. He felt like Thomas just came in out of nowhere and took centre stage in his life. Ben used to get given the sales. Ben used to get offered on lunches with Jack. Ben would be the number one person to see for any fantastic holiday offer and now he heard today from Gerry that Jack was arranging an upcoming birthday present for Thomas.

Some lads trip somewhere to play golf and have beers. Why was nothing mentioned to Ben? Why was he left out? Gerry said he was told to keep his mouth shut about it which made Ben feel even more resentful. Gerry was not invited either and said not to worry about it but no offense to Gerry, he barely drank. Jack knew how much Ben liked a beverage. Gerry then tried to backtrack and soften the blow and said that it was probably because the relationship between Ben and Thomas was strained so Jack would not want to put Ben in an 'uncomfortable position'. Uncomfortable position? Ha. Bullshit.' he laughed out loud.

Ben grabs his phone from his pocket and brings up Facebook. As if by habit, he cannot resist but go straight to the search bar typing 'Agnes Grey'. He hovers over the message bar, opening and closing it several times. He looks for the green dot to indicate she is online but there is nothing. He misses her but he just can't deal...

After another swig of alcohol, Ben checks his bumble profile 'No new notifications' He goes on to check if anyone has accepted his friend requests. No new requests. Just then, an email from 'payday loans' advising another missed payment, he swipes left quickly to delete. Ben swallows hard 'Hey another top up over here!' slamming his beer glass down. Ben clicks back once again to Facebook, clicks on Agnes and begins to type: 'hi I know it's been a long time but I need some help, I am running short on funds and......'

Ben freezes mid message, a grin spreading across his face as he looks up at the tv above the bar. 'MTV's Catfish' another poor sucker taken for all they are worth.

Ben signs up and logs on to an old profile. A profile he hasn't used in a long time. 'Kellie Hawke'

She is 28 years old. Born and bred in Portsmouth. Her picture is actually someone from the USA, partying hard with cocktails in hand. Attractive. Attractive to other people unlike Ben. The profile has 859 friends but has probably only spoken to five of them. No one needs to know. Kelly Hawke needs to make some money. Fast. Who can we message? Who would fall for a poor but gorgeous girl in need of money to 'help her grandmother get the care she needs?'

Ben changes the profile picture. Kellie is now in a boob tube top covering nothing. Perfect. Ben smirks and he scrolls through 'friends you may know'.

'Gerry Hobbes' hmmm retirement fund? Nah... too in love with his wife. There is only one person who can help him. The number one womaniser. Jack O'Neill.

***

In the office the next day, Ben keeps his eye on Jack over his computer screen. Jack was absolutely loving the conversation between 'Kellie' and himself. Why wouldn't he? She's sexy, she is young, and she is seemingly interested.

Ben just wants what he is owed.

'You look a bit worse for wear today Ben' commented Gerry as he collected his paperwork from the printer. Ben pursed his lips 'you know how it is Ger... out late with friends watching the footy.'

'Who was playing last night? I am looking forward to going to some matches when I am out of here' Gerry smiled.

Ben's smile faded. 'Oh.... I err.... Can't remember ha-ha!'

Gerry waits, a strange look on his face.

'Manchester City! That's who its was' Ben laughed. 'My brain is like a sieve'

He looked down at his phone feeling more relaxed when Gerry did not press further.

Message to Kellie

'You definitely need to come in to Safe Travel.... Come and see what U can do for you 😕

Ben looked over to Jack who was smirking down at his phone as Shania walked in with the coffees and Ben witnessed Jack lock his phone quickly, and put it under some new brochures.

Jack put the blinds down and closed the office door.

He typed another message to Jack:

So maybe if I did come in to the work place, I could book some 'extra activities' but first I want to know more about you'

Ben hesitated as he went to press send at the same time - a text message received advising of a maxed overdraft.

'Shit!'

Ben hovered, his conscious playing a weird game of tennis. He shouldn't be doing this right? ...Yes, he should...he was just doing his research...he needed to be sure before he made his next move. When would his next move be? No... this was completely the wrong way...but.

He thought about the final demand letters. The warning of eviction. The late credit card warnings....

It's now or never.

He pressed Send

Message sent.

Ben sat back, heart pounding. He just needed to sit back and wait for the reply.

It came almost instantaneously.

'What would you like to know babe?'

'Are you married?' Ben typed.

Jack replied:

'I am but its legal only. No love anymore there babe.'

'Do you have kids?' Ben typed furiously.... he sat almost with his nose to the screen.

This time the reply took a few moments.

'No. Never had kids. Never wanted them hun. Too much expense! I would put my balls in vinegar before having kids. Complete waste of time haha....so back to you babe.'

Jack clearly wanted to get off the topic. Ben let him. However, there were certainly a few topics he would make Jack talk about with 'Kellie' again...

NINE

Thomas sat on the bus the next day; eyelids heavy from his lack of sleep. He noticed several missed calls from Emily on his phone from last night. He had been so engrossed with Earth Cam, that he completely forgot to text her to say he was home safely. He began to reply when he looked up and noticed the man in the trilby hat getting on to the bus. Thomas groaned and looked outside in the hope the man would not notice him. 'Good morning young man, you look tired?'

Thomas lifted his head and the old man had sat on the seat just across from him. Thomas politely looked across and managed a smile. The man's eyes were so heavily lidded and weighed down with wrinkled folds that it was almost like talking to someone asleep, yet he was quite alert. 'I do feel tired today and I know I look it' replied Thomas. A couple of people turned around in their seats to almost examine if what he was saying was true. Thomas smiled politely back at them feeling slightly irritated that they were listening in to his conversation.

'Don't worry son, you still don't look as old as I feel' the old man laughed which then made him cough quite fiercely. 'You remind me of my son,' said the old man. 'I do? How come?' replied Thomas. 'He is overworked too with the weight of the world on his shoulders it seems. I don't know. In my day, it was much more work AND play but these days ...' the man paused and Thomas waited for the man to continue. 'These days it's all about the shilling earnt, nothing but greed and the cyberspace' the man continued and Thomas noticed the deep worry lines protruding in his forehead. 'You mean pounds earnt' Thomas smiled softly but it seemed like the man did not hear him. Thomas noticed that the people on the bus had moved several seats down the bus. 'Do I smell or something?' he grinned to the old man who was rummaging in his shopping trolley for something. 'Here son, spray some of this old spice. I used to have to fight the ladies off with this stuff' he offered. Thomas did not want to appear rude so took the bottle from the man and sprayed his wrist. He got a huge waft of cinnamon and it definitely smelt like it had been in the man's trolley for at least 20 years. He grimaced. 'Thank you' said Thomas handing the bottle back to the man and he noticed the age spots all over his hand. The bus rocked from side to side as they travelled down the familiar roads. 'Where are you off today?' asked Thomas. 'I go to the cemetery to visit my wife several times a week. It gets me out the house,' replied the man and Thomas smiled thinking to himself 'that is such dedication'. They were reaching Thomas' stop when the man asked 'son what is your name?'

'Thomas', he said, shaking the old man's hand. 'Yours?'

'My name is Stanley. Stanley Addington. Call me Stan if you like' replied the man.

'It was nice talking with you Stan, I'll see you soon'

As Thomas got in to work, he saw Shania leaving a note on his desk. 'Hey Shania, I'm here, what's up?' 'Oh, hey babe, I'm just making arrangements for Gerry's leaving party, we need to get some dates in the diary' Shania said. 'I didn't even know he was leaving? Has it been announced? Said Thomas surprised.

'Oh, Jack told me, sorry I thought you knew' replied Shania, chewing her gum loudly and looking a bit red faced. 'Shania, I tried a new aftershave on today, have a whiff' Thomas said grinning and waiting for her to grimace in shock.

'Babes, I cannot smell anything on you I'm afraid! You may want to get your money back'. She walked off swiftly in her high heels heading straight for Jack's office. Hmmm there is definitely something going on there Thomas thought to himself. He was surprised Gerry was leaving. He did just celebrate his 64th birthday so Thomas guessed he was finally going to take some time for himself.

Ben walked in late as usual but did not seem to have a care in the world. He was getting worse with this recently. Thomas was not sure if it was even possible but Ben seemed even more slow moving today. He got himself a coffee from the machine and sat down with his phone texting away so quickly that Thomas could only imagine that it was either a potential love interest or another useless and time-consuming game of crushing candy or whatever it was called.

The whole team piled into the meeting room with Jack as usual at the head of the table. Shania sat very close by just looking at Jack up and down like he was a slab of cake and she was on a sugar free diet. You could tell that Jack was enjoying the attention though as he loosened his collar a bit as if the heat was getting to him. He kept staring down Shania's blouse as if he did not care who was watching.

Ben sat slumped in his chair clearly uninterested whilst Gerry looked pretty relaxed. 'So would I be if I was about to become a man of leisure' Thomas thought to himself.

'We have a couple of announcements' said Jack picking up the paper in front of him and straightening the corners. Firstly, Gerry is leaving us, he is retiring to enjoy more time with his family' said Jack 'so we are arranging a small gathering at the Dolphin pub in town, hoping for tomorrow night if you can all make it? I know it's late notice, sorry about that kids' he smirked. Jack was clearly too busy womanising than to keep us in the loop Ben muttered. Thomas turned and looked at him, surprised by his comment but for once he agreed with him. Shania gave Ben a dirty look and shuffled in her seat awkwardly. Gerry laughed, enjoying the banter between everyone.

'Secondly, I would like to give our Thomas a massive pat on the back for his meaty sale this week with the Marshalls. Not only did he secure the trip but all the additional extras they took on, will mean we get a good bonus from this. Thomas I could not be prouder of ya kid' Jack smiled. He handed Thomas an envelope and everyone around the table knew what this meant. Joy comes in such wonderful different flavours and Thomas wanted to savour this moment. For the first time in a long time, his body relaxed and instead of tingles in his hands he would normally get from anxiety, he just felt warmth and a buzz run through him.

'Drinks on you tomorrow night then Tom?' Ben smirked. He had a murderous look on his face as he put his head down, Thomas noticed as he thanked the team for the support. 'I tell you what team, if I did ever get stuck with a sprog, I would want this guy' Jack gripped Thomas' shoulder with pride.

Oh gawd, its Mother's Day coming up again! Every year I struggle with what to spoil my mum with. Like... I take her to the oh so fabulous nail salon every year which she loves but....'

'Shania, Mother's Day is at the end of March' Gerry laughed. 'You have plenty of time to panic! Join me the day before like everyone else!'

'Plus, can I just say that sounds riveting' Ben sneered as he slurped on his milk shake.

'Shut up Ben, it's called being prepared AND it's the thought that counts.' Shania stomped off. 'I'm taking 10 Jack' she grabbed her Chanel purse and headed for the door.

Thomas looked up from his desk, studently hesitant to carry on this conversation.

'You know, you can put the ladies off Ben making snide remarks like that.' Thomas said hoping to swiftly get passed the subject of mothers.

'Treat 'em mean and all that Tom Tom' Ben fired back.

'Ah yes I remember this rule,' laughed Gerry. 'If a boy is horrid to a girl in the playground it means he likes her. Except Ben, this is not a playground and you want to impress her not piss her off' Gerry winked.

'Speaking of Mother's Day....' Gerry starts

Jesus, why are we bringing this up again

'My mum is in her 90s so I will probably go visit with Denny before hitting the town, scoring some drugs and partying like you kids do. Jack, do you still get discounts in MNS?' laughed Gerry.

'I am sure your mum will appreciate an MNS voucher eh Thomas' Jack cackled as he threw a half-eaten muffin in the bin.

'You don't talk about your family much Thomas, what does your mum do for a living? Gerry said lightly.

Why does it feel like he is stirring the pot? Is it my imagination?

'It's um… it's a complicated one actually' said Thomas, struggling to continue.

Gerry, Ben and Jack were quietly sat almost waiting for him to carry on.

'We have a dysfunctional relationship to be honest'

Ben looked interested then turning to face Thomas with almost a genuine look – as if triggered by the conversation.

'I haven't seen her in a long while…we don't…. ger on. If I do see her, it's always difficult almost like I have to be pretend everything is fine as if to not …. set her off. Like I am wearing a …'mask' Ben and Thomas said simultaneously then and looked at each other with surprise.

Jack rolled his eyes as if bored of this topic now 'Hey Ger, can we discuss handovers'

Gerry reluctantly got up from his chair as if disappointed to be missing something.

'So, you really aren't a fan of your mum then?'

Thomas didn't respond.

'It's funny really. Agnes…. My…my mother, we are not close either. Not for the last few years anyway' Ben wheeled his chair over taking Thomas by surprise.

'With my mum, Dolores… she never…. I mean, nothing was ever good enough' Thomas added. 'She drank too much, all the time. I had to grow up and find my own way pretty quick.' Thomas looked down sadly and Ben's facial features softened as he listened.

'I know what you mean about having to find your own way. Especially as I could only count on myself in the end' Ben said quietly.

Thomas sat forward in his chair 'oh god, I'm sorry… in the end? Did she…. is she still here?'

'Yes, she is still here but I chose to walk'. 'It was my choice' Ben added.

Thomas refrains from commenting too much.

Can I trust him? Are we actually bonding right now?

'Agnes was the centre of my world for so long but when I began to ask questions about where I really came from... who my father is....'

'.... Which you have every right to do' nodded Thomas.

'Sometimes I think Agnes is right. She said I will be led down a black hole of lies and disappointment if I look into the past.' Ben stopped and took a deep breath.

'So, were you?' Thomas said.

'What?'

'Disappointed?'

'Oh, I definitely am....'

Thomas frowned as the followed Ben's eyes over to Gerry and Jack coming out of the office.

TEN

Jack could be a frustrating man but Thomas felt like he was under endless obligation to please his boss. He could not keep hold of a job for longer than a month before he met Jack. Thomas was working in a local newsagent when Jack had come in to buy some travel magazines. They started talking at the till point about a magazine about travelling to Italy. Thomas immediately impressed him with his knowledge of Italy: Venice - the great city of canals...the great renaissance masterpiece of Michelangelo's 'David' located in Florence... Thomas explained to Jack that he could plan an entire itinerary inspired by a single interest, from the Renaissance art to enjoying the natural attractions of the dramatic coastline, lakes or the outstanding, picturesque mountains. Jack stood there a stunned, impressed look on his face and offered Thomas an interview at his local travel firm (STH). 'You are just what I need at my place, what was your name, Mr Knowledgeable?' Thomas grinned and accepted the interview and received the phone call within the hour from Jack. He joined the team a week later and quickly established himself as a high flier, both with his colleagues and the customers, instantly much to the look of disgust of Ben, Jack's golden employee standing nearby.

'Tell me Jack, how did you and Ben end up working together? It does seem like a bit of an odd pairing' asked Thomas as they packed up. Everyone else had returned to their desks and Shania had gone on one of her 'coffee runs' which was more like heading to a few shops, marinating herself in the department stores' latest perfumes and coming back with cold caffeine.

'Well, it was simple really, he came in at a very busy time. We were snowed under and he was desperate for a job,' laughed Jack.

'So, was he always ... like this?' questioned Thomas.

'I have noticed a change in his mood and work ethic. I have to say lad' replied Jack. 'Ben was always a hard worker like yourself. He always looked to please. He booked the holidays and hit all the sales targets! He used to be my golden boy… ha till you came along'. Jack continued 'The kid never did well with any competition.' Jack hesitated 'Between you and I Thomas, it's not just you he is in competition with. He hates the fact that the ladies flock to me as well. You can see it on his face when they come in to see me specifically. What can I say, I'm a silver fox' Jack laughed. 'Oh, I forgot to say Tom, the security lad that looks after Petersons has been questioning when we are going to sort our security cameras out. Obviously, we do not leave any money here overnight but I have asked Shania to look into some for us and left her a list of websites to find the best price. Make sure she doesn't go for the most expensive, eh? Whilst I am away, can you keep an eye on the place? I'm sure it will be fine but I was thinking you could use that Earth cam of yours if need be? At least until we get this equipment rolling.

Thomas rolled his eyes and said 'are you still taking your wife to the cabin this weekend then?'

'I sure am lad, there is plenty of me to go around.' Jack winked and walked out.

'Ben what are you doing at my desk? Thomas asked as he walked out of the meeting room. Thomas did not like anyone near his desk.

A desk is like a personal space for someone, almost like a bedroom, everything set out perfectly. What the fuck is he doing invading my space

'Back off Thomas, I was only answering your phone. I noted the message on this post it notes? See' Ben said sharply, holding up the slip of yellow paper.

'Sorry Ben…thank you for taking the message' Thomas nodded. Ben looked frustrated but calmed down after Thomas thanked him. 'Did you see Jack and Shania? Ben said. 'Could they be any more *obvious*?'

'We just have to let him get on with it, Ben. You like Shania, do you? Thomas questioned but Ben did not answer and just slumped back in his seat.

That's a yes then Thomas thought to himself. He understood why. Shania was a good-looking woman that was for sure but nobody compared to Emily in his eyes. Maybe Shania could bring something positive out in Ben though?

He was trying to stop himself from cleaning Ben's desk. Not just a cursory clean up either, he wanted to bleach the whole thing and go through files, shred unwanted papers and get rid of those used coffee cups.

Thomas snapped out of his daydream of cleaning when the office door opened. 'Hi there, can I speak to Jack please? It's urgent'. A tall, tanned, dark haired woman walked in clearly on a mission and walked towards Jack's office confidently. Immediately, Thomas and Ben looked straight at Shania who had a face like thunder. She followed the woman with the eyes of a hawk as she entered Jack's office. Jack held the door open with a massive smirk on his face and proceeded to shut the blinds. Thomas felt bad for Shania and simultaneously bad for Ben who was clearly into her. Seeing your crush completed besotted with someone else must hurt.

'I remember batting the women away in my day,' laughed Gerry. Shania looked at him blankly, clearly not appreciating the comment.

'Sorry Shan but I have seen a lot of women go into that office the last few months. Some even leave messages and phone numbers for him that he's barely even met. You are a young, beautiful lady. Get yourself out there' Gerry said kindly. Shania started reapplying her lipstick whilst keeping one eye on the office door.

The phone rang and Ben picked up the call with a smile on his face knowing that if he could arrange a customer coming in, he could get a sale under his belt.

'Hi Mr Dunn, how can I help you?'

Mr Dunn was currently on a work trip with some clients. Ben arranged the itinerary and the whole office knew about it because he boasted about it for a week or more. 'What do you mean the...?' Ben immediately sat up from his slump, heat travelling up his neck.

'That is what was arranged Mr Dunn! It was a 4-star deluxe....' 'I don't understand... well back at you! shove it up your ass Dunn' Ben shouted loudly much to the surprise and horror of everyone.

Jack was just walking out his office with the sun kissed beauty to hear the end of the conversation and see Ben slam down the phone. She hurried out the door clearly having got what she came for.

'BEN GREY. IN MY OFFICE NOW, SON!' Jack roared.

It was minutes before the door burst open again and Ben came out in tears of rage.

What the fuck do you mean you have to let me go? screamed Ben.

'YOU CANNOT SPEAK TO OUR CUSTOMERS THE WAY YOU JUST DID!

'AFTER ALL THE HARD WORK I'VE PUT IN!!'

'Lad, don't think I don't notice you swanning off to Starbucks for an hours at a time. You used to be so dedicated, now I just don't know you anymore!'

'This was YOUR idea' Ben turned to Thomas and yelled. 'That's why you stayed behind in the meeting room today isn't it? You were discussing getting rid of me! This is what you wanted all along'

Ben was spitting venom as Thomas sat in shock.

'I I I didn't know any of this Ben honestly' he spluttered. Ben had completely lost it and had become a victim of his inner storm. He was triggered and it was too late. Every move he made; was like he had a clock ticking inside his head. Possibly another countdown till the next explosion. He started kicking the tables and throwing chairs until he saw Jack's beloved portrait picture on the wall. Jack loved that thing.

It was one of those pictures that could not be possibly taken on a phone, printed and framed. Jack had a professional photographer come in and spent hours getting just the right pose. Afterall, his face was the face of the business and 'made the ladies come in for a visit' in his words.

'BEN NO!' Shania screamed but it was too late. Ben surveyed Jack as if waiting for a reaction, daring him to do it. He grabbed the frame and violently smashed it on the floor, shards of glass scattered everywhere.

Jack stood there with an unreadable expression but Thomas was waiting for him to blow up in anger. Jack looked tense with a tightness in his face, unsure what to do or say next.

'FUCK YOUR JOB!' Ben shouted and stormed out, leaving a ringing silence.

'LOOK, I'LL GIVE YOU TWO WEEKS' NOTICE. YOU CAN RESIGN, OK?!...BEN... BEN!!!!!

Jack for one seemed speechless. His face was now an ashen grey and he kept open and closing his mouth like a guppy. He suddenly was far from the attractive man he fashioned himself as.

'What are you all looking at. Back to work' he said very quietly, going back into his office and shutting the door.

Shania burst into tears.

'Don't get upset, love.' Gerry consoled her. 'Look, the shop is due to close in half hour anyway.

'Should we go after Ben?' asked Thomas.

'I will go after Ben. You two, get your coats, we are closing. I doubt Jack will object.

It was up to Thomas to see Shania safely on the bus home. He back tracked back to the office, debating whether to check on Jack, then decided against it.

His eye then caught Gerry. He had clearly managed to track down Ben. Gerry had his arm around Ben's shoulders and was steering him into a nearby pub.

For some unknown reason, Thomas felt a terrible flash of dread, like something terrible was about to happen. Very quickly the feeling vanished. He turned on his heel and left for home

ELEVEN

'Can you believe he is firing me, Gerry? I mean what the hell? I do not deserve that' cried Ben as he punched his fists on the bar.

'You are not exactly helping your case throwing furniture around like a teenager in a strop' said Gerry sharply. His eyes searched Ben's and softened 'I know Jack's relationship with Thomas has bothered you massively, it would me if I learned he gave a pay rise to all of you and not me'

'He what?' Ben raised his voice listening intently. 'He hasn't' Gerry backtracked. 'I am just trying to make a point son'.

Ben pressed his thumbs to his skull and was unsure what to think anymore. 'You still need to come to my leaving do and stick at my side; I'll look after you' Gerry said. 'The truth is, If I was in your shoes, I would be pissed too. Thomas seems to think he is the big shot but of all my years in the business, I would describe him as a very average sales person'.

'People like Thomas will always try to rise to the top and they will do whatever it takes no matter who gets in their path.'

'So, you agree this is all Thomas' fault?' said Ben bitterly.

'I wouldn't say that, Jack is older and should know better but I have honestly never met a man that has made so many bad decisions' clarified Gerry. 'The bloke can't even stick to one woman so Thomas is like the new toy to play with. He is the flavour of the month you know?' 'Jack is the one to not be happy with here really? I remember when he said something derogatory about Denise, I was so angry with him' Gerry said 'let's just say my wife is not a fan of his'

'What did he say?' Ben replied. Gerry did not reply but went on to explain:

'Did you know, long before you joined the business, Jack and I were equal partners? We went into the business together and I put in most of my life savings to make it work. I paid for the premises, the training, the computers, you name it. Jack came to me as a fresh entrepreneur who had studied Travel and Tourism. I was working for 'Going places' at the time and was desperate to open my own company. Jack had come in with many of his women through the years and eventually we got talking on a more business level. At the start it appeared that we had the same vision. In most successful businesses, you have one person who is the visionary leader, so one with the ideas. Then you have the 'get stuff sorted' person.' explained Gerry. 'He had the gift of the gab and the sales ability and described us as the Ying and yang'

'Which one were you' said Ben listening intently. He looked up to Gerry and he always felt like he could confide in him.

'I had the knowledge and the money as I had been saving for years but Jack just knew people. He was younger and he convinced me that I needed him. It did not take long till he wanted more of a share, more than the 50% agreed. What was strange was that he knew my wife and I were struggling for money and soon after she became quite unwell so I had to take time off. He would make digs about putting in 15-hour days and I did not do my share. Of course, I could not put in my share whilst Denise needed me at home. In the end he convinced me that he would take on the business himself as 'reputation was everything' to him. During my time away, it became a bit toxic and Jack could not handle it all. I could not think of ways to increase profits when I was busy making sure Denise had the shopping she needed, making sure she had her medication and ensuring she got enough sleep. 'Can I tell you something Ben?'

Ben leaned in: 'Of course'.

'I had a feeling there was some fraudulent behaviour at one point, something unethical but whenever I questioned it, I was made to feel guilty after all 'we were in a bit of a mess' because of me and in the end, I decided to let him buy me out.' Gerry said thoughtfully.

'That's awful mate. To put such worries on you when Denise was unwell. You must have been devastated to give up your share' Ben said emphatically.

'He promised I would always have my job and as I got older, I was almost grateful to not have the stress Ben, and I never did lose my job and then eventually you came along and became his favourite'

'You must have hated me' Ben replied

'I had and have no reason to hate you Ben but my point is, everyone is just a number in this world and no matter what happens, you can always be replaced. A small ant in a big colony. One thing is for sure though, one day, Jack's number will be up one day'. Gerry took a long sip of his whiskey, his eyes narrowed, drilling into Ben. He swallowed hard. Oh yes. Up. One. Day.

TWELVE

It was the evening of Gerry's leaving party. Emily had strewn newly ironed clothes across the bed. She had finally decided on her dark purple silk top and jeans and was now sat at the dresser, winding her hair into curls. Thomas winced at the clothes and his fingers twitched, longing to hang them in the closet. To distract himself, he settled himself on the edge of the bed, knotting his fingers together. Their eyes met in the mirror.

'You look nice' he smiled, watching her hair ribbon over her shoulders as she tugged the curling iron through. She paused for a second and a sad smile came upon her face.

'Thank you...you haven't said that to me in a while.'

'I know. I should say it more often.' He meant it.

She turned back to her reflection. 'Are you going like that Tom?'

Thomas looked down at his jeans and polo shirt. 'I was going to. Why, don't you like it?'

She shrugged. 'It's fine but...it's a leaving do. You look a bit every day. Why don't you wear that nice red shirt I got you for Christmas?'

Thomas obediently went to the closet, using it as a good excuse to scoop some of the clothes off of the bed and hang them up. He had an uneasy feeling about tonight. He felt tired. Distracted. He wasn't even looking forward to tonight and wished he and Emily were ordering a Just Eat and binge-watching Netflix...

'Are you looking forward to coming tonight, Em?'

'Well, it will certainly be interesting to see everyone' Emily said brightly, now applying mascara. 'Is Ben making an appearance by the way?' she asked cautiously, glimpsing around at him. 'I can't believe he tried to blame you for Jack's decision' she added.

Thomas, in the middle of buttoning felt his hands become clammy. *Jeez I can't be assed to face all this crap.*

'Yeah, he is coming' he replied. He is still fired apparently; I think Jack managed to calm him down when they went out for lunch'. *Jack always has the gift of the gab*

'I just cannot help but feel guilty' he cried suddenly.

Emily looked at him in the mirror again. 'Tom, whatever for??'

'Ben has been there a lot longer than me and I feel like I'm well...kind on. To blame' he replied sadly. 'I sold the holiday to Iceland. I get the recognition. Everyone kisses my ass.' he was pacing now 'That's what made Ben lose it. Now he's out on his ear. I should have just let him make the sale and he's still had a job!' He began digging his nails into his palm. *That's it. Let me feel pain. I deserve it.*

'Thomas! Tom! Stop it! Emily spun herself from the chair, went to him and grabbed his wrists. Look at me. You're freaking me out. Do not EVER apologise for being good at your job Tom'. Her hands went from his wrists to his face. They were cool, comforting. *That feels so good.* It's not your fault that Ben turned into such a lazy twat. If you ask me, I think, frankly, that he has an anger issue. The way he went on at you like that!?' Thomas stood half

listening, his hands were now over Emily's, pressing her to him.

'Why do you immediately assume it's your fault? She whispered to Thomas, pulling him down next to her to sit on the bed.

Thomas pressed his head to her forehead. He had a strange, almost menacing desire to grab Emily, throw her on the bed and begin making mad love to her. She was his comfort. He did not want to go down this rabbit hole. He'd spent so many years keeping those memories in check like a bubbling cauldron. Forever simmering. Forever leaking. But contained. But now here, the words began tumbling from his mouth like water...

'I suppose it's where my mother used to blame me for absolutely everything that went wrong when I was younger'. He swallowed, whispered. 'If she felt lonely, it was my fault and I was not spending enough time with her. If she forgot an item when home from food shopping, it would be my fault because I distracted her'.... it...it...' Emily clutched him tighter and he felt her encouragement in her grip.

'It was even my fault when I was up in my bedroom and she burnt herself on the oven. I...I. know she was not well, she's still not well of course. It is the constant mocking, the looks and the judgement with Ben but it reminds me of the memories back in my room at home. I would hide from my mother at the back of my wardrobe. She would come upstairs with her slipper just to hit me when she felt someone needed punishing. It was mostly mental abuse with her but regardless the scars remain the same' Why am I telling you this. You will want to run away. Leave me. I don't blame you.

'Well, you know I've only met her a handful of times' Emily said quietly. 'When was the last time you went to see her?'

'Well, I think it's best you keep your distance from her, don't you agree? Thomas snapped, suddenly out of his trance. His fingers tightened around Emily's fingers, prising them from his face that had become alarmingly damp. Wiping his eyes furiously, he stood up, turned his back on her and went to grip the chest of drawers, breathing hard.

'Tom'. Emily whispered. 'Tom, I don't like this, you are scaring me.'

Remorse flooded him. He couldn't lose Emily. He'd forgive her this time. Screw it. Let's get hammered. He turned to face her smiling.

'Sorry' he whispered. 'I just. It's not the right time to talk about ...this...now... and anyway' he made a pained attempt to smile at her. To restore the balance. We've got a leaving party to attend to. He held up his aftershave. 'Will Hugo Boss do?'....

Half an hour later, Thomas and Emily were walking hand in hand and arriving at the Dolphin pub. The air was warm and the pleasant sound of gulls and sea spray carried their way. Southsea pier was a bit further up and already the streets were beginning to fill with the first of the University's student revellers. The Dolphin was a bit shabby to attract students but was nicely priced with a friendly enough proprietor. The floor was old, dusty and the decoration was sparse. A chipped dartboard hung on the wall surrounded by some middle-aged men. A creaky jukebox was on the other side of the room, playing some old 90's hits.

Old chipped wooden tables, worn mats and torn seats were arranged without any real pattern and was occupied with mostly groups of middle-aged men and women. At the back of the room was a crescent bar. Thomas and Emily made their way to the back of the room where there was a small 'function' section with a tatty rope segregating the area. Two large tables had been set up, labelled 'Safe Travel Holidays 8pm' with limp looking sandwiches and other 'party food fare'. The pub had tried to compensate by hanging some balloons by the large windows. Thomas's colleagues were already there and seated with drinks on the table. Gerry was in the centre, smiling amiably, and nodded as they took their seats.

'Hey Gerry, so you're free'. Grinned Thomas.'

'I am indeed, dear boy!' Gerry raised his whiskey up. He was already looking red in the face. He had brought the leaving card from everyone and placed it at the centre of the table. 'Lovely messages. What a great team. I'm going to miss you all.' He beamed at them although the beam seemed to dip a bit when it reached Jack, Thomas thought. Shania was wearing a ridiculously low-cut top and a skirt that was practically a belt. Her ear lobes drooped with the sheer weight of her earrings. She had doused herself with perfume which almost knocked them out as she reached towards Gerry.

'Gerry. BABES!!! What's 'STA going to be like without ya?? I'll miss my office dad!'

'I'll miss you too lovely. Gerry said, blowing a kiss at her. 'Hey Thomas! Don't just sit there, go and get your lovely lady a drink!'

'Emily grinned and turned to him. 'You heard the man, let's go!'

They got up and Thomas risked a glance at the corner of the table where Ben was sat, silent, looking at his phone. Thomas desperately wanted to make eye contact. To smile. To let him know that he was sorry for Ben. But Ben did not look up and feeling like he was in purgatory, Thomas followed Emily to the bar and ordered a pint and a Gin and Tonic....'

* * *

As the evening wore on, the colleagues got more and more raucous. Pint after pint was downed. Shrieks were made to the bartender for more Jägermeister shots which made Thomas almost throw up. He threw up his hands in the air' No more. NO more'. He slurred but Shania was already winding her way back to the table with another round.

'TWO FOR ONE BABES!!' She screamed. 'TOM-TOM, YOU BORING B-BASTARD... GET THEM DOWN YA!!!! WHOOOHOOO!!!!' Emily had gone to the Jukebox and put a fiver in and it was now vibrating playing the best of the 2010's. At this moment, Bruno Mars was wailing about a grenade...or it could be a braid... Thomas wasn't sure he knew anymore. His stomach was swirling and he was feeling very dizzy. But this was good. Very good. The cauldron was bubbling. It couldn't ever flow over...'

Across the table some other colleagues were playing a drinking game, capital cities of Europe with Gerry!

'Right Gez! Let's see how a career in travel has educated you! Capital of Germany?

'Ea-easy' Gerry slurred. 'B-Berlin'.

'Denmark?

'Copenhagen'.

'Argh, you're too good bro. How about.... LITHUANIA???

'Gerry screwed his face up...V-V-Vi...no, RIGA!!

'WRONG!! VILNIUS YOU OLD GIT!! AND YOU WORKED IT TRAVEL??!! CHUGG CHUGG CHUGG!!!'

There was already the odd evil glance and one comment made by Jack which turned into a hurricane of insults from Shania which ended with her stormed off to the bar. 'Women eh Thomas. Sometimes I wonder...' Jack laughed.

Emily, who was on her tenth G&T had slumped in her chair and was propping her head up with her elbow. However, Thomas could tell she was still sentient; she had watched the exchange between Jack and Shania silently but with narrowed eyes as if to say: I beg you to finish that sentence and you will have me to deal with next.

Jack really did not help himself, Thomas concluded, sipping his pint. The guy meant .... hell no, the guy didn't even always mean well. He was so...combative... constantly batting out opinions and making misogynistic comments to get a rise out of people; he didn't care about being liked, as long as the spotlight was on him. The worst thing was that women gravitated towards it; they mistook the arrogance for confidence and saw him as a wild beast to tame. However, Thomas thought ruefully. One minute you are a predator, the next the prey...

Oi Thomasina!!! Jack left his chair and staggered to the one next to Thomas. He reeked of real ale. 'Come...s-see!' He leant over Thomas and held the phone in front of Thomas's face. It was not only real ale, sweat was leaking from his pores, making the alcohol in Thomas's stomach lurch.

'S-Scroll, Thomasina-scroll.' Thomas obediently placed his finger on the screen. The place looked very inviting with the two people in the photo grinning as their legs intertwined under the water of the hot tub, holding up glasses of champagne. It looked very private, very romantic, especially with the low lights placed just perfectly behind the couple. Despite his internal monologue, Thomas felt slightly jealous.

'Look Thomasina, this will be me and the Mrs, all day in the tub, drinking till early hours, plenty of.' Jack winked. 'I ...'

'I think you should concentrate on getting things back on track as you say, get out that doghouse, eh?' Thomas muttered impatiently. 'After all, that's why you wanted it booked right?'

Shania did not look impressed as she walked back to the table and Thomas wondered if she had heard his comments. She looked at Thomas with scrutinising eyes that frowned under her perfectly shaped eyebrows. She had clearly done a few shots before she walked back to the table but it seemed that all was forgiven very quickly. Jack had quickly lost interest in the conversation between him and Thomas and had now turned his attention back to Shania and the flirty banter between her and Jack started up again. 'Jack, your stubble is tickling my neck' she giggled as he whispered something probably inappropriate in her ear.

Ben was staring across the table at Jack and Shania, but Thomas could not read what Ben was thinking. He was getting way too drunk. He glanced at the clock. Eleven O'clock. Must be last orders any minute. He could hear murmurs of his colleagues talking about going to Time & Envy. He had a sudden urge to go dancing, to immerse himself in the beats of club music, to forget...

So, Emily, have you always wanted to work in accounts? Do you ever miss the social side of pub work?' Ben was clearly trying to not pay attention to the lion and its 'prey;' across the table. However, he was still making a point of not looking in Thomas's direction.

'I don't remember mentioning about being a barmaid?' replied Emily sharply. She appeared to realise she had sounded abrupt and furnished her comment with a smile. Ben appeared to look a bit hesitant but shrugged 'Oh. Well Tom has erm spoken about it at work before I'm sure' he concluded.

'Oh. Right. Well, I miss it sometimes, definitely. Life seemed a lot simpler back then and you are right, the social side was great' she smiled. They exchanged a look which felt shallow and a bit awkward so Thomas spoke up 'Hey how are you doing Ben?' he asked quietly. He did not want to make a scene if Ben lost his temper again.

'As well as to be expected I guess you could say. Tom-Tom.' Ben muttered, his eyes narrowed as he picked at a beer mat and looked directly at Thomas for the first time that evening.

'Well, if you need any help, I know that 'Total Jobs' website has always been helpful to me? Maybe we could...'

'Well, you don't need to worry about using it now do you, boy-of-the-hour.?' Ben interrupted.

Thomas felt his face burn and looked down at the table feeling defeated. 'Tell us more about your job Emily? Thomas says you are a fully established accountant? That's very impressive' Gerry smiled across the table. He was very red in the face now.

Emily seemed grateful for Gerry being there. He always helped her feel at ease. 'I specialise in Forensic Accounting and quite often have to deal with legal proceedings for companies. It can be shocking what you get to see. It keeps me busy and it's always interesting' she explained.

Jack overheard this. 'Oh, really Emily? Could we convince you to come work with us? Maybe shave off some costs?' he winked.

'You couldn't afford me Jack' she grinned.

'I love a negotiation' smirked Jack.

Thomas was grateful that Ben was engrossed once more in his phone. Didn't Jack just use that as one of the excuses to fire Ben? That the company isn't making the money it needs? Thomas thought.

Jack was ogling down to Emily's chest 'Always thought an accountant more of a man's job myself. Waste of a bird's beauty, on numbers.'

Emily looked gobsmacked 'Excuse me…WHAT??…'

Shania jumped in 'J, I am thirsty….?' hinting and looking at him with wide eyes. I'm just going to the ladies' room T; I need to freshen up' said Emily clearly looking uncomfortable now.

'HOW ABOUT ANOTHER ROUND OF DRINKS KIDS?' shouted Jack.

'Guinness for me please boss' said Thomas.

'Fosters for me' Ben smirked.

'You know my favourite J,' shouted Shania.

'I'll catch your Mrs on the way back and see what her poison is' Jack nodded to Thomas, swaying slightly as he stood.

Ben went to vape in the pub garden. Taking his opportunity, Thomas followed him.

'Ben...we didn't get to finish our conversation.'

Ben sucked on the vape, not taking his eyes off Thomas. 'Everything is going to be good for me... soon'

'I'm glad you are feeling more positive' Thomas said sincerely, leaning on the wall for support. 'I'm guessing you have a plan for when you leave then?'

Ben's expression remained vacant. 'Nothing set in stone yet but a few leads'

'Do you think you will stay as a travel agent? It will be so odd you are not being in the office. I know we haven't always...'.

Ben mumbled something clearly not listening 'he will pay anyway' he said but not looking at Thomas.

'Oh, you mean in your pay-out for leaving?' Thomas asked.

Ben smiled. 'Something like that Tom-Tom. Something like that.'

He sucked hard on his vape and exhaled deeply. 'Well, I guess, we'd better go re-join the party. Golden boy.'

'Stop calling me that'. Thomas snapped. 'I'm not 'golden boy' or 'boy of the hour'. Stop putting this crap on me Ben. Look, I'm sorry for the situation, alright. I really am. But it's not my fault. It's crap you got fired but it's not my fault.'

Ben laughed although Thomas couldn't tell if it was genuine mirth or mockery. 'Sure, Tom.

They were accosted by Shania when they returned to the table.

'Guys, I'm just going to see what's keeping our drinks' she tottered off to the bar in her heels. Ben watched her get up and adjust her bra under her tight-fitting shirt.

'She such a confident bird, isn't she? so self-assured, apart from when it comes to Jack-Sprat of course. I wonder if his wife has any idea how much he plays away? I reckon someone needs to tell her,'said Ben.

'Absolutely not, we do not know what goes on behind closed doors but it's also none of our business' replied Gerry.

'I agree, it's best not to get mixed up in relationships.' said Thomas.

'You would agree' Ben tutted but Thomas was not listening. He noticed Emily coming back to the table, she looked white as a sheet. It was like there was a sudden stillness on both sides. Her arms were crossed and rigid as she ran over.

'Tom, I am feeling unwell, do you mind if we leave? I honestly think I might pass out any second' Emily cried. She looked awful. Her mascara was now smeared, rimming her eyes like bruises, her hair was coming out of its elegant curls, looking limp wan. Thomas felt a rush of concern. No. There's no chance of going out dancing. The night was over. Enough.

'Sure, Em. Gerry I am so sorry, we will have to catch up with you soon though'

'No problem at all, I'll let Jack and Shania know' Gerry hiccupped. It's b-been great to work with Thomas. You are a top kid.' Gerry shook his hand with as much strength as he could muster. He was now completely wasted, surrounded by empty pint glasses. Thomas hoped his other colleagues would see him home safely.

'God knows where the drinks are' moaned Ben but Emily was already heading out of the door. 'It must be a bug, sorry guys' Thomas said, rushing after Emily.

'Are you ok Em?' '

'I just want to go home' replied Emily quietly.

'Has someone upset you?' Thomas demanded.

'No T. I just feel really faint. I just need a shower and my bed. Actually yes, I am upset. It would have been nice for you to step in and actually stick up for me tonight' Emily was getting tearful. 'He is absolutely disgusting and creepy...'

'Oh darling, just ignore his comments. Sorry, we are just so used to it, it goes over my head now' said Thomas feeling guilty, pulling her into a hug.

She returned his hug and buried her face into his chest so his heart beat against her cheek. 'Someone should make him pay' she concluded.

THIRTEEN

There was a strange atmosphere in the office the next day. Much to Thomas' surprise, Jack was not in yet. Perhaps he was nursing a hangover. Gerry was packing and Ben was hovering in the kitchen.'

Shania walked over before Thomas could even take his hoodie off. 'Babe, I need to talk to you urgently' she said still looking wide eyed like last night. Perhaps she too was suffering this morning.

'You should tell your Emily to keep her hands off my man' she whispered. He could smell the strong scent of her peppermint gum whilst she smacked her lips. 'What on earth are you talking about?' replied Thomas. His heart was racing now almost as loud as a train on the tracks.

'I went to find them last night because Jack seemed to be taking ages with the drinks. He wasn't at the bar so I thought I would go and surprise him and wait by the toilets. Oh! Don't look at me like that babe, you and the whole world flipping know what's going on with us! Anyway, that's where I saw them, by the exit door in the back'.

'What exactly did you see?'

'She had her hands on his chest looking rather red in the face' Shania continued. 'She obviously wants a piece of him like all the women in this town. Does no one understand that he LOVES me?''

A thought pushed itself into Thomas' mind and he knew that it had to be ridiculous. He tapped a palm against his forehead as though that would dispel the thought.

Anger started rising within him now

'Emily was incredibly upset last night. She would have told me if he had tried it on with her? You must be mistaken' Thomas said shaking his head. Shania got out her phone and showed Thomas a text from Jack:

'Babe what women are you talking about? You are the only woman for me. Yes, I have the ladies come to see me at work but that's just business I promise. Emily just had too much to drink and I was making sure she was ok. You are my future <3 I've got a headache so I am going to take the day off babe. I'll try my best to see you tomorrow. I'll make it up to you. J xoxo'

'You know where Jack is this weekend don't you?' said Thomas angrily. He felt his voice rising now.

'He is with his wife at Finlake trying to piece back together his wreck of a marriage'

'No, he is not. He promised me he was going to get out of it and spend the weekend in bed with Moi' her pink talon nails now tapping loudly on the desk. Her pitch went up irritatingly high at the end of her sentence.

'Shania, I am sorry but you need to wake up. You are not the only woman on his radar and you will not be the last. I need to speak to Emily now' Thomas went to get up from his chair and Shania stood in front of him now, her perfume so overpowering, he thought he might choke. Ben smirked then. Perhaps he was enjoying that it was seemingly over for Shania and Jack and was enjoying the drama unfolding.

'He LOVES me, Thomas. It's your girl that's trying to ruin things.'

Thomas got his phone out of his pocket ready to call Emily and trying to ignore Shania when he noticed a text from Jack:

'Hi pal, I decided to go down to Finlake early. I hope Emily is feeling better? Sorry you both had to run off like that. I think Emily may have had a few too many shots but I'll explain when I get back. Remember to keep an eye on that Earth cam of yours just in case and I'll see you on my return, okay? Keep the office going whilst I'm gone and if anyone asks, I've pulled a sicky. Jack'

'You say he isn't going to Finlake?' Thomas turned the phone around to show Shania.

'Jack has explaining to do for both of us it seems, now I need to call Emily'.

Shania had tears in her eyes 'maybe he wouldn't have gone if you hadn't put the idea in his head about making it work with his wife'

'I didn't realise you heard that conversation Shania? I am sorry but I think it is for the best?'

'What to ruin my plans with him and our future?' she sniffed sadly. Thomas rose from his desk. He felt guilty showing her the text message but she did need to know. His main priority now was talking to Emily and getting to the bottom of this.

Thomas had tried to call Emily but her phone was turned off. This conversation was not something he wanted to have over the phone anyway. He trusted his girlfriend. He has no reason not too and he just needed to hear from her if she was ok and what had been said.

'Thomas, just take a deep breath. Nice slow deep breaths. Don't lose your shit.

Thomas walked to the kitchen to make himself a coffee, he needed it rich and dark with a creamy oat milk. The aroma helped with the headaches and one was definitely on the horizon. He tried to call Emily again. Voicemail. 'It's times like this I wish house phones were still popular' he muttered as Ben came into the kitchen 'Hey is Emily, ok? I have been worried about her. She left so suddenly last night...'

Shocked by Ben's concern, Thomas couldn't help but wonder if Ben had gotten out of bed on the right side for once. 'Nice of you to care' Thomas said unsure whether to carry on this conversation. 'I am going to leave the office early and go straight to hers if that's ok?'

'I was about to suggest the same thing' Ben smiled.

Thomas felt like he was speaking to an alien with the sudden change in attitude from Ben. 'Il goes out and grab us a lunch deal. We could use some fuel' Ben said, grabbing his wallet to leave.

Thomas was grateful that Ben was grabbing some food for them all as he didn't realise how hungry he actually was until Ben mentioned lunch.

As Thomas walked past Shania's desk, her head was deep in her chest of drawers as if she was looking for something. She remained like that for nearly 10 minutes and finally emerged, looking flustered.

'You OK, Shan?' Thomas asked.

'Wah- oh yeah fine.'

'You lost something?'

EU. OH...right...yeah, my my ...stapler. I've found it. 'Babe, I'm sorry for earlier, okay? I was speaking to Gerry in the kitchen and he actually talked some sense into me. He said that I really need to start respecting myself more and I need to move on from Jack...'

Thomas felt irritable then, 'I am sorry but not everything revolves around your stupid relationship with Jack. I need to make sure my girlfriend is ok and right now; I can't even get a hold of her'. Shania looked hurt then and Gerry spoke up 'Hey Thomas, there's no need for that is there. I think you need to go home, speak to Emily and get some rest, eh? We will be ok here'

Thomas couldn't argue. He apologised to the team and left the office in a hurry without even picking up his hoodie.

FOURTEEN

Jack had one hand on the wheel and the other on Caroline's knee as they drove to Finlake.

The wind pushed on the car and Caroline sighed deeply 'of course it's going to rain whilst we are away, typical British weather'

'Let's enjoy it anyway love. A quiet, secluded cabin where no one can hear us eh' Jack purred. It was clear what was on his mind.

Caroline played with her wedding ring with her thumb and index finger, the jewels glistening back at her despite the clouds in the sky. Did the ring mean anything anymore? Time will tell.

'I am glad we are having a couple of days just us Jack, we need it'

Caroline looked over to Jack but he did not return it. His eyes remained fixed on the road, he was looking straight ahead to the empty, winding road deep in thought. Caroline was aware that she was not the only important person in Jack's life. They never decided to have children but were both happy with this decision. She had taken a gamble when she married Jack, they enjoyed their holidays, their Sundays spent together.

It was then she discovered the affair.

She had taken him back. Despite herself. But the affair had proven an electric shock to the heart. She had begun learning Portuguese. Re-inventing herself. His infidelity stained their relationship like poster paint on an oil canvas.

They arrived at the cabin and Caroline hoped for no distractions, no technology especially phones, a cabin so remote that no one would be able to find them. They could have a proper talk and hopefully find a way past this situation.

As they got out of the car, Jack was already reaching for his iPhone from his pocket. 'Jack, really? I thought we were leaving work behind this weekend?' she said, trying to be calm.

'Caz, it's just an important email, it will not take long' he rolled his eyes kicking the pebbles underneath his feet.

'If it's an important email, why are you grinning like a Cheshire cat Jack. How do you expect me to trust you?' she hissed.

Jack turned red and shoved his phone back in his pocket but he did not answer.

The inside of the cabin was beautiful. The sliding doors led into a spacious living room area, a log fire, cosy sofas and even a fully stocked bookcase. As Caroline walked through to the bedroom, she noticed further spectacular decking and a hot tub surrounded by fairy lights.

This should be a romantic getaway for a happy couple, not an attempt to fix what is already broken.

Jack brought in their bags and immediately locked himself in the toilet whilst Caroline poured herself a glass of wine.

As he came out, he was smiling at her 'you know I love you Caz, don't you?'

Caroline considered the question for a second before answering 'do you?'

Jack handed over his phone 'you can have this and look through it till your heart's content'

'You must think I am an idiot? You have just deleted any incriminating evidence?'

'Don't be silly babe. Here keep it. You will see there is nothing to worry about'

The water was slowly coming to the boil on the stove, the meat seasoned and was sitting on the butcher blocks. Jack stood dicing an onion whilst the other vegetables waited their turn on the counter. Caroline began to feel relaxed and it did seem like she finally had Jack's full attention. She kicked off her heels and put her feet up on the sofa, she felt like she was self medicating through the alcohol but she felt nervous. Maybe after a few drinks, they could have a proper conversation like they used to do in the early days.

'So how is the business going?' she said, glancing up at Jack who she had to admit, looked incredibly handsome, cooking in the kitchen. There was something so attractive about a man that could work a kitchen.

'I thought we were not here to talk about business Caz?'

She wound her hair around her finger and bit her lip hard, she could not help herself when it came to talking about the business. Afterall if it was not for Jack's investment in Safe Travel, they would not live as comfortably as they do now. Caroline loved the money.

'Business has been quiet but that's expected for this time of year Caz but the numbers will soon pick up.

'I bet it's going to be weird without Gerry being there isn't it. I cannot believe he is retired, I thought he would work till the day he died' Caroline giggled.

'Everyone did, but it was time he let go'

'What do you mean let go?'

'Well, he never really got over handing everything over did he. At least with him gone now, I can finally breathe again without his jibes or making me feel guilty'

Caroline got up from the sofa and walked towards Jack suddenly really wanting to hold him.

It was a difficult marriage. She was torn between loving him, hating him and yet still fought for his attention and craved it badly.

Jack's phone pinged then but he did not jump or hesitate in anyway, still, this did not help Caroline's nerves.

'It's a number unknown' she said as she unlocked the screen with his code - his birthday, not even her birthday. *Ha. probably because he never remembered* she thought.

'Probably a client or something, or one of the guys asking how it's going' Jack said calmly.

Jack did not panic as when he ran into the toilet, he did remove anything that may get him in trouble but also blocked the many numbers that may try and get in contact. It's okay. He knew once Caroline was asleep, he could unblock and copy and paste the many apologies he needed to send to each of his 'friends'. He always referred to them as 'Babe, Baby, Honey or Sugar' as he forgot names so easily.

Caroline was an attractive lady, with her honey blonde hair skimming her shoulders. Her perfect red lipstick never out of place and her curves of softness. Why couldn't he stay faithful?

Caroline's face went scarlet as she read out the text: 'Meet at your office Sunday evening?

I've got a little something to show you, I think you will like it ;) '

'Babe it's probably Thomas messing around' Jack shouted defensively.

Who was he kidding? One of his past conquests trying to get back in his bed.

'Babe seriously, I bet the poster arrived of me. The photographer e-mailed it over the other day. It's probably been blown up and put on the way. But only you get the real thing you sexy devil.'

Caroline's eyes were still on him. 'So, I can delete it yes?'

'Sure, you can.... hey come here.'

Caroline's eyes narrowed. 'In a bit. I'm going to run a bath. She disappeared into the bathroom. It was hours before she came out and when she did, she didn't join Jack in the hot tub but slunk straight to bed, her face as black as thunder. Jack sunk back into the tub, and sunk another whisky, feeling like a lobster that was slowly being cooked alive...

FIFTEEN

Thomas arrived at Emily's quicker than he thought. He walked up to the door and noticed that she hadn't picked up her mail or her milk delivery. As Thomas waked in, it seemed even messier than usual. He ran up the stairs two steps at a time and found her in bed. The curtains were still drawn and the dust filled his lungs. Emily led there with her eyes wide open like when a rabbit is caught in headlights. 'Em, talk to me darling, Shania spoke to me at work and....'

With that, Emily burst into tears as she finally sat up. This was when Thomas could see the red marks on her chest and the bruises on her arms. He froze. His blood is boiling like water in a kettle. 'Jack attacked me, Thomas. He put his hands on me and when I said no, he grabbed my arms' she sobbed.

Thomas couldn't even speak. 'I am sure Shania saw but she chose to assume I was hitting on HIM' she cried.

Thomas grabbed her and held her close realising just how small and vulnerable she felt in his arms. 'I think he was drunk; I don't want to report him or anything....'

'We must report him Emily, he has assaulted you!' Thomas spluttered. 'Did anyone else see anything apart from Shania?'

'No, I don't think so and it was so dark by the toilets. He was giving me looks across the table. He clearly ignored all visual cues to leave me alone and I kept feeling him leaning across the table. I know it sounds ridiculous and I am sure I was the only one to notice'

'Why the hell didn't you tell me last night Em. I knew he had upset you but not this....'

'This wasn't the first time it's happened' Emily swallowed hard.

'What do you mean? Jack? Or your university experience?'

'No no, when I was a teenager in care, one of the 'dads' ... he would try and creep into my room at night to 'check on me'. I would pretend to be asleep, but he would always know I wasn't because tears would escape my eyes. He would touch me, himself or both and then whisper abuse and threats in my ears' tears streamed down her cheeks now. 'He would shame me with his words as if that would make me stay quiet and not call for help. He was right in his thinking because I knew the family or the social worker would just think I'm lying.

'I tried to report it eventually when I gathered some strength or perhaps, I was led into a false sense of security by one of the workers, but my fears were confirmed and they thought I was an attention seeking child. I was never taken seriously' Emily's cheeks were damp with tears.

'I think we need to get you to the doctors anyway before anything to check you over' Thomas said, trying to contain his anger. His palms were hurting from where he pressed his nails in so hard.

How did I not pick up on this before?

'No, honestly Tom. What good would it do?'

'What good would it do? Emily. You're my girlfriend. Jack is my boss. How am I meant to carry on working there?'

'Tom, I can take care of myself. I've...'

She trailed off.

'You what?'

'Nothing. Just leave it Tom.'

'I'm definitely not leaving it. I'll have to speak to him. As soon as he is back from Devon.'

'What about your job?'

Thomas took a deep breath. This was a living nightmare. How could this be? Jack was his mentor. His friend. Why did every one he put his faith in turn out to be a complete...

Forget this nice guy bullshit. He's had enough.

'If I have to walk away from Safe Travel, so be it. What kind of person would I be if I continued working for a man who assaulted my girlfriend? But that won't be enough. He has to be accountable.'

Emily hugged him. 'I don't know what I'd do without you. I know you would do anything for me.'

'Of course, I would.'

She looked exhausted. 'I just can't think about this anymore tonight. I need some sleep. Call me tomorrow.'

'I should stay.'

'I'd prefer to be alone.'

'I'm -I'm worried about what you could do...'

'You mean...top myself??'

'You know what I mean' he shouted. 'We are two of a kind. We get each other. Both fucked up childhoods. You get what I'm saying.'

'I get it. And I'm not in that place yet. I will be fine. Now. I love you.'

She smiled as if to herself and walked slowly to her room, closing the door.

***

Thomas got home, bubbling with rage and threw his bag on the floor. Oliver came through from the lounge and Thomas was grateful that he wasn't alone.

'What's going on man?' Oliver walked over. He always looked the opposite to Thomas: well-groomed with a fashionably stubbled chin, piercing blue eyes and olive tanned skin even in the winter, bastard.

'Jack attacked Emily whilst we were all out last night at the pub'

'What the hell? What did you do?'

'Well, I only just found out today and...'

'Have you confronted him?'

'He is away with his wife'

'Let's fucking go there'

'I need to talk to him alone when he's back although his wife should know about this'

Thomas punched the wall in front of him. He knew that when his anger boiled up, he needed to take the saucepan off the heat and open the lid. He needed to breathe.

'He's got to pay Thomas.' Oliver said, his voice in Thomas's ear.

Thomas nodded. 'I will make him pay.'

SIXTEEN

It was Sunday evening and Thomas felt cold as he tried to settle in bed. He knew that Jack would be back at some point in the next few hours. He knew he would have to face him tomorrow. How would he possibly stay calm? What was he to say?

The doctor had advised on some counselling sessions for Emily and some short-term medication. They spent some time googling different practices and reading reviews of local sessions available.

They looked at talking therapy as well as books on cognitive behavioural therapy that they could perhaps work through together. Emily needed to talk about it to heal but he felt he could not be the only person she would talk through this with. Not because he did not want to help her, of course he did but more so that this absolutely needed a professional.

This plan eased his mind slightly but he kept mesmerizing about hitting Jack straight in the face before he had a chance to make excuses or try and get out of what he'd done.

Lying in bed, his head ached with the need for sleep. He flipped open his Kindle and tried to read but the glare just hurt his eyes. It was no good, his body wasn't going to obey; he would have to occupy himself until morning. He knew the answer. EarthCam.

Thomas padded to the kitchen, made himself a cup of tea and made his way back to his bedroom. He noticed Oliver's door was closed. He didn't normally close it at night. He usually says he likes 'the air' and doesn't like to be shut in. He eased himself into his chair in his small room. Travelling the world for a few hours was a good way to kill time. Then he remembered he needed to check on the shop, not that he owed Jack ANY favours he thought to himself. He was more worried if the team had locked up properly before they left. He was so preoccupied about getting to Emily on Friday that he forgot to mention about the double locking. He would have a quick look and then check out Times Square in New York. another place on his bucket list.

EarthCam was very similar to google maps except instead of a still image, everything was live. As the page loaded, it was slightly grainy when coming into focus. The streets were completely deserted. It was as if God had stopped time and removed all the distractions so he could see the town for real. How it really was. He decided to zoom in on the street where Safe Travel Holidays was located.

That was when he noticed a figure walking by the shop, a silhouette almost.

There was a light on in the office and immediately Thomas started to panic. *'Wait, is that a light that stays on all night? I doubt it. Jack wouldn't want the electricity bill. Did one of the team leave it on?'*

it was too late to call anyone now. That's when he saw the second shadow.

Are they together? Are they breaking in? Someone is walking out of the shop?

Thomas wanted to grab his phone but he was almost glued to his seat. The person walking out the shop was now walking closer to the computer screen. They didn't seem to have anything in their hands? But he did notice some headphones, an over the head pair. They walked along the pavement with their head down clearly not hearing or paying attention to anything or anyone around them. Thomas' heart was hammering. He felt the bile rise in his throat. He was swallowing hard.

The second shape came up behind now and Thomas realised they were not actually together. They were holding what looked like a hammer and were speeding up behind. For a split second, the attacker hesitated and it seemed like they said something to their victim or maybe had a change of thought?

Thomas jumped out of his seat and yelled at the top of his voice 'NO!!!!!' then of course realising that they wouldn't hear him. They swung the hammer hitting the person to the ground. Is this some kind of a joke? Thomas yelled to Oliver but got no response. In the soft yellow glow of the street lights, he could see the dark liquid pouring from the shadow on the floor. 'This was a fucking murder. Live!

OLIVER!!!! Where are you? Get in here now!!!!! What the fuck!!! Oh my GOD'

Thomas gagged as he took his eyes off the screen to grab the phone and sat on his bedside table. He glanced at the time 2:05am. He went to dial 999 when suddenly, the realisation hit him. The perpetrator wasn't even trying to clear up the mess, they just stood still looking at their victim, no sense of humanity. They made it look easier than peeling an orange. What a little effort it had taken. Thomas couldn't take his eyes off them and thanks to the glow from the street light, that's when Thomas recognised the letters on their clothing 'Eat, Sleep, A T History. Repeat.

SEVENTEEN

It was 2:46am and Thomas sat, hands shaking violently. He couldn't bring himself to call the police. 'That was his hoodie the killer was wearing? It had to be right? It was dark. Maybe it wasn't his hoodie? It couldn't be just a co-incidence, could it?

What? The same letters missing in the exact same spot Thomas come on!?'

His mind was swirling. He knew he needed to call the police. He knew he needed to report this crime. What if the police thought it was him? If that is his hoodie? Nah how could they? He would be ringing to report it therefore he wouldn't be in the firing line, would he?

Plus, he couldn't be the only person in the world with this hoodie.

Oliver walked in the room fully dressed.

'Where have you been!' Thomas yelled hysterically. 'I have been screaming for you! I've just witnessed a murder on EarthCam and....'

'You what?' said Oliver sharply, starting and running across to grab the laptop.

'They were wearing MY hoodie Oliver I'm sure of it. I saw...I saw the fucking letters on the back clear as day. Where the hell have you been?' Thomas was shaking. His T-shirt was soaked with sweat.

'OK.OK. Thomas. Calm the fuck down. I couldn't sleep so I went to Gunwharf Quays...took in the late showing... are you sure you haven't been dreaming. Perhaps you fell asleep and...'

'No, I haven't been dreaming!!!' Thomas opened the laptop back on to EarthCam. He couldn't see anything on the screen now.

'Why would the killer have been wearing your hoodie, Thomas? Is someone out to hurt you? Who would have done this? I can't see anything?' Oliver's voice was raised. Thomas was almost grateful that Oliver too was starting to panic now as he felt less alone.

'Can't you see that blood on the floor there?' Thomas shuddered.

'That could be a spilt drink? You can't tell that it's definitely blood?

EarthCam just showed an empty street now. As if nothing had happened.

'Maybe wait till the sun comes up then we can go check it out?' said Oliver.

'I know what I saw. I need to call the police now.'

'No, you don't said Oliver firmly. 'You need to wait'. His eyes fell on the large bottle of red wine on the desk. 'You've been drinking again. For Christ's sake Tom, you've got to stop doing this. The police will just see you as another pisshead, only in his room not on the pavement. We will go first thing then call the police if we have to.'

'But...'

Listen Thomas, there is nobody there. Are you sure he was dead? He may have gotten up and walked away to get help. Or someone could have helped him. You've probably just witnessed a mugging'. He got up from the bed. 'Look, I promise I will accompany you to the station tomorrow. Just-try and get some sleep for now.'

But sleep was not an option. Thomas tossed and turned, eyes burning from exhaustion but his mind going too fast. It didn't help that the red wine was now giving him a dull headache and nausea. It further didn't help when he ruminated on Oliver's assertion that he had caught a midnight showing at the cinema, when the cinema shut at 11...

EIGHTEEN

It was a busy morning at the police station when Jonathan Marsh arrived. He was starving; he had shared a watermelon with his wife who was on Slimming World and had embroiled him into the new healthier lifestyle. God it was boring. He headed straight for the station canteen and picked up a sausage sandwich. He was all set for a morning of checking his e-mails and chasing up sub ordinates on ongoing cases. Little did he know.

'O'Rourke. You are needed in the briefing room?' his colleague Healey said.

Marsh bristled. 'I've got a busy morning ahead. When is this?'

'As in now'

Sighing, Marsh crammed the rest of his sandwich into his mouth, picked up his notebook and dutifully headed for the briefing room.

'A body has been found in front of Safe Travel Holidays over at Southsea. '

'What do we know so far?'

'The body is Jack O'Neill. Owner of the business. 52 years old.

I'm putting you in charge Marsh. But there will be too much workload on your own. I'm giving you a partner.'

'Oh yeah. Who?'

'We would like you to work with Seamus O'Rourke. He's newly qualified and I think being put under a strong mentor such as yourself will bring out both of your strengths.'

Marsh had met O'Rourke a couple of times since he had joined the team but O'Rourke struck him as a little…what was the word…'

'O'Rourke I'm sure is a fine Detective Inspector but I think for this case, I would be suited to someone a little more…. I think O'Rourke tends to lead by emotion a little too much.'

'And you tend to lead with logic. I think you will complement each other well. My mind is made up.' The Sergeant walked away.

Marsh sighed and rubbed his eyes. This was going to be a long day. He opened a Google search page. Marsh likes to be logical, thorough. The results for 'Jack O'Neill' brought up a flurry of images: a young, arrogant looking man holding up a trophy for *Entrepreneur of the Year – The South*, his arm around an attractive looking woman, and another one, and another one…this bloke was a player. Wait a moment, he had a wife?'

'Excuse me', Marsh looked up and a younger man in his late 30's was standing with two coffees. He had layered brown curls, blue eyes and a tall slim build. His voice was soft and had a slight Irish lilt.

'I am Seamus O'Rourke. I am working with you on the O'Neill case.'

'Right. Yes.' Marsh gestured to his screen. Started on the preliminary research.'

'Sensible plan. I brought some coffee. I just got it black but got some milk and sugar for you.'

This guy belongs in hospitality, not Detective Work.

'Thanks' Marsh muttered. 'I'm going to book out the breakout room.'

They carried their drinks and notebooks in to the room to begin brainstorming. Marsh brought out a large whiteboard from the side of the wall.

'They will need us very soon at Safe Travel Holidays. But first, I need some details.

Marsh scribbled the name 'Jack O'Neill.'

So, our victim. Jack O'Neill. Owner of Safe Travel Holidays. Suspects-0 at present. Our next steps are to go to the shop and gather some evidence.

O'Rourke was patiently writing things down. 'How about Mrs. O'Neill? Has his wife been informed?

We are still awaiting some formalities.

I was still only 07:30 and it was still pitch dark in the late January morning.

'We will have to rope off the area before the employees get here.' Marsh instructed. 'Someone will have to wait outside the shop and turn them away.'

'I've got the names for you if you need them' O'Rourke said, consulting his notebook.

Marsh looked mildly impressed. 'You do?'

'Yes, once I got the news, I'd be on the case with you, I did a quick check of Facebook. Safe Travel has its own page. Looks like it's a very small establishment. Only four full time employees, sir.: Thomas Walker, Gerry Hobbes, Shania Simmons, Benjamin Grey.

'Good work. Do you print off any pictures of them?'

'Yes, sir.

'Good work. '

Marsh took the pictures to the forensics team who were combing the area and instructed the team to turn the employees away once they started arriving.

'So, what do we have so far?' Marsh asked the forensics team.

'Well, the door to the office was locked. The victim had his key on his person. Therefore, he either was just about to go into the office or he had just come out. From the angle of his body, we concur that the victim did indeed go into the shop and had just come out when he was accosted.'

'What appears to be the most likely scenario so far?' interrogated O'Rourke.

'IT seems to be a robbery gone wrong. The victim has suffered severe trauma to the temple. Strangely though, his wallet, keys were all on him. The attacker clearly had the advantage but then didn't take what they wanted.'

'Strange.' Muttered Marsh. 'Now, are there any security cameras?'

'Unfortunately, not. Too much of a quiet area.

Marsh winced in frustration. 'I was expecting that. Life is never that simple, is it?'

But a priority is to comb the inside of the office'. Said the forensics team member. 'See if O'Neill left any clues as to why he was at his place of work at 2am.

'What time do you think the murder occurred?'

'Last night around 2am-3am, judging by how long the body has been in rigour mortis'.

'O'Neill owned the company so he has got the perfect right to go into the office when he liked.' Marsh observed. Still, why??? What couldn't wait until morning?

'Can we see the surrounding area? Asked O'Rourke.

Marsh and O'Rourke scouted around the side of the shop. A narrow alleyway led to the back door of the shop, probably the break room. A smattering of cigarettes littered the floor where the staff had their fag breaks. There was a tin dustbin and a large green recycling bin which took paper. They opened it eagerly but it was just full of out of season brochures.'

Still can't expect the killer to be that much of a twat.' Remarked Marsh.

Leaving the forensics team to carry on their work and to await the autopsy results, they headed back to the station to the breakout room.

'So, our suspects so far Marsh said, picking up a squeaky marker.' All of the team at Safe Travel Holidays.' He wrote each name on the Whiteboard and magneted the print out of their faces next to each name...and...he put a large question mark and underneath it rote 'Nutter.'

'O'Rourke smiled. 'You are a little...unconventional, sir.'

'Being bland and conformist never solved a case.' Muttered Marsh.

'Sir, that's not a slight at me, is it?'

'What. No, not at all.... O'Rourke!' Marsh looked flustered. 'Right, so now we wait for the results of the autopsy'. In the meantime, we gather evidence on as much of the 4 employees as we can. I will leave that up to you. Go on their social media pages. Contact who you need to. I want a full profile of each one by the end of the day.'

'Right you are.' O'Rourke got to his feet. 'I'm hoping they will cope today when they hear the awful news.'

Marsh picked up his cigarettes. 'Certainly not the best start to a Monday morning.

NINETEEN

Thomas dragged himself out of bed, grateful for the morning so he could finally do something about his anxieties. He forced himself to have a very quick shower,

'Oliver, come on let's go' Thomas shouted. He walked into the hall but he couldn't hear anything. He knocked at the door of the bedroom. No reply....

The only sound Thomas could hear was the sound of his heartbeat. All he could do was replay last night in his mind. He felt like he was stuck in an intricate web and needed to weave his way free. He had so many thoughts in his mind that he couldn't work out what had actually happened or if it had been a dream. Like waking up from a really, heavy night sleep and you feeling unbalanced.

Thomas knocked at the door again and let himself into the bedroom. Oliver wasn't in bed. He really did not want to do this alone. Where the hell had he gone? Especially after last night's events. Maybe he did not sleep either.

There was no time to talk anymore about the events of last night. He needed to go and see for himself. Right now.

Getting hastily dressed, a strange, constricted sensation in his stomach, he grabbed his bag, phone, keys and headed to the bus stop.

As he sat on the bus, he surveyed the other passengers. Due to the early start, there was only one nurse who looked like she was so exhausted, she may fall asleep at any moment and miss her stop. On the other side of her, was a rough looking man who looked like he may be drunk. Or still drunk from last night. He was murmuring to himself and picking the skin around his nails.

The back looked unoccupied so Thomas went and sat down and tried to concentrate on what he saw last night. His head felt so heavy so he tried to close his eyes but there was nothing he could do to relax. Outside was still just past dawn and there was a pearly glow in the sky. He thought about texting

Emily but he did not want to put anymore added stress onto her. He urged this journey to go as quickly as possible.

When the bus finally came to a stop, Thomas walked the remaining block to work. As he came closer, that's when he noticed the bright white and blue tape surrounding the area. He stopped dead in his tracks. This was not his imagination now. He was fired up and was wide awake. A hornet's nest of Police and forensics were swarming the area.

Thomas moaned in horror and anguish. Horrific visions of the mutilated body danced before his eyes. He tried to force them away. He got to the corner and looked down to the shop.

A police officer came towards him quickly. 'Excuse me sir, this is a crime scene, we have cornered off the area, you need to...'

'I w-work at..at.. Safe Travel' said Thomas stuttered. The world seemed to be wobbling on its axis.

'The police officer was going through a sheaf of papers. 'Can you confirm your name please.'

'Thomas. Thomas W-Walker' .'

Someone wake me up from this nightmare. Oh my God.

The police had clearly been prepared for his arrival. Thomas caught a glimpse of his colleagues' photographs in the police officer's hands.

'Not today you don't I'm afraid sir, can we take your contact details as we will be in touch as soon as we can but for now, please go home. Can you tell your colleagues or anyone else you may know that works in the area NOT to come to work today. If they are already on their way as I'm sure they are, we will give them the same message we are giving you.

'Who is it?' What's happened? Does anyone know?' Thomas asked urgently.

'We absolutely cannot confirm for sure anything until the next of kin has been informed and we officially identify the victim. I am afraid that's all I can say for now.'

The policeman kindly but firmly took Thomas by the elbow and steered him away. Thomas saw the chalk outline in the shape of a splayed figure on the pavement.

TWENTY

So, it was all true. He DID watch a murder on screen. Last night. And he had done sod all about it.

With trembling fingers, he fumbled for his phone; his hands shaking as he dialled Ben's number. There was no reply.

Next, he tried Shania.

'Hey babe you, ok?'

'Actually no, have you left for work yet?' Thomas asked urgently.

'Just about to, babe, are you not feeling well? You sound terrible.'

'We can't go in today…. the police. They…. they….' His breath caught in the cobwebs in his throat.

'Thomas, I'm not understanding you? What's going on?!' she shouted.

'The whole street has been cordoned off. There has been a murder'.

'Oh my God! Are you sure?' SHIT THE FUCKING BED!!!!!'

'I have just been there. They told me to go home. I don't suppose you've heard from Jack?'

'He was texting me this weekend, whilst with her of course but no, I have seen sense, I haven't replied.' Shania said.

Thomas was surprised at this, despite himself but now was not the time to veer down that path.

'We need to get a hold of him though. I need to call the others. Meet me at The Six Bells in an hour? We will get everyone to meet there'.

'Right. OK. Be there soon' she gabbled. Fuck me'.

***

An hour later, Thomas, Gerry, Shania and Ben were sitting around a large wooden table. Shania was chewing her nails, a panicked look on her face. Gerry was sipping a lemon water seemingly calm; Ben had his head down staring at his phone. He hadn't said a single word to them all yet.

Thomas looked at each of them, from one to the other considering if he should tell them what he witnessed last night. Every time he drew breath to utter the sentence, the words got caught in his throat.

He texted Oliver

'I couldn't get into work today. Police everywhere. I was right. You at home?'

'Has anyone heard from Jack?' Shania spoke up trying to keep her voice steady as she gazed up at them all.

'His phone is off and I don't have a number for his wife? Does anyone else?' replied Thomas.

'Maybe he is still travelling back? said Gerry. 'Took an extended vacation?'

'He's definitely back' said Shania quickly.

'You know that for sure?' said Ben sharply.

'I mean, he said he would be back today for sure as he wanted to go over some new posters for the window.' Shania said and put her head back down. Her face betrayed her, flushing red.

'I reckon it was probably a bar fight gone wrong. You know what kids are like these days...too much to drink' Gerry said calmly.

'On a Sunday night?' added Shania.

Gerry gently shrugged. He did not say anything but Thomas wondered if that was truly what he was really thinking. Thomas thought he saw a flicker of a glimpse pass between him and Ben.

This was no bar fight. That psycho had a weapon. Was it a knife? A golf club? Who walks around with a golf club at 2 in the morning?!

'Do you reckon we will be able to get back in the office later? Thomas questioned. He was desperate to look for his hoodie.

'I don't think so. The police have our details so until they've investigated, I don't think any of the shops will be able to open.' said Gerry. 'Wait till Jack hears about this; he will have a field day if STH gets on the news'.

'I'm just wondering who the poor person was' said Shania.

Ben continued to look extremely pale.

When it got to lunchtime and it was clear there was no news, the team decided to all go to their homes.

'Let's keep in touch on the WhatsApp group, eh? Said Shania shakily.

Gerry offered a lift to Thomas.

'You look so tired Thomas, I think you need to go home and get some sleep' said Gerry, looking concerned.

'Yeah, I didn't sleep well, I guess I could use a nap. I must check on Emily first and see how she is doing. Would you mind dropping me there?' Thomas said. He was still feeling incredibly nauseous. He had felt a fever coming on all morning.

He checked his phone but no reply from Oliver.

He should be up by now?

'So, what will you do now with all your time off Gerry? '

'I've got a few ideas' said Gerry vaguely. 'I'd love to take a drive on Route 66 in the States. Denise isn't the most adventurous of people but I'm sure I can persuade her. Just having some more time to myself really. I've given a good number of years to Safe Travel. Now I want to be the one doing the travelling!'

'Sounds perfect to me'

'So how are you and Emily doing? Gerry asked. Thomas suddenly felt another wave of nausea and held a hand over his mouth hoping for it to subside.

He needed to talk to someone. Anyone.

'I was meant to talk to Jack today.' Thomas said cautiously.

'Oh? Anything important?'

Thomas inhaled deeply and pushed his head back on the head rest.

'Jack attacked Emily. When we went to the pub, he tried it on with her and when she said no, he wasn't impressed.'

'Excuse me...what?!'

'Emily begged me not to call him or the police so I've just been sitting on this all weekend.' He felt his chest tighten.

'This must be reported' Gerry spluttered. 'Did he touch her?'

'Shania fortunately went to find Jack and found them before it could go too far. She actually thought Emily was into Jack. Can you believe that?'

Gerry paused and Thomas felt the heat start prickling at his skin.

'Actually, this is Jack and he is a womaniser so I am afraid I can. There isn't any skirt on this planet that Jack wouldn't chase. I do feel sorry for poor Caroline. She's an attractive woman you know. She could have her fun too if she wanted too. But no, she chooses to stay faithful and this is how she gets repaid over and over again.'

There was a softness to his voice that was laced with venom.

Thomas sat still and Gerry continued.

'That's not to say I believe Emily would ever do that to you Tom. I am relieved she was not hurt. I just know Jack and what he is capable of....'

Gerry did not have to tell Thomas what he was thinking and they continued the drive silently, the mood heavy.

They only said a brief goodbye when they arrived at Emily's.

'Well, keep in touch over Messenger Tom. Whilst we wait for further news.'

'Yeah. Cheers Gerry.'

Emily was working from home this afternoon and her table was cluttered with files and receipts. She smiled when she saw Thomas.

'I've got some chicken and chips for us. Nothing too flash but I'm so busy and ...well...I've not been in the mood to do much, if you know what I mean.'

'Sure, no problem.' Said Thomas distractedly.

'So, you decided to work from home today' he said.

'Yes. I just could not sleep last night and the thought of commuting in the freezing cold, with thoughts of Jack's grubby hands on me...I – I needed my own space. Thomas, just whilst the food is cooking...I – I just need to finish up on something, that OK?

'Fine.' Thomas mumbled. He kissed her cheek and went into the lounge and once again left a message for Oliver.

'Oliver, where the fuck are you mate? I need to talk to you urgently! The murder I witnessed on EarthCam. It really happened!!! I'm witness to a goddamn murder. A murderer who got into the ruddy shop and nicked my hoodie. I'm at Emily's now but call me as soon as you get this!'

He paced the floor constantly checking for messages until Emily called him in.

***

'Thomas, I wish you would put your phone down and try to relax. I know today has been distressing. I am sure we will know more soon!' Emily said, her voice rising.

Thomas had not mentioned what he saw on EarthCam. Emily was already feeling so fragile with the instance with Jack; he couldn't bring himself to cause any more upset.

'Yeah. Yeah. I know OK I get it.' He snapped.

'Are you tapping your foot Thomas.'

'No?'

'Yes, you are, I can see your leg wiggling under the table'

'I feel like I am not allowed to even blink without you snapping at me?' Thomas said irritably.

The air felt stifling, with all the thoughts they were not saying to each other. Thomas pulled out his phone yet again to check WhatsApp.

'Someone must have heard from Jack by now'. Emily sighed and rubbed her eyes as he looked through his call history.

He noticed a missed call from an unknown number and his hear raced.

'I wonder if it's the police or something'

Thomas got up briskly and redialled the number.

'Hello? is that Thomas?'

'Y- yes, hi who's calling? '

'This is Caroline, Jack's wife?

'Hi Caroline, we have been wondering where Jack is, we tried to call....'

'Jack is missing, Thomas. We came home from our weekend away and...' she choked back tears. 'He said he had to rush out so left me to unpack the suitcases. He hasn't returned Thomas!!' she was hysterical now. 'I've been trying to call him God knows how many times. I think something terrible has happened to him!!!'

Thomas turned to Emily but she was already looking at him as if she heard every word. Her face white.

TWENTY-ONE

Thomas held his breath until his throat burned. He hung up the phone and faced Emily. 'It's Jack. He's missing.'

Emily's eyes widened 'for how long?'

Thomas' heartbeat was beating so hard, he could feel it in his ears.

'Since last night. Apparently, they got home from Finlake he went out and…. Didn't come back'

'He is probably doing what he does best, shacked up with some woman.' He had never heard her voice like this before. Hard as steel. A zero-fucks given voice. It gave him chills.

'What if it was him? Who has been murdered? No one has heard a goddamn thing from him, he's missing and someone has met their maker on the street that our office is on! It's not looking fucking good, is it???!!

'OK. Thomas. THOMAS!!!! you need to calm down'

'I don't think I do actually Em, how can you be so calm about this?!'

'We have to just try and relax and wait for the police to advise us. I'll be honest, I couldn't really give a flying rat's ass where that bastard is.

It was time to tell her.

'Em, listen…there's something I haven't told you.' He croaked.

'What do you mean?'

'Okay…okay… this is going to sound bizarre but I… I saw the murder. I was on EarthCam and….'

'Thomas darling, you spend too much time on that computer, I am worried. You are obsessed. You said you haven't been sleeping well? What did you actually see? Were you dreaming perhaps?'

'You are not listening to me!!' he shouted in exasperation.

'I AM listening Thomas' Emily actually got up and took him by the elbows.

'I need to go home. I'm sorry Em. I just need to go'. He wrenched his arms from her grasp and made towards the door.

'Thomas, stay here! Please'. THOMAS!!! Her voice carried on the wind at his retreating figure.

Thomas ran out the door to Emily's and headed for home. 'Why did I try to tell her? I knew she wouldn't understand. I knew she would contradict me'.

He started to pick up speed, his breathing increasing and the adrenaline running through him. 'I need to speak to Oliver. Oliver understood.'

Thomas looked around the inky black streets. Where the fuck was, he?! He decided to walk home via the sea front. Walking home via the streets made him feel alone.

***

'Oliver why didn't you text me back today?' Thomas said breathlessly as he got through the door. Oliver was lying sprawled across the couch, his eyes bloodshot with tiredness.

'Sorry man, it was a rough night wasn't it. I've been asleep.

'Well, you weren't here this morning! Where the hell have you been?!'

'I've just- I just had a few things to take care of man. I'm here now, OK? So...was this EarthCam vision all bullshit?

'NO! Haven't you listened to my message! What I saw was REAL!!! There has been a bloody murder in front of Safe Travel Offices. To cap it all off, my boss is missing and so is my bloody hoodie!!'

'Oh shit!!' Did you speak to the police? I really thought you may have dreamt it man.'

'I fucking wish I did. I tried to tell Emily but I think she thinks I'm going mad. I need to get hold of Jack. Do you think it was him? It has to be right?' Thomas said, losing all reasoning.

Oliver did not give off much of a vibe. 'I really don't know Thomas but we need to locate that fucking hoodie.'

Thomas felt a sense of relief again when Oliver said 'we'.

'I couldn't get into the shop today.' He said miserably. 'And tomorrow it looks like it will be closed too.'

'Well, give it one more day mate. If you still don't hear anything, you need to break in to the shop. You have to see if your hoodie is still over your seat. We will go together. I will keep look out if I have to.'

Thomas nodded weakly. He felt a little better after having talked things through with Oliver.

Oliver got up, walked over to Thomas and hugged him. 'Mate. It will be fine, brother.'

Thomas felt too miserable to be embarrassed. He hugged Oliver and felt a tear roll down his cheek.

'Here mate. Lay on the sofa.'

Thomas obeyed.

'I'll fix you a drink.'

Oliver went into the kitchen and came back with a tumbler of Fanta.

'How did you know? That's my favourite childhood drink.' Croaked Thomas.

Oliver smiled. 'I know that, bro.'

He draped a throw over Thomas. 'I'll be in my room OK.'

Thomas was already dropping off to the sound of the TV and a strange dream of him sipping Fanta in a childhood playpark with a boy who looked very familiar....

TWENTY-TWO

Tuesday

Thomas woke to bright sunshine streaming through the window.

He stared motionless at his phone, six texts from Emily. He felt bad that he just left her last night especially after what he blurted out. He laced his fingers together and stretched out his arms. He went to dial Emily's number but jumped as it started vibrating.

Caroline.

He couldn't make out the voice. A loud sobbing could be heard down the phone. 'Caroline? Is that you?' Thomas groped for words. Words that he could not find. 'Jack, have you...'

'He's dead' Caroline croaked.

'What?'

'I had to go and identify his body this morning, the police called me. I cannot get his...his...image out of my...my mind.' she sobbed.

Thomas sat there completely frozen to the spot, molten terror spreading through him. His legs like jelly.

'This can't be happening. This can't be fucking happening. I watched the murder happen and I did fuck all about it.

'I know they are still investigating the area. Can you tell the others, I can't bear it? I just want to be sick' she coughed.

'Have you got family with you?' Thomas asked.

116

'My sister is flying in on the red eye from Lisbon. 'I've got a family liaison officer in the meantime. I know Jack thought a lot of you Thomas. We will get together soon to discuss the business and what happens from here but for now, I just need to take this in. Oh, my husband.' She broke down again in a fresh wave of sobs.

'Please don't worry about anything other than yourself right now. Thomas whispered. I – I will take care of things.'

As he pressed the red button to cancel the call, he had to make a run for the toilet where he was violently sick.

***

Thomas seriously considered locking the door, going back to bed, putting the covers over his head and staying there. He remembered how he used to hide as a child when his mum was in one of her moods. He tried to pour a coffee but could not stomach the smell and his body tried to retch once again. The steaming hot liquid spilled over the sides of the mug as he lacked concentration. Thomas paced the room, digging his nails into his arms, an old habit when he tried to calm himself down. His arm started bleeding and he could feel the pounding in his chest getting stronger. His mouth felt as dry as sandpaper as he walked down the hall to Oliver's room but there was no sign of him this morning and his bedroom door was shut again.

Thomas paced back down to the kitchen trying to catch his breath. He looked at the time. The morning news would be starting now. He switched on the TV:

'A local man has been found brutally murdered just several feet away from his workplace. He was found by local bin men in the early hours of Monday morning. The body has yet to be identified.

Exhaling hard, Thomas leaned against the kitchen counter.

I saw Jack get attacked and I did nothing. Could I have saved him if I had rung the emergency services? What was he doing there anyway? What the fuck was Jack O'Neill doing in the office at fucking two in the morning?

***

Emily was staring at her phone, terrified.

She had checked her social media and there was a strange message waiting for her. From a young woman, requesting to message her. Buy the name of Kellie Hawke.

She clicked accept.

'The message was short and brutal. 'Hey hun how are you?'

Emily's heart began pounding. She typed in 'Sorry, do I know you?'

The reply was nearly instantaneous.

'It doesn't matter who I am. '

Emily typed back: 'If this is an MLM, sorry I'm not interested.

Another speedy reply.

'I'm not into all of that. No, I want you to tell me what you know about Jack 'O'Neill.'

Emily's heart pounded. She began to tremble. 'He was my boyfriend's boss. And for the record, I find him a creep. Why?'

'I'm trying to get some information about him.'

'Are you a journalist?'

'Not exactly.'

'I can give you plenty.' Emily spat. He owned a back-end travel business, Safe Travel Holidays, he's married but acts as if he's a God dropped from Mount Olympus. He was complete sleaze. Why? Why do you want to know?

She waited for the reply but the status changed from available to offline.

Emily began shaking. She crouched down and put her head between her hands and wailed in despair and panic.

TWENTY-THREE

'So, Jack O'Neill is definitely the victim then?' said O'Rourke.

'Without a doubt. His wife came to identify the body this morning.'

'Hs she been offered pastoral care?'

'Of course, she has O'Rourke. That is protocol. Sad as the situation is, we are not here for the sentimentality. We are here for the facts and logic.'

'Facts and logic cannot be twinned with empathy and compassion.'

'Both good qualities but rarely bedfellows. We have a case to solve. And we will do that with facts.'

Marsh brought out a suitcase, unzipped it and brought out a chessboard. He eyed O'Rourke as he did this, putting all the pawns in neat little rows, the knights, the rooks, the queen and then finally the king.

'O'Rourke raised his eyebrows. 'You want a game of chess now?'

Marsh smirked. 'Do you play?'

'Badly.'

'I happened to be junior chess champion when I was thirteen.'

'Impressive.' O'Rourke smiled.

'I have brought this out as part of your tutorial under my wing.' Said Marsh. 'Now, when I approach a case...I tend to see it like a chess game. Pull up a chair.'

O'Rourke obeyed, looking mildly amused.

'You see, you have the pawns. They are sent out into battle first. They do the dirty work and are taken out first. Then you have the knights and the castles with their fancy schmancy moves. You have the King, who is the weakest prick on the board, everyone falls over themselves to protect him, kiss his ass...'

O'Rourke laughed.

'And then you have the queen. The most powerful piece on the chessboard.

'Am I detecting an analogy here for Mr O'Neill?' O'Rourke raised his brows.

I approach all cases through the lens of a chess game. Mr O'Neill isn't necessarily the King. People play all sorts of roles in life and especially in a murder case. We have to sort the pawns from the knights from the Kings to the Queens.'

'Right, well I will take White which means I go first. 'O 'Rourke smirked.

'Good man. And as my new pawn, what do you propose your first move should be.'

'I have full details. Addresses, numbers of all the employees. I should start making some enquiries. '

'Indeed. And start asking questions of their whereabouts. Take them one by one.'

O'Rourke nodded. He looked at the board. 'I will start with Thomas Walker.'

TWENTY-FOUR

Thomas' phone started vibrating again and he wondered if the team had caught the news as well.

'Hello am I speaking with Mr Walker?'

'Yes, who is speaking please?'

'This is Detective Sergeant Seamus O'Rourke; I apologise for the unexpected call. Could we ask you to come down to the station this morning? We have a few questions for you regarding your boss Jack O'Neal?'

The officer had a calming lilting Irish voice.

'Oh um. Right.'

'You can Google the directions. Or do you know where the station is?'

'N -No I know.'

'Good, are you available to come to the station now?

* * *

He decided to call a taxi and stood shivering outside. He needed to speak with Oliver about his plan to go retrieve his hoodie. His phone vibrated once again. It was the work WhatsApp group. Ben.

'Guys have you had a call from the police station? I have to go in this morning about Jack? 11am?'

Gerry then responded 'I'm in at 12 noon.'

Shania messaged 'I too have to go in but not till 2pm. How about we meet at the pub again? 5pm? I -I think we need each other right now.'

Thomas felt selfish but secretly relieved, the news would be travelling fast now. It would not just be him in the station today it seemed. Perhaps it was just protocol.

It was howling with wind and rain and the roads were clogged with traffic. The Police Station looked foreboding as Thomas stepped out of the cab and hastily paid. The raindrops were chasing him in, punishing his cowardice of not going in by getting him wetter and wetter. Thomas ran his hand up the slippery railing as he walked through the double doors into the warm reception. The receptionist looked up to see a pale face.

'How can I help?'

'I'm here to see Detective Sergeant O'Rourke please.

'One moment please.' The secretary called the extension and gestured for Thomas to sit in the waiting area.

Thomas looked around at the posters on the wall; wanted people, numbers for Alcoholics Anonymous and Crime Stoppers, leaflets for people whose loved ones were in prison. Officers came and went through the doors. The room smelt of bleach and everyone's footsteps clanged and echoed.

Finally, a youngish man in his late thirties came out. He smiled.

'Thomas Walker? Detective O'Rourke. Would you come this way please?

He followed the detective to an interview room. His phone phone pinged once again. Was this time Oliver? but it wasn't a reply from Oliver, it was a text from Emily. Shit! He had become so distracted with the phone calls and the news; he had not responded.

'Hi T, I've seen the news. I can't believe it. Please call me as soon as you can, I'm so worried about you. xx'

Thomas quickly responded *'I am so sorry for running out last night. Yes, it is all over the news, I'll call you as soon as I can. I love you. xx'*

Emily was going back to work today after taking some stress leave after the attack.

They arrived at the interview room where a second man was sitting. This man was older than O'Rourke. Late forties by the look of it. He looked sterner.'

'Mr Walker. I am Detective Inspector Marsh.

Thomas swallowed and nodded.

'Would you like a water Thomas?' asked O'Rourke.

Thomas nodded and took the cold plastic cup in his hand gratefully.

'I know this must be difficult sitting here today' Marsh stared back at him.

'Could you just sign here to advise you are happy for us to take a witness statement from you.'

Thomas' hands were shaking as he took the pen to sign. He wondered if the police would pick up on his nerves.

Marsh gave the date and time on the tape recorder and began questioning.

'How long have you worked for Safe Travel Holidays, Thomas?'

Thomas paused and genuinely had to think how long it had been 'I would say it's been 14 months.'

'Would you say you had a close relationship with Mr. O'Neal?'

'I mean, we got on well. I am so grateful that he gave me a job so quickly, I was very lucky. I was in the right place at the right time, I - I guess'.

'Did you ever see Mr. O'Neal outside of work?'

'Sometimes. If there was a team night out or someone's birthday then yes'

'How about your colleagues? Would you say you have a close relationship with them?'

Thomas paused before answering. 'We all get on reasonably well'.

'Only reasonably?'

'I mean it's like with any office isn't it. Not everyone is your cup of tea but you try to get along with everyone regardless' Thomas swallowed hard, hoping they didn't hear.

'Where were you on Sunday night into the early hours of Monday morning?'

'I was at home in bed' replied Thomas quickly as his hear roared.

'How did Mr. O'Neal seem before he went away last week?'

'Same as ever really. He was looking forward to it and spending some time with his wife'

'Would you say Mr. O'Neal had been worried about anything recently? January must always be a quiet month for sales.

'We actually had a successful sale last week so Jack – Mr O'Neill. had been very pleased but I mean yes, it has been quiet. With this job, you do get peaks and troughs.'

'We will be looking kore closely into the business accounts.' Said O'Rourke. 'Of course, you would not have had anything to do with them but I want to be transparent with you.'

Thomas nodded. O'Rourke seemed kind. Dare he tell him what he saw on EarthCam?

'So, let's go back to how you met O'Neill 'said Marsh, jerking Thomas's attention away from O'Rourke. Thomas sensed an inkling of frustration on O'Rourke's part.

'I was working at a newsagent. Mr. O'Neill came in to buy a travel magazine. We got chatting. He – he was impressed by my knowledge. He offered me a job at Safe Travel.'

Marsh frowned. 'That's a bit unusual. Wouldn't he go through the usual channels of agencies, indeed? Isn't that what the internet's for?'

'Jack liked...head hunting him. His people.' Thomas mumbled.

'Interesting' Marsh muttered. 'So, you were headhunted and have been working for the agency for 14 months. You get on reasonably well with your colleagues. No grudges as far as you know. So, tell me your whereabouts on Sunday evening again into early morning Monday. I need you to be a bit more concise.'

Thomas swallowed. 'I was at home. I did some tidying up. I watched some TV. Spoke with my flatmate. I was up quite late, browsing the web.'

'Ah you have a flatmate?' said O'Rourke. 'What is their name?'

'Oliver.'

O'Rourke nodded but looked puzzled. 'Noted.'

'I think we have everything we need for now; we will be speaking with your colleagues this morning as well. Thank you for coming in and cooperating with us Thomas.' Marsh said unsmiling and Thomas did not know how he should take this so he nodded politely.

'We will likely be in touch again soon.' Marsh said sternly. Can we ask that you stay local for a bit?'

'Of course.'

His nerve had failed him. He had not mentioned EarthCam.

O'Rourke accompanied him back to reception. 'Thank you for your time, Thomas. We will be in touch.'

It was still pissing it down outside. There was obviously no work today. But he didn't want to go back to the flat. He wished he had someone like...a parent to talk things through with. But Dolores and he were so far from that place. Their relationship was non-existent. All of a sudden it hit Thomas that apart from Oliver and Emily, he was quite alone in the world...

'Hey, Tom!'

'Oliver!'

Oliver bounded up and hugged him. 'Got your message man. How did it go?' Did you spill the beans about EarthCam?'

'I couldn't. I'm such a fucking coward.'

Thomas couldn't help it. He suddenly burst into tears.

'Ah mate. It's been a rough few days. Oliver put an arm around his shoulders. How's about we go for a walk along the beach, eh? Don't you remember you loved skimming the waves with the stones?!'

'Thomas wiped his eyes.' I don't remember me telling you that. I must have been drunk.'

'Ah, I'm your man, my bro.'

***

Back in the station, Marsh and O'Rourke were dissecting the notes from the conversation.

'I had a feeling that kid was going to say something to me.' 'O'Rourke said grudgingly. 'And Marsh, you then deflected his attention back to work.'

'I don't understand. What do you think he was going to say?' Said Marsh.

'I don't know. It just looked like he was on the brink of confessing something.'

'Wow a confession first interview. That's wishful thinking O'Rourke. You need to lower your expectations. Seems like a pretty non-descript kid to me. Bit spaced out if I'm honest.

'He's not a kid! He's 28.'

'Everyone under 30 is a kid to me.'

'There's something else that's puzzling me too. Walker said he had a flatmate. But when I was doing my research into his address...there is only a record of one person living there.'

'He is probably subletting. You know what these people are like.'

'Mumm'

'I'll be in the breakout room. Need a quick break before Mr Christian Grey- er I mean Mr Benjamin Grey comes in.'

He left, leaving O'Rourke mulling over his thoughts and putting a question mark next to Thomas's name.

TWENTY-FIVE

That evening, Thomas arrived at the pub and noticed Gerry, Shania and Ben all sat waiting, looking uneasy. Shania was very tearful but her compact mirror was nearby and a tissue as she kept checking her eye makeup.

Thomas felt bad and decided to go straight to the bar first to try and calm down, replaying the interview in his mind and all he could think about is that he needed to find his hoodie. He was still hopeful that it was coincidence and he would find it safely on his chair on his return to work.

Ben came up to the bar and made his way over to Thomas cautiously and Thomas held his breath, his back was arched and taut with tension. *I cannot deal with his snappy moods today* Thomas cursed in his mind.

'I can't believe this has happened Tom, can you? Talk about making us all feel guilty or what? Who would want to hurt Jack? I mean, nothing makes sense' Ben said in a low voice.

Thomas felt sorry for him then, after all Ben, had worked with Jack a lot longer than he had and this must be so hard for him as Thomas was pretty sure, this was Ben's first real job. Jack had carried him basically all this time and now he was gone.

'It really is dreadful. I wonder if it was some sort of mistake? I can't imagine Jack having many enemies? Except maybe....' Thomas stopped then.

'Go on?' replied Ben.

'Well, he wasn't exactly quiet about his affairs, was he? Maybe one of his lady friends finally had enough and went 'Fatal Attraction' on his ass?' Thomas was becoming used to the vitriolic poison in his thoughts.

'I don't think he owned any bunny rabbits' smirked Ben.

Shania walked up to the bar now noticing their conversation and looking very distressed and Ben was all too quick in throwing his arm around her, comforting her.

'Who would do this to Jack?' she sobbed. I just cannot believe it'

Gerry was last and walked up to them both 'You boys, ok? I know this is a shock for all of us so we need to stick together right now and I really think Shania needs us too' he looked over to her. Her flushed cheeks and puffy eyes picking at the skin around her usually perfectly manicured nails. 'I think this has hit her more than any of us' Gerry said softly.

'O'Rourke followed me out earlier and said 'Please make sure you don't go too far eh...' talk about patronising' he said sipping his beer.

'What did they mean don't go too far' whispered Ben.

'So, what did Marsh and O'Rourke question you on?' asked Shania.

'Ben shrugged. 'They wanted to know how long I had worked at Safe Travel. How long I had known Jack. What was I doing on the evening Sunday?'

'Same' said Shania.

'Same' said Gerry.

'Did you – tell them about your secret bunking up with Jack?' Ben asked Shania bitterly.

'Shania set her drink down and her lip wobbled.'

'You didn't!' Ben shouted and pointed at her. 'If Marsh and O'Rourke found out you kept information from them, your ass will fry!'

Shania trembled. 'It – it has nothing to do with anything!! Who who ever killed Jack was a random lunatic. It was a mugging gone wrong.'

'Interesting that's the narrative they are pushing.' Mused Gerry, sipping on his drink. 'A mugging gone wrong. Must have been the shittest mugging in history- Marsh and O'Rourke let slip that nothing had been taken from Jack. Not even the shop keys. And who walks around with a weapon at 2am?!'

'Lunatics!' squealed Shania.

'Not lunatics Shania. Pre meditators.' Gerry explained patiently. 'This was no random attack. This was a planned attack.'

'You – you are saying that the attack was pre meditated? That Jack was the intended victim??'

'It wouldn't surprise me. Jack has got a long list of haters.'

'Oh My God!' Shania took a big gulp of her drink and wiped her brow.

'So, the point is Shania. You had better be transparent with the police. It will look bad if you hide information like that.' Said Gerry.

Ben looked panicked. 'They- they won't; I bang Shania up, will they?' He had gone incredibly pale Thomas noticed.

Shania began to cry. 'Look, I know he was a dickhead but I'd – I'd never do that. I was ...well I thought I was...in I...

'No, don't you dare say it!' Ben shouted. He knocked back his shot and headed outside pulling out his cigarettes.

Shania sniffed. 'Oh God.'

Thomas felt a strange pang of sympathy for both of them.'

It's because he likes you.' He said quietly. 'He's pissed off because you liked Jack...and not him.'

Shania looked puzzled. Ben ...likes me likes me?'

Thomas smiled despite himself.' Surely you can't be that slow on the uptake? We all see the way he looks at you around the office.'

Shania looked towards the door. 'He is a nice bloke. Ben. Underneath'.

Thomas couldn't quite bring himself to agree but nodded.

If we weren't all suspects right now, I'd open up. But I can't.

'Thomas. You've always been nice to me. There's something I need to say.'

Gerry cut in. 'You both need to see what's happening about your jobs. Whether Caroline will carry on running the business.'

'That's another thing to worry about' Shania agreed. 'Shall – shall we message her Thomas? I don't want to look like a twat right after her husband died. And... well...I don't know if she knows about me...and...you know...'

'I will message her. I've spoken to her a few times. 'Said Thomas.

And whatever Shania was going to confess, was forgotten.

TWENTY-SIX

Denise was working the graveyard shift again at the hospital. She would be working until 5am. Uploading records in the basement. Alone. She could disappear for hours and no one would know she had gone.

Michael the technician had finally helped her get her head around the system. He had shown some shortcuts that could make uploading documents easier. She was in for a long night and had got herself a black coffee from the machine for the staff working in the lower ground floor. They were a special breed her colleagues who worked on the lower ground floors. Sallow skin, chipped nails. Never seeing daylight, going home in the dark. It was a wonder they all didn't start craving blood and raiding the blood stocks at the full moon. She laughed at her own private joke.

She was ready to get started on the pile in front of her. Tonight, she was especially jittery. She knew tonight it was likely she would come across what she was dreading.

It actually didn't take her that long before she came across it. The autopsy reports. For her husband's former business partner. Her best friend's husband. Her friend in a way. The autopsy report for Mr Jack O'Neill. She couldn't help it. Hands on fire from the heat of the plastic cup, nothing registered on her brain. She began to read....

TWENTY-SEVEN

Thursday

Back at the station, Marsh and O Rourke were putting bios and pictures on a large notice board.

'So, our suspects. Thomas Walker. Ben Grey. Shania Simmons. Gerry Hobbes. Caroline O'Neal, Denise Hobbes'.

'O'Rourke was interested. 'So, you think Mrs Hobbes could be a suspect?'

'I'm certainly not ruling her out just yet.'

O'Neal took out a marker pen.

'So, here's what we know. Mr O'Neal went on a break to Devon with his wife Caroline. He returns and for some unknown reason, decides to visit Safe Travel Holiday offices in ungodly hours. Fair enough. It's his business. But what in the hell could not wait until the next day?? We don't know if he managed to get in the shop or he had just got there and someone sets on him with a hammer. A few blows to the back of his head. Finished. Now, first thoughts would be a mugging gone wrong but this doesn't ring true. Firstly, Mr O'Neal's wallet was still on his person when he was found. Secondly, who carries a hammer around with them?! Muggings are usually opportunistic and involve knives.

'Agreed' said O'Rourke.

'I'll call the bank up; get a hold of company account statements.' Said O Rourke.

'Excellent.'

'History lesson for the morning. O'Neal and Hobbes founded the business together. O'Neal then took over, apparently with permission from Mr Hobbes who took a back seat, bought a premises in Southsea. Hired Miss Simmons, Ben Grey came knocking on the door apparently looking for a job. Thomas Walker was an 'accidental hire'. He and O'Neal met when Mr Walker was working in a newsagent. Matthews showed off his expertise of geography and O'Neal thought he'd be a good salesperson.

'How do you know all of this extra stuff?' asked Marsh impressed.' We didn't cover all of this in the interviews.'

'Wiki' O'Rourke grinned. 'Mr O'Neal was always updating the Wiki page. He set up a Twitter account for the shop too.'

'What kind of...excuse me...backend travel office needs a Twitter feed?' laughed Marsh.

'Marsh. I'm a millennial. Social media is the dogs now for business promotion.' Grinned O'Rourke. 'Look'. He showed Marsh on his smartphone.

'Hashtag this. Hashtag that. Hashtag Safe Travel. Hashtag Hashtag Hashtag. Oh, give me a break the guy was 52.'

'So what? Gen Xers can't be down with the kids. I'm defending the bloke. Good business sense.'

'I'm not complaining. The Twitter account seems like a gold mine. Mine in for all its worth. I also want you to look up all of Mr O'Neal's social media accounts.'

'Will do,' said O'Rourke.

Marsh checked his e-mails. 'Oh, that's efficient. The hospital has e-mailed over the autopsy report.'

'Excitement rose in O'Rourke. 'Excellent. Do you have time to read it now?'

'No time like the present. Are you happy to have lunch here?'

'Certainly.'

Marsh went to the canteen and came back with steak pies, chips and beans... and some soup.

'Wait a second.' He spoke. He took out his phone and snapped a picture of the soup.'

'How the Slimming World going?' grinned O'Rourke.'

'Urgh, we have a meet this evening and we have to show pictures of what we have eaten today. So, I am photographing this lovely...er...soup.' Marsh grimaced. 'I'm not lying. I will just omit the pie and chips!'

O'Rourke smiled. 'In a court of law, that's lying by omission.'

'Yeah well....' Marsh smiled in spite of himself. 'Right, this autopsy.'

They pored over it.

'Victim male 52. Estimated time of death 2:30am.... Bruising around the wrists... presumably where he was held down...poor bloke.... Skinned knees where he fell to them...so where...what was the Cause of death...here we are. Cause of death: blow to the cranium with metal object. Most likely a crowbar or a hammer.'

'Blimey' said O'Rourke. 'So, this definitely puts paid to it being a random attack.'

'It certainly does. No one would be walking around a quiet area of Portsmouth just armed for no reason. If it was a bar fight, they would at least be down Guildhall Walk with all the students. No, no, this is significant. Whoever this person was, was specifically after Jack O'Neill.'

'And this could explain why O'Neill was at Safe Travel Offices at such an ungodly hour!' O'Rourke said excitedly.

'Absolutely. I think O'Neill knew his killer!'

'I think he was there to meet his killer!'

'Precisely!'

They each sat back in their chairs, looking excited and pleased with this development.

'How would O'Neill have been contacted?' do you think? Asked Marsh.

'By any means. Phone, e-mail...'

'Right. Phone records. Check O'Neill's phone records. The calls he made at the weekend in Finlake with his wife.'

Marsh added weapon: Hammer to the board.

'So, we have our suspects. Now we have a weapon. Which of their pretty little faces will crack first??

TWENTY-EIGHT

The cool, professional receptionist calmly took the guest passes from the two women and issued locker keys, towels and bottled water.

'Have a lovely afternoon' she smiled.

Denise had taken Caroline out to the upmarket spa that Gerry and she were members of. She had telephoned and asked for an emergency guest pass.

'My best friend's husband has been murdered. I think that's a pretty valid reason to need some de cleansing.'

She hadn't said that to the receptionist of course. She was way too timid. She had always been timid. But this was too important. She needed to keep close to Caroline (ambiguous-close to be a friend but close to keep track of how the trail was progressing)

The heated floor in contrast to the cool spray of the ice room was making her head feel light. They found a quiet corner to lie on the hot stone beds.

'Thank you for taking me here today, Denz.' Caroline said coolly.

'Anything to get your mind off of things'. Denise didn't know how to navigate this minefield. She had brought Caroline here to relax but....

'How are your Portuguese Lessons going?'

'Mmmm, they are going well. Language learning...it's a good distraction.'

'Which language school is it again?'

'The one next to the college. The college rents out the computer room.'

'Also look. Caroline showed Denise the landing page of her phone. 'I've downloaded Duolingo so I can keep up the learning on the go. I can string some sentences together.'

'Will you be going to see Petra in Lisbon?

Caroline's sister Petra had emigrated to Lisbon about 5 years ago. She said she'd never return to live in Britain, not with so much sun, sea, sand and cocktails.

'Petra did offer to fly back but what's the bloody point?' Caroline rubbed her eyes.

'Your sister wants to show you support.' Squeaked Denise. 'Why don't you go see her?'

'I can't leave the country. Marsh and O 'Rourke are still mapping their leads. They will need me on hand to answer any questions.'

Caroline's face crumpled. 'Oh God. I can't believe this is happening'.

'Denise's heart began hammering. How was she to react?

'Oh Caroline, I'm so sorry this has happened to you. Is there anything Gerry and I can do at all for you?'

At the mention of Gerry's name, Caroline seemed to bristle for a second. 'Thank you. I will let you know.'

They led in silence for a few minutes, listening to the trickle of the indoor fountain.

'Ha- have you?'

'Safe Travel Holidays? Nothing as yet. Marsh and O Rourke are still ripping the accounts a new rectum. Combing everything for clues. To be honest, I feel like getting shot of the whole damn business. Whether or not Gerry will come away with a dime from the place I'm not sure. I can't be damned with the whole legal spider's web....'

Denise had flinched at Caroline's language...but didn't say anything. Who could blame the woman? She was a widow now....in the most brutal way...

'How had the four of us come to this?'

I – I was actually going to – to ask if – if the police had heard the results yet of the autopsy?'

(THE AUTOPSY WOULD HAVE BEEN CARRIED OUT BY SOMEONE OTHER THAN DENISE. DENISE HIDES THE ORIGINAL, MORE COMPREHENSIVE ONE THAT LISTS THE STRANGULATION. RE WRITES IT SO SHOWS DEATH AS BLOW TO THE HEAD)

'Marsh and O Rourke told me we will have the results in a week'.

Caroline looked sideways at her friend. 'Has Gerry said much at all?'

Denise stuttered. 'Er.er no, no nothing why?'

'He and Jack were business partners. I know things went a bit tits up business wise but I'm hoping Gerry will show me so, me solidarity.'

'Oh Caroline. Why – what do you mean...that's all water under the bridge?'

'Let's be honest Denzie. It wasn't. We both know there was a lot of unfinished business between your husband and my husband.'

'Denise's heart was hammering. 'Caroline, what are you trying to say...'

CAROLINE IS ENJOYING GAS LIGHTING HER

'I'm not trying to say anything. Look I know the type of person my husband was. He always liked control. Gerry is...more of a peacemaker... (CAROLINE IS TRYING TO WIND DENISE UP, MAKING DENISE THINK SHE KNOWS THAT SHE KNOWS!)

'Gerry gave up his share of the business happily!'

Caroline sipped her drink. 'Listen, let's not get too far into this. You've been very kind bringing me here. Just for a few hours. I want to put my grief aside and ... she settled back and opened her magazine (CLUE TO THE READ THAT CAROLINE CAN BE VERY DETACHED)

This unnerved Denise. This was not how the spa visit was meant to go. They were in a room of ice but her hands could not stop sweating....

Later, Caroline sat at her table, alone. Looking at old photographs of her and Jack. Trying to decide which photographs to use for the funeral. A blank page lay in front of her, the pen on its side. She was meant to be writing an obituary but she couldn't concentrate. Petra cooked dinner for them both and was now busying herself doing housework. Her sister always looked so healthy with her golden tan, highlighted hair, a few crow's feet from soaking up the Portuguese sun...

Caroline sighed and stretched her arms up. She picked up her phone and clicked on the Duolingo app. Have a Portuguese lesson to distract herself? The app asked her what she would like to practice today. She selected 'Friends and Family.'

Eu não tenho amigos. Eu não tenho família.

I have no friends. I have no family. She muttered to herself, tasting the Portuguese on her tongue. It was a nice language. It suited her.

Putting aside the obituary, she pulled another stack of paperwork towards her. Jack's documents for Safe Travel Holidays. He had never kept them particularly organised. Piles and piles of statements, expenses. Caroline had sifted through, trying to make head and tail of the situation of the business. But it was no use. She had tried unsuccessfully to hack into Jack's computer. She had tried all means of passwords including all the memorable places and dates they had shared. All came back 'Computer Says No'. It reminded her of when he and her would watch Little Britain and laugh at David Walliams. She put her head in her hands and squeezed it hard. Where had it all gone so wrong? She knew she had married a player but she was the one who was going to change him. Jack loved her. 'My philandering ways are behind me 'he said to her the day after their wedding. 'You're the only woman for me.' She had believed him.

She had fought hard to keep him. From the day they had met when he was a student studying Travel and Tourism, trying to keep him to herself was like trying to nail jam to the wall. She still recalled that horrifying incident when that crazy woman had accosted him, saying he had fathered their child and demanding money. Jack had told her where to go, thankfully. He had re assured Caroline that there was no way he could have been with the woman at the times he claimed they were together.

She's a crazy fantasist, they all are, those types of women. They are bitter and twisted. They see a powerful alpha male and they want to drag his name through the mud because all they can get is the betas. She was jealous of you because you had snagged the alpha babe. Don't let her come between us.

Caroline had believed him and they had gone on to marry. She kept trying to forget that woman. She didn't even know her name of who she was, whether she was out there raising Jack's child…'

No, she wasn't going down that rabbit hole tonight. She was going to focus on selling Safe Travel Holidays. Another loose end to tie up. She was sure Jack, being as wiley as he was, had a load of money tied up in the business. He was always going on about turning it into a dynasty. She would sell it and take the money. Well, it was the least he owed her.

TWENTY-NINE

Shania sat alone at her flat, still feeling drunk from all she had sunk at the pub. God, this was such a bloody mess. She thought about calling the cop station and asking for Marsh and O'Rourke – well, O'Rourke. That guy was a bit nicer.

They had asked her the usual questions. She had told them she had shown up for interview with Jack and the moment she had left the shop he had called her, telling her she was hired.

She had left out that he had instigated contact on Facebook, commenting on the attractiveness of her photo. A flurry of messages had begun. Shania had been so drawn to him. Jack was at least 25 years older than her but – and she grimaced – a diet of watching shows like The Batchelor., Love Island...she wanted to be aspirational when looking for love, why settle for the pimply 21-year-olds. 'I don't want no Scrubs' as TLC had sung.

It had flattered her when Jack had shown such an interest. In their conversation, he mentioned he was a business owner. He was married but unhappily, looking to leave his wife soon and was looking to fall in love again with the right woman and whisk her off in the sunset. God, he had actually used that line.

She really thought he and Jack had had a chance. She would change him. She was young, vivacious, fun. A breath of fresh air. Well, she had tried to be.

It had been fun in the office in the office for a while. She felt like Bridget Jones admiring Daniel Cleaver. They would send each other flirty messages through e-mail. He'd frequently called her into his office and they would have a fumble and a giggle. She knew it was wrong but...'

But there was no way she could let the detectives know any of this. It would put her in the firing line as a target.

Sometimes love makes you do crazy things.

Her biggest panic at the moment was remembering what she had left in the office....and the fact that it was very likely that she had been the last person to see Jack O'Neill alive....

THIRTY

Wednesday

Marsh and O'Rourke bought breakfast and headed to the still cordoned off shop of Safe Travel Holidays where forensics were still being carried out.

O'Rourke had treated them both to buttery croissants.

'I won't tell if you won't 'he smiled.

'Cheers' Marsh muttered.

'Lose any weight last night.'

'Nah I gained. Everyone in the circle was very sympathetic'.

O'Rourke smiled. 'Well, I'm not entirely surprised with what you put away.'

They greeted their colleagues in the forensics. The office stank of bleach. A lot of anything DNA based would have been collected Monday and yesterday. Today, there was a big search at the office looking for anything incriminating.

'It's shame that O'Neill never thought to put a camera up.' Marsh said, looking at the bare walls.

He stood by the door.

'OK. Roleplay. I'm Jack O'Neill. It's 2am and I have just walked into the office. What would I be here for?'

'I'd go to the desk.' Said O'Rourke.

The forensics team had already bagged a lot up.

'O'Rourke began opening the drawers.

'It's strange. No pictures of anyone. I know he didn't have kids, but there's no pictures of his wife. Only himself.'

'Classic narcissist' Marsh muttered.

'I'm still waiting for O'Neill's phone provider to provide me with a list of calls and texts he made on Sunday evening.' Said O'Rourke.

'Yes…look over here. 'Marsh gestured for O'Rourke. 'There's a stain on here. What looks like…lipstick…or…chipped polish?'

'You think this belongs to Simmons?'

'Quite possibly.'

'Well, she probably went in to O'Neill's office frequently. Maybe doing photocopying. It's interesting but not incriminating.'

'Hmmm'.

Jack's office was down a narrow corridor which at the end had a fire exit door.

'That leads to the back alley.' Said O'Rourke.

Across from O'Rourke's office was a small kitchenette and an extension with some faded couches where the team would take their breaks.' They presumed. The sink was loaded with cups and cereal bowls.

'Have these examined too.' Said Marsh to one of the team who obediently went to bag it all up.

'O'Neill's computer will have to be pulled apart too.'

Shania's and Gerry's desks were at the back wall. Across from Shania's desk was Ben's desk and Thomas's, opposite Gerry's. Thomas and Ben's desk were the one's nearest to the door.

'Blimey. there's a big mess on Grey's desk.' Noted O'Rourke.

He went over. It looked as if the whole desk had been ransacked. O'Rourke found paperwork for holiday destinations, invoices, queries from customer... and...wait a minute.

'There's a whole load of print outs to do with O'Neill here.' He spoke.

'Really?' said Marsh. 'Well, maybe O'Neill asked him to help him with a campaign.'

'I don't know. 'said O'Rourke thoughtfully. This seems more.... personal.' Look'

There were print outs of historical articles on Jack O'Neill, records of awards he's won. Safe Travel's Wiki page. Also, as the detectives flicked through, also print outs from Ben's own social media pages.

'MMM, does seem a bit odd.' Said Marsh. 'Let's take them back to the station.'

'Agreed.'

'It's intriguing that all the other employees were headhunted by O'Neill but Mr Grey, according to his interview, persuaded O'Neill to hire HIM.'

'I wonder what it was about Grey that made Mr O'Neill take a chance on him?'

'I need to make some calls and get some bank accounts checked.' Said O'Rourke firmly.

***

Rourke disappeared to make the calls to the employees' respective banks. Marsh took the paperwork back to the breakout room to peruse.

'So, no murder weapon found on the premises. That wasn't a surprise. No video footage. This was going to be a hard case to crack. But Marsh was determined.

He knelt down in front of his chess set. It helped him think. Certainly, at the moment, O'Neill was the king. But who was the piece on the board that wanted to get to O'Neill? It was either a colleague or a family member...

O'Rourke came back in 2 hours later?'

'What did the banks say?' Marsh rubbed his eyes.

'Interesting stuff. God, even as a detective you are on hold for ages!'

O'Rourke read out his notes.

'Both Walker and Simmons are solvent but Grey is nearly maxed out his overdraft. He has a payday loan coming out of his ears?'

'Do you think he was trying to rob Safe Travel?'

'But no money is left on the pre mises.'

'Maybe he was trying to blackmail O'Neill by getting juicy gossip on him.'

'A possibility. Doesn't make him a killer though.'

'How about Mr Hobbes' account?'

'Solvent too. I noticed some slightly unusual transactions to *Caixa Geral de Depositos.* That's a Portuguese bank. It didn't allow me to see who the beneficiary was.'

'Hmm, the guy is looking to retire. Could be paying for a rental property or some holiday out there?'

'I'm going to follow it up but that will take some time. One other thing. Walker.'

'I've researched the owner of the property rented by Walker. I called him up pretending I was interested in renting the house. The bloke said he already had ONE tenant. So, one thing is certain. Walker is illegally subletting his apartment.'

'That's a civil matter though, not a police matter.'

'Well, the threads are branching out. We now need the company accounts. '

'Safe Travel…bit of an ironic name it becoming, isn't it?'

THIRTY-ONE

Thomas headed for the bus stop, he clenched his arms across his chest, wrapping them around himself as tight as he could. His fingers tingled. He got out his phone and made sure to call Emily before he put her off any longer.

'Hi darling, how's your day going?'

Emily answered with a sharp tone to her voice. 'How is MY day, Thomas, your boss is dead, the same boss that attacked me just days ago. Oh, and NOW the police have just rang me wanting to speak to me tomorrow about Jack? Why would they want to do that? What the hell Thomas, did you tell them that Jack attacked me? What were you thinking?'

'Woah, what the hell? No, I didn't even mention you at all. I don't understand'

'This is the last thing I need, my first day back at work and now tomorrow, I have to take leave just to go and see them. You are the only one I've talked about the attack. I don't know what else this could be about?

Thomas sighed 'Well the following morning after the pub, Shania came in ranting at me saying you had tried it on with Jack so naturally I wanted to set her straight but I doubt she would mention this and...look can we talk about this tonight? In private? I don't want to do this on the phone. When do you have to see them?'

'I've got to go Thomas; I am meant to be in a training session. God knows how I am going to concentrate now' Emily hung up the phone so quickly, Thomas did not get to say goodbye.

Fuck. Why did they want to speak to Emily and who told them?

Ben was in the office when Shania and I had the discussion? But I also told Gerry in confidence when in the car with him. Not just that though, if the police do know about the attack, it also puts us both in the firing line with a motive.

The bus was full of people, everyone soaked from the rain. The steam was condensing on the windows. The smell was pungent of body odour and wet clothes.

Thomas groaned as he walked towards the back of the bus. Then he found himself smiling. The old man in the trilby hat sat looking out the window. 'Hey Stan, how are you? Is it ok if I sit here?' Stan looked up, the lines on his forehead growing deeper. Thomas needed the distraction with some mindless chatter.

'Thomas, my boy! It's good to see you, yes please sit down. Thomas immediately smelt the old spice.

'You never did tell me what you do for a living?' asked Stan.

'I work as a holiday agent in town' Thomas couldn't hold his gaze as he noticed some of the people turn around staring at them. He was waiting for Stan to mention Jack and guessed that's why a few people turned around also as the business was all over the local news.

Thomas swallowed hard but Stan did not mention Jack.

'Ah that must be fun for you' a trace of a smile still on his lips. 'Have you been to the cemetery today then Stan?'

'Oh yes, rain or shine, I go and see her. I would feel guilty if I didn't go' he smiled sadly.

'Guilt is a very destructive thing' said Thomas with a crack in his voice then.

'What do you have to feel guilty for?' Stan asked.

'Oh. Nothing. Nothing.'

Neither one of them spoke as Stan turned and gazed out the window. 'Nothing really' Thomas said quietly.

'You don't sound sure' Stan persisted.

Stop it Thomas, stop being so paranoid. How could he know anything at all?

'Guilt lives within all of us' Stan said quietly. Thomas waited for him to continue.

'I should have taken the medication described to me when I had the chance but I am stubborn and I thought I knew better. My son begged me to listen to the doctors and do what I'm told but I was stuck in my ways'

'Can you not start now? Now you know? 'Thomas paused.

'I'm too late my boy, the damage has been done' Stan concluded and then sat in silence for the rest of the ride.

Thomas noticed that when everyone got off the bus, they were all deliberately avoiding his eyes....

THIRTY-TWO

Emily answered the door as soon as he buzzed that evening and immediately, he could sense the tension between them.

Thomas' eyes drifted to the mess of the flat, food packets on the floor, crumbs, mud was smeared next to some trainers on the floor. Why did he care about this right now? This should be the last thing on his mind.

Emily hung her head to one side and smiled softly at him 'are you ok? Relief ran through Thomas when he realised it was not going to be a heated discussion.

'I am sorry I got so stressed earlier. I was thinking, I will go and see them and whatever has been said about any disagreements with Jack, I will just downplay it.'

'What?' Thomas blurted out, incredulous. 'He DID attack you Em and that should not be ignored for Christ's sake!'

Emily shook her head, her gaze trailing over his face.

'Yes, it did happen and it was awful but Jack has gone Thomas, in a horrific way. Listen Thomas, we do not want them to think we had a vendetta against Jack days before his death'

'I understand what you are saying but it's not like either one of us bloody did this'.

'I honestly cannot believe it's happened! It's a waking nightmare! How is everyone?' Emily said ignoring his comment.

Thomas's mouth hung open as he struggled to answer, his thoughts still elsewhere and the musty smell in the flat greeted him. 'Everyone is um, everyone is in shock of course. To be expected I guess' he could feel his nails digging into his palms again.

The anxiety was crippling.

He needed to talk to her properly and be completely honest. He felt like a spare part in this flat, even though he had been here a million times before.

'Let's make a cuppa shall we and chill out for a bit, you look like you need something stronger though?'. 'A tea would be fine, thank you' he replied.

He followed Emily into the kitchen and noticed the pizza boxes still sat there from the other night.

She placed her hand on her hip as she put the kettle on and when she looked up, she saw the distracted, distant look in his eyes. His hair looked as if he had been running his hand through it for hours.

Seeing Emily made him realise just how much he missed the closeness between them. He just wanted to hold her, close his eyes and wait for all this to disappear.

'I know how mad this sounds okay but you need to just listen. I saw Jack's murder Em. I was on EarthCam. Remember he asked me to look out for the shop whilst he was on his weekend away? Do not ask me how I happened to be watching at that exact time but I was and...'

'Thomas, you tried saying this the other day and did we not agree you may have fallen asleep at the computer and dreamt this?'

'No, you tried telling me that you thought I may have dreamt this but I am telling you know I did not. I saw this with my own eyes'

'Ok ok, please calm down. Just talk to me'

'I saw two people. The first one being Jack coming out of the shop and then a second figure behind him. I thought they may have been together for a split second and then of course the attacker came up behind and hit him and knocked him down. It was obviously very dark and grainy but I had this compulsion to keep watching....'

Emily stood in complete shock and completely ignored the kettle that had finished boiling.

Thomas was crying now 'it was startling, it was fucking awful Em, I felt like I couldn't breathe and then that's when I noticed.'

'Noticed what?' Emily grabbed a hold of Thomas' arms then and urged him to finish.

'The killer...they.th...ey were wearing my hoodie'

'What do you mean your hoodie? How could you possibly? I mean you are not the only person to own a hoodie Tom''

'It was my Uni hoodie with the missing letters. I left it at work when I rushed out to come and look after you and now it's gone.'

'And that stopped you calling the police?' she whispered, comprehension dawning on her.

'I bloody panicked Emily. wouldn't you? Now they want to speak to you and I... I feel claustrophobic. I need to find my hoodie'.

Thomas wrung his hands; he felt the tears pricking the corners of his eyes.

'I'm scared, Em, I'm really fucking scared. 'How about if that was my hoodie... Em?!'

Emily looked frightened.

'If it was...I would say that...that...whoever killed Jack...if they were wearing your hoodie...they'd be trying to frame you....'

THIRTY-THREE

Thomas waited until Emily was asleep and sat in silence for a moment procrastinating over his decision. He watched for the gentle rise and fall of her chest and she was cocooned within her duvet, safe and warm. He still had his work key in the bottom of his bag and his curiosity got the better of him. He needed to go back to the office to see if he could see the hoodie. He wanted to prove himself wrong and that his hoodie had nothing to do with what he saw.

The moon was dim and the air cold as Thomas ventured outside, the darkness hung like a curtain around him. He carefully shut the front door to Emily's flat desperate not to wake her. Nothing stirred and nothing spoke.

The taxi driver did not ask questions or make any kind of conversation and Thomas was grateful for the silence as he urged the car to go faster. The only words he uttered to the driver was to drop him at 'Beehive walk' which was a couple of streets away and there lived a block of flats. He thanked him politely in the hope he did not draw any unnecessary attention to himself.

As he walked the remaining way there, he finally reached the top of the street and he headed for the back door of the shop. He noticed the police tape was still surrounding the outside. The place was deserted; it felt very haunting. The bins were kept around the back and Thomas could not believe the odour coming from them as he sealed up his nostrils with his jumper and begged his brain to conjure memories of sweet-smelling perfumes. After a quick glance over his shoulder and one more to make sure, he used his key and opened the back door to the shop. He felt his heart quicken as he snuck through and immediately, he was hit with the smell of chemicals and a complete mess. His love of cleaning was urging him to tidy up but he knew he just had to look for the hoodie and then get out of there as quickly as possible.

Careful to not touch anything, Thomas snuck over to his desk. He could not turn any lights on so was careful to manoeuvre around the furniture. It felt strange being there. Just last week, everything was normal, happy even.

He walked over to his desk and looked straight over to the chair where his hoodie would be draped. Nothing. No sign of it. Fuck. He looked under the desk, in the draws, under the tables, there was no sign. He saw something out of the corner of his eye and jerked around, thinking he had been caught. His breath left his throat and his heart roared in terror as saucer eyes and a manic, joker like grin was staring right at him. It took a second to register that it was the poster of Jack, unhinged and dangling absurdly from the wall. It must have come unstuck whilst the deep clean was taking place. Jack's face no longer looked cheeky, it was ghoulish, grotesque, his left hand still on his hip but the right hand that was usually raised in a palm splayed Haven holidays wave, which according to comments from customers on STH website looked 'cheesier than a stilton factory...', had been slashed off. Thomas took a quick gasp which was partway between a laugh and a sob. It had obviously fallen down during the police search and now Jack's eyes were staring into his soul. With one last look, Thomas crept towards the back door and out into the alley.

THIRTY-FOUR

Gerry heard Denise crying again.

'Love come on. You can't keep letting your emotions get in the way.'

'Oh Gerry.' Denise sobbed. 'I can't sleep. I am going out of my mind.

'Shah shh love it's OK.'

'That Detective duo, Marsh and O'Rourke called me in today.'

'And you told them all about how you were friends with Jack. That's the truth. How can they question that?'

'They will see the business history between you and Jack. They will begin to draw lines. Gerry, I can't lose you!'

'You won't lose me darling.'

'You are so noble Gerry. So loyal. But you must stop sticking your neck out for – '

'Darling. All you need to do is tell the police what they need to know. Nothing else.'

'Oh Gerry!'

She broke down and sobbed in his arms. Gerry held her close, looking hard at the wedding ring around his finger with the imprint of a horse.

THIRTY-FIVE

The following morning, Thomas woke up in Emily's bed. He Couldn't remember what time he eventually got in but looking at his phone, he has slept in. There is no sign of Emily, just her empty side with ruffled pillows.

His phone began to vibrate on the bedside table. Still disorientated he answered the phone 'Emily?'

'Hi Thomas?'

Thomas froze.

'This is Detective Sergeant Jonathan Marsh, we met you back at the station?'

Thomas sat up with a jolt. 'Of course. Hi, how can I help you, Detective?'

'Thomas, we wondered if we could come by your flat today? We just have a few more questions and we could use your input if you do not mind?'

Thomas hesitated and pressed his fingers into his closed eyes, feeling a sting.

'Was I not much help the other....'

'Of course, you were, it's just a couple of things we wanted to run by you' Marsh replied sharply, cutting him off mid-sentence.

Thomas had no choice and he could not exactly say no 'Yes of course. What time should we expect you?'

'We? I have you down as living alone actually?'

'No, I live with my roommate Oliver Creswell'

'There was a 10 second pause from the Detectives end.

'Well OK then. We can confirm you live at – '

'No problem at all' Thomas swallowed. 'See you then'.

Thomas called Emily.

'Hi Tom, I...'

'Em...the police want to see me again. I thought we were going to discuss what we were going to say.'

'I know Tom, I was called to the office. What time are they coming?

'Three. God, should I mention the hoodie?'

'No. God no. Listen, as I keep saying, if it was your hoodie the person was wearing when you saw the attack, then the killer would have had to have been able to get into the office to get the thing. But you – we need to make sure...quite sure that the hoodie is not in the agency. It could still be.'

'I know that it's not! But that is what Oliver...'

'Excuse me who? Oh Lord, I have to go, Tom, just tell them the bare minimum. Keep things vague until we can find out more. I love you, OK?'

She hung up.

***

3pm came around quickly and there was a sharp rap on Thomas' door as he was pacing around his kitchen waiting for the dreaded visit. He took a quick look in the mirror and groaned. He tried to dress well with a smart shirt and clean jeans but he still looked wan and pale.

'Good afternoon, Thomas'

'Good afternoon'.

Thomas tried to stay calm but he could feel sweat gathering on his hairline which he tried to wipe off with the back of his hand as they entered the kitchen. 'I am well thank you; can I get you both a drink?

'A water will be fine thank you'

'Oh yes please, water would be good' said O'Rourke who spoke very softly compared to his colleague.

'It is routine that we take a look around.'

Thomas swallowed. 'No no, go ahead.

Marsh and O Rourke started poking around.

'Is this your flatmate's room?' asked Marsh.

'Yes.'

Marsh turned the door handle. The room was pristine. The bed was folded neat and crisp. Thomas knew Oliver was a minimalist but...there was no hint of any personality at all.

'Well, your flatmate is certainly houseproud. Marsh remarked.

'I'm not often in his room.' Thomas stuttered.

He thought he saw Marsh and O Rourke exchanging glances.

'Let's focus on Mr O Neal. Do you have any idea why Mr O'Neal would want to go to work at that time in the morning?'

'No, I really don't' replied Thomas still looking around. 'Although...he was a workaholic.'

'But 2am though' Marsh said sharply. Thomas felt Marsh's eyes bored through him. 'Even a banker in London may balk at those hours.'

'We will of course be checking the agency's accounts' said O' Rourke. 'We have reason to believe that Mr O'Neil was in a great deal of debt.'

Thomas opened and closed his mouth like a goldfish. 'I -I didn't know that.'

'Mmm, interesting, isn't it?'

Thomas said nothing.

'You must have been very angry when you heard that Mr O'Neal had attempted... shall we say relations with your girlfriend?'

'I was going to have a chat with him when he returned from his holiday, just to clear up any misunderstandings.'

'Was this chat in the middle of the night near your place of work by any chance?' Marsh pressed him then.

'Of course not!' Thomas frowned and pressed his nails into his palms hard.

There was a painfully awkward silence and then O'Rourke finally spoke up 'Thomas this is a nice picture with Emily here?'

'Oh yes on graduation day' Thomas replied, his throat closing up.

'Ah what University is that? I am just trying to make out your hooded jumper?'

Thomas froze, his stomach dipping 'um The University of Portsmouth. I stayed local'

'What does it say on your hoodie?

'Eat, Sleep, Art History, Repeat. Everyone was given a hoodie when we left' Thomas pursed his lips.

'Do you have the hoodie here? I would love to see it?' O'Rourke asked.

'I am afraid not, I left it at work. I quite often forget it' he said quickly.

'No problem, well I think we have asked all of our questions for now Thomas. If you think of anything else about Mr O'Neal or anything, please give us a call?' Marsh said unsmiling.

'Will do' Thomas said, realising when he moved that his back was soaked in sweat.

Thomas shut the door to and fell flat with his back against the door. His hands rubbed his burning eyes as he choked back tears. The four walls were closing in on him and his already knotted stomach twisted itself tighter. He thought he was going to be sick so he ran to the bathroom and grabbed hold of the edge of the basin. *Breathe. Just breathe Thomas.*

He splashed some cold water on his face and perched on the side of the bath.

'Oliver is that you?' Thomas could hear talking coming from the kitchen. 'Thank God you are home; the police have been here and...' there was no one there. Dead silence apart from the quiet hum of the fridge.

Meanwhile, Marsh and O Rourke were having a catch-up meeting at the local Costa.

'Do you think it's relevant to the case...him illegally subletting?'

'Not directly but the fact that he is capable of deceiving his landlord could point towards something else.'

'So,' Marsh said excitedly. 'What did you get on the Safe Travel Holiday company accounts?'

'Very juicy stuff. The company was in a lot of...to put it delicately...merde!'

'How much...merde?'

'It seems Mr O'Neal liked living the high life. Loads of bills to swanky restaurants, a new suit from Savile Row. Let's just say that Mr O'Neal was charging a lot to the company account when it should have been coming from his own money.'

'But Mr O'Neal owned the business.'

'It's still bloody unethical. Another interesting thing…. there are repeated payments to account 070499/62439800. I recognised the number. That account belongs to Miss Simmons.

THIRTY-SIX

Emily rushed over as quickly as she could when she received the call from Thomas. 'You sounded hysterical on the phone, what did the police say Tom?' she let herself in and rushed over to him as he stood staring into space. 'They saw the picture of us at graduation Emily'

'Okay, so?'

'I was wearing the hoodie in the picture! They asked to see it which means they must know something. Otherwise, that is one hell of a coincidence! I know I left that hoodie at work when I rushed to see you. Next thing I know, SOMEONE kills Jack wearing the hoodie which means they must have taken it from work and that could be anyone! Now suddenly, the police are interested in it? Why didn't I just call them that night or even tell them when I first went to the station?'

'You were frightened, you were in complete shock and you said it all happened so quickly that you barely had any time to register it. We have to keep our mouths shut. It would look incredibly suspect now. Saying anything is not an option.'

I feel like my own mind is blackmailing me. My own hidden, dark companion.

If you don't clean up this kitchen before Emily leaves, something bad is going to happen.

'Thomas you are shaking, please hold my hands' Emily tried to calm Thomas down and by holding his hands, he would not be able to scratch or pinch himself. 'Please sit down with me?' she said softly.

'Me, I think I just need to go to bed, will you stay with me tonight?'

Why is it when you are in desperate need of sleep, no matter how exhausted you are, you cannot drift off

Thomas led in bed, getting more and more irritated as his mind would not let the thoughts lie. He had got into a new habit of checking Earth Cam at night, throughout the night. Thomas felt like if he did not check EarthCam and visit at least ten places, something bad was going to happen to someone else he cared about. Yes, he was obsessed before but not in a negative way, he used to use the site as 'homework' for holidays and ideas for his clients. Now, he needed to check everything was alright with the world. He needed to check that he was not going to let somebody else die and do nothing. Thomas felt he could not even tell Emily about this new ritual he had picked up; she was already worried enough.

Something is wrong with me. I am losing my mind. This might convince her that I am actually in need of locking up.

He looked at the clock on the bedside table, 03:12am, Emily stirred then 'Thomas why are you sat on there for? Come back to bed'

Thomas turned to her and said 'I couldn't sleep so was just thinking about holiday ideas for us'

Emily smiled 'the best ideas do not come out of tiredness or exhaustion'

This dysfunctional sleep was almost like an invitation to think deeply about my life and what I can do to make things better. What will make it better? answers?

THIRTY-SEVEN

Jack's funeral was above all a celebration of his life and accomplishments. The coffin was pulled from the hearse by six strong men, but even they almost buckled under its weight. Of course, Jack had to have only the best - a solid gold coffin. It must have cost a fortune. The coffin gleamed in the early morning light that streamed through the windows of the crematorium. He could not help thinking: Jack was beyond this world now, why the damn fuss? Then he remembered the poster in the shop window and how long it took that poor photographer to get the perfect shot. Jack never did do things by halves.

On top of the coffin were a huge arrangement of beautiful flowers, almost as if to hide the reality many hearts could not bear to think about. Guns and Roses started playing 'Live and let Die' as everyone found a spot to stand.

That is quite a choice of song... I bet I wouldn't have this amount of people here if I died.

Thomas looked around at the sheer amount of people that had turned up; it was making the room incredibly stuffy. Towards the back were elderly people, tight lipped and stooping low, grandparents perhaps? There didn't seem to be a sign of any weeping parents, Jack had never spoken of any parents come to think of it.

Notably, a few rows from the front were a line of crying women, clutching ridiculously tiny handbags, all of them probably half of Jack's age and Thomas did not believe they were all family members. Thomas strongly suspected Jack would have given anything to see this day and his very obvious fan base. 'Which missus?'

I wonder if Caroline has noticed.

That is when Thomas spotted Marsh and O'Rourke standing against the back wall.

Shit, are they here for me? For us? They are out to get me. They want to bring me down.

Thomas felt sick and his heart started to hammer. His first impulse was to hide within the crowd and warn the others but then he realised they had probably already seen him and any commotion would cause them to strike.

Ben stood next to Shania with his arm around her and did not remove it even when the service began. His jaw was tight. Gerry stood with his wife Denise a few rows back and his expression was unreadable as he whispered to her.

Thomas waited with baited breath throughout the service. Jack had not been religious so there were no hymns but some quotes from famous comedians read by some old college friend. He did have parents alive after all; his father Mr George O'Neal got up to tearfully provide a reading:

No parent should ever bury their child, no matter what age. Although there was a time when things were so bad at home, it crossed my mind if I wanted to keep fighting in this life.

As everybody lined up to pay their respects to Jacks' close family members, Thomas held his breath and let himself swallow but it felt like a big pill had become lodged in his throat.

'Thank you for coming Thomas' she said softly before tears started to fall down her cheeks. She was the picture of a broken woman and could not mask her grief before an old and frail looking woman came and linked her arm for support. She smiled back softly

'This is Jack's mother Iris O'Neal. Iris this is Thomas - one of Jack's workers at the agency. 'I am so sorry to have to meet you in such dreadful circumstances Mrs O'Neal' Thomas said, almost choking up himself. Iris nodded politely, her hand shaking as she held her tissue. It seemed as if she was in a daze. Expected. The lights were on but it was like nobody was home.

I also watched your son get murdered but did not call the police when I should have about it.

Gerry was next in the queue and pulled Caroline in for a hug and a kiss on the cheek. Thomas forgot how close they must have been, she would have known Gerry a long time.

'We are so dreadfully sorry for your loss Caroline, Iris' nodded Gerry. Denise who seemed as quiet as a church mouse took her turn and threw her arms around Caroline. They held each other for what felt like a long time.

Ben and Shania did not join the line to pay their respects. Instead, they walked over to the smoking area for Ben to get his fix of his vape.

It would have been completely inappropriate anyway

Thomas glanced back over at Caroline only to see her looking tormented and red with anger. For a second, Thomas wondered if Caroline did know who Shania was but she was not looking at her. She was looking at a tall, blonde, young woman standing in front of her. Thomas noticed it first in her eyes, then the rising tension in her muscles. An inability to think clearly was soon abundant. Suddenly her ability for emotional generosity was gone and she stood as cold as stone whilst this woman spoke to her,

'What did you say about my husband? How DARE you even come here today?'

The woman stood tall, looking down at Caroline clearly not worried about the upset she was causing.

'I had a right to be here Caroline, it's an open service. It seems you couldn't keep him happy, by the looks of it not a single one of us could' she shouted looking around. 'One woman just wasn't enough for Jack!'

Thomas' mind quickly filled in the blanks as he realised that he had heard correctly.

People started to turn around uncomfortably as Caroline let her hand take over and swiftly reached up and slapped the woman hard.

'Get out of here. NOW' Caroline screamed as Marsh and O'Rourke were quick to escort the woman off the premises.

Shania was gripping tightly on Ben's arm; her face was frozen and she was wild eyed.

'Does anyone else have anything to say about my husband!?' Caroline yelled. 'How many more of you tried to ruin my family?!'

Thomas walked over and grabbed her hands and spoke softly 'It's okay Caroline. It's all going to be okay'

How can I promise this when I have no idea what 'okay' even is anymore?

'Here Thomas, I'll take it from here.' Gerry came over and took Caroline by the arm and steered her away out of sight.

It wasn't lost on Thomas to see Denise watching Gerry and Caroline intently, tears streaming down her cheeks and her eyes burning as if with rage…or fear….

THIRTY-EIGHT

The two detectives got back to the police station and went straight into one of the meeting rooms. Marsh could not even be bothered to shut the door properly 'What a time to be spouting off about an affair eh? Marsh turned to O'Rourke shaking his head. 'The question is, Mrs O'Neal seemed like she already knew the blonde lass talking to her'

'What's your point? I probably would have slapped her too' replied O'Rourke.

Marsh pulled down on the blind needing urgent privacy 'you aren't getting it are you?'

O'Rourke paused and stared back at Marsh closing his eyes and leaning back in his chair

'It is clear Mr O'Neal had a lot more interest in playing away than he did with paying attention to his wife at home' Marsh said smiling.

'I think she knew about the affair/s'

'If she knew, why would she have stayed married to him?' O'Rourke replied, his interest quickening.

'Could be anything, money? Security? Domestic violence? He may have been threatening her? Want to hear something even more interesting?'

O'Rourke leant forward eagerly

'Mrs O'Neal booked a plane ticket to Portugal a couple of weeks ago. Guess when she is meant to leave? Next month.

'I mean, that could be anything. I'm due a holiday myself, perhaps I'll join her'' O'Rourke laughed.

'It may not mean anything but think about it, she finds out about the affairs, she is a scorned woman. She bumps off her husband in her jealous rage before sunning herself abroad...'

'So cliche. So easy'.

'Did you also notice how Thomas was quick to go over and comfort her?' Marsh pushed.

'Yes, I did' O'Rourke countered, enthusiastically but with less conviction.

Marsh nodded like an energetic puppy. 'Something could be going on there?'

'Isn't she old enough to be his mum?'

'Well, at Thomas' age, I was necking my boss who was twice my senior.'

'Necking? Like some sort of vampire? O'Rourke laughed loudly now.

'Maybe she paid Thomas to bump him off so they could run off into the sunset together with O'Neal's life insurance.'

'You have been watching way too many films Marsh'

'We need to get his conquests in to provide a statement I think and have a conversation with Mrs O'Neal'

'Now that we can agree on'

'Who else is on the list?'

'His conquests remind me of that Mambo number 5 song! I wish I had got his secret' O'Rourke laughed. 'A little bit of Monica in my life, a little bit of whoever by my side' he sang.

Marsh gave him a round of applause and then looked serious as he said 'let's pay a visit to Mrs O'Neal'.

***

Caroline answered the door looking worse for wear, she looked like she had not slept in days.

'What can I do for you detectives?'

'Hello Mrs O'Neal, we are sorry to disturb you at this difficult time but may we come in?'

'Please call me Caroline' she opened the door and they followed her through to 'the office' which could only best be described as a windowless storage cupboard.

O'Rourke held his breath, the place had less air than a flat tyre and he felt light headed.

'Can I make you both a cup of tea?'

'No thank you' they both said in sync.

'Please take a seat' Caroline said as she sat down weakly on an office chair. The desk had a small computer screen and a picture in a small frame of Jack and Caroline. They were smiling whilst sitting on a beach somewhere sipping cocktail. O'Rourke felt sorry for her then.

'Could you remind us of the night of Mr O'Neal's murder? What time did you return home from your weekend break?'

'We got stuck in traffic on the way home on the M275, I would say we did not get home till at least 7pm.'

'What did you do when you returned home?'

'I went for dinner at my friend Denise's house'

'Was it just the two of you?'

'No, her husband Gerry was there too. Jack was supposed to join us but said he had a headache after the long drive home so was going to take a nap'

'Taking a nap after 7pm really is hardcore. I would never be able to sleep later if I napped then' O'Rourke said and Marsh gave him a black look.

Marsh listened intently 'Is there a reason you came back so late? Don't these places kick you out by 10am?'

O'Rourke laughed trying to keep it light 'Yes they do because It always meant I could not spend the last night in the clubhouse whilst the wife got the kids to bed'.

Caroline did not smile at this 'Jack always had connections because of his job, they always gave us an additional afternoon before we had to leave.'

'Lucky for some' Marsh replied.

'So, Jack just did not turn up to the dinner?'

'Obviously not, detective' she said irritably.

'What made him decide to go to work anyway; it was such a late time?'

'He was always obsessed with checking his mail and making sure the shop was still standing - it was his baby'.

'Did you not find this odd?'

'I just assumed he was still asleep if I am honest, I was enjoying the company of my friends'.

'How long have you known Denise and Gerry?'

'A long time. I met Gerry when he first got the agency with Jack, wherever Gerry is, so is Denise so we became a bit of a foursome'.

'I thought I already explained this when I first spoke to you both' she added.

'Thank you for your patience, we just needed a bit more detail, I know this has been such a terrible time for you'

Caroline paused then, playing with her wedding ring which still had its pride of place on her finger. She appeared lost in thought.

'That must have been hard for you at the funeral; a woman jumping at you like that... saying she had been sleeping with your husband'.

Caroline looked up then. 'The intrusion was not appreciated' she said sharply.

'Is there any truth in her statement?' Marsh continued.

'Of course, there probably is, it's no secret that my husband liked to play away on occasion'.

'That must have been really painful for you?' Marsh questioned.

'His guilt and ability to make it up to me used to help.' she smiled sadly.

'Are you saying you did not mind?' O'Rourke jumped in, surprised.

'I am saying that we had our routine...look...are we done here? She mumbled and gave a tight smile.

'There was one last question actually... we believe you have booked a flight for a holiday? Is this correct?'

'Yes, that's right. My sister lives in Lisbon. Portugal. And thinks I could use the break away after the trauma'.

'Of course. Well, thank you for your time, Mrs O'Neal, we will let you get on with your day'

They barely had time to turn around to say goodbye when the door shut in their faces.

Marsh and O'Rourke travelled back to the station, glad to be out of the claustrophobic room.

'What do you think?' Marsh questioned.

'I want to speak to Mrs O'Neal's friend. Mrs Hobbes. I want to find out more about the dynamics of this friendship gone wrong.'

'Between Mr O Neal and Mr Hobbes?'

THIRTY-NINE

As Thomas made his way to STH, he felt his stomach churn with molten dread. Caroline had rung and wanted everyone to be at the agency that morning for a meeting. He knew it was important to go, after all he had to find out what was happening to the business and if he would be returning to work anytime soon. He walked up to the glass door and caught his reflection within it.

I look fucking awful. Like I haven't slept for months. Why am I here. I cannot cope!

The office still had that clinical, hospital smell; it looked like Caroline had got someone in to clean, there were hoover marks on the carpet and there was a faint smell of pledge. Clinical.

Certainly not a place where people would be inspired to book a getaway. He walked over to his desk and chair. There was no hoodie draped on the back of it. He swallowed hard. He glimpsed up and his colleagues who had all arrived before him; everyone looked subdued, lost in their own thoughts. Gerry, who should be officially enjoying retirement was also here for support of the team. He too, wanted to learn the fate of the business. Shania did not look like her usual groomed self. She looked incredibly pale. Her nails were bitten down to the quick and she looked painfully thin. The stress must really be getting to her.

Ben walked over to Thomas' desk 'Listen man, I know it's too early to say right now, but with Gerry officially retired and now Jack has gone, maybe I should stay on for a while?'

Thomas was surprised.

'Well, sure, Ben. But I think that's got to be up to Caroline.'

Ben looked angsty. 'I hope in light of everything, she will let me keep my job. Look, I know me and you haven't always seen eye to eye.

'We need to wait and see what Caroline has in store for us...but yeah, I would like that.' Thomas offered his hand and shook Ben's and they both nodded together. Thomas smiled.

It was another 40 minutes before Caroline came in through the door looking flustered. The team had already made a second round of tea and tipped the remains of packets of biscuits onto a plate in the waiting area.

Gerry got up to take her coat.

'Hi all, thank you for waiting for me. I am so, so sorry I am late.' she said breathlessly.

'Caroline. Relax. Come and have a seat.' Gerry grasped her arm, walked her to the table and helped her into a large chair which strangely made it look like she was 'queen' of the table. 'Here. Have a tea.'

'Thank you, Gerry' she said shakily, holding out her hands for the mug and sipping it gingerly whilst everyone smiled nervously at her.

'How is everyone?' Caroline smiled weakly whilst trying to make eye contact with them all.

'I think everyone is about the same' replied Ben. 'It feels weird being here.'

'How are you, Caroline? 'Thomas asked knowing full well she would be far from okay.

'I have been better, thank you for asking Thomas.' she took another sip of the tea and swallowed hard.

'I have brought all of you here today to discuss the business and where we go from here.'

Shania stared down at her lap clearly feeling uncomfortable and Thomas couldn't blame her.

Ben sat forward tentatively. Thomas sat wondering if they did get another chance here, will it be much better for him and Ben this time around? Maybe they could actually make a good team...

Gerry sat calmly with no expression on his face.

'So there comes a time when the bird needs to leave the nest, as they say. The storm has passed through and ...'

'You are getting rid of the business, aren't you?' Ben interrupted.

Caroline paused and bit her lip before answering 'I am, I am sorry but I need to let it go. I hope you can all understand.' she said sadly.

'Without Jack, there is no business anymore' Shania said softly.

'That's not true' Ben spoke up. 'We made the business what it was. We completed the sales. Yes, Jack was the face but us little guys kept it going'

Thomas was shocked and had to agree with Ben but he also did not want Caroline to be under any more pressure. He did not want so speak up now though against Ben and risk the new shaky foundation of friendship that was building. He ended up making a weird croaky sound and his views went unspoken. His heart was also beginning to hammer...

What will I do now? No job? Try and not panic

Everyone sat in silence. They could not argue with Caroline. She had to do what was right for her. Where did that leave them?

Ben spoke up then 'will we get redundancy compensation? I mean, essentially Jack canned me so I am not going to be entitled to anything am I?'

'It's okay Ben, I want to speak to you about that anyway, we will discuss this after the meeting.

'What about the existing customers?' said Gerry

'Of course, they are ATOL protected so anything already booked will be okay' Caroline said confidently. 'I am so very sorry to all of you, this is very difficult for all of us but listen, we have a couple of potential buyers so all is not lost and if they do wish to go ahead, you could well be in with a chance still for a job so I don't want to worry you yet' she said kindly.

The colleagues left the meeting room except for Ben who hung back to talk with Caroline. This seemed to distract Gerry; he kept glancing at the office door, an anxious expression on his face. Ben and Caroline spoke for about 15 minutes and when they came out of the office, Caroline was smiling and Ben looked more relaxed.

'I have a few errands to run so I will leave you all here to…. sort your personal belongings for now until we know more. If they are coming in to look around, you do not want anything valuable sitting around. Thomas could you possibly write an email to the big clients about our situation and of course record a new answerphone message for any returning clients. I am sure whoever takes over the place will take good care of everyone' Caroline's eyes were glazed over and everyone could tell she did not want to be in the office longer than she had to be.

'I will walk you out Caroline' said Gerry, following her to the door.

Shania had kept her head ducked the entire time. Thomas couldn't blame her. He didn't know if Caroline had ever found out about Jack and Shania. He had another thing on his mind.

The hoodie was not in the office. The hoodie was not in the office. This mean that with almost certainty that Jack's killer had been wearing HIS hoodie when he murdered Jack. This meant that the hoodie had been taken from the office to give the killer some camouflage. This meant the killer had a key to the office. Which could also mean…It didn't bear thinking about. Ben, Shania, Gerry…were one of them guilty??

He would have to do some digging.

'Hey, does everyone want to come to my place tomorrow? Maybe have a few drinks? I know I could use it?' Thomas said, trying to be positive as they went back to their desks to pack up.

'That sounds good thanks Tom Tom' Ben brightened then. He actually seemed genuine.

After a few moments and clearly comforting Caroline outside, Gerry walked back through the doors and looked around.

'These walls have been my cocoon for the years I needed their sanctuary and I thank them. I thank you all actually. It will be weird having somebody else taking over this place you know? I thought Jack would be here forever.'

He put his head down and sniffed.

Shania walked over to him, put her slender arm around him

'We all did' she whispered.

'I will be taking many memories with me and I understand why Caroline would rather let go.' Gerry replied.

'Caroline said she has a lot of buyers interested.... Ben said thoughtfully.

'You thinking about putting in an offer Ben?' giggled Shania.

Ben smiled as if to himself. 'Maybe.'

Thomas couldn't tell if he was joking or not.

'This is the first place I finally felt at home and like I was good at something' Thomas said softly. 'I remember when I joined, the walls were a bright sea blue' said Ben looking up and down the office. 'The sun has faded them massively.'

Ben switched his attention to Shania who was gathering her desk ornaments, bright pink fluffy pens and notebooks. A ridiculously girly pen holder and smelly gel pens like back in school.

'It's going to be weird not seeing you every day' he smiled to her. 'I will miss my messages on the ever so colourful post it notes from you.'

Shania smiled then. 'I always felt like Jack's puppet on a string truth be told' she said 'I was good for when it suited him' she recounted.

'He never deserved you' Ben said quietly. 'Anyway. Fresh start for us. Fancy being my date to Thomas's party?'

She looked surprised but pleased. 'Er yeah. Sure.'

'Gerry, you are invited too.' Said Thomas.

'Thanks Tom. I'll be there.'

Thomas surveyed his colleagues. So much left unsaid. So much he was cared to say. It was like his mother used to chastise him when he tried to open about things. 'Are you on drugs Thomas??' she'd yell. Without any siblings to offload on, he resorted to having lots of conversation in his head. But they remained in his head. Never escaping. Never making themselves known....

FORTY

'When are we going to see Mrs Hobbes?' asked O'Rourke.

'Later on, today. But I think something else needs to take precedence. The fact that Miss Simmons was being paid money from Safe Travel's account.'

'What did you think of Mrs O'Neill's reaction at the funeral?'

'It's not completely out of character I suppose. The woman's husband has been murdered.'

'I find her a bit...detached. There's something odd about her.'

'Does she know the dire situation of Safe Travel's finances?'

'She soon will do. I chatted to her briefly at the funeral. She's calling the employees together to say she is selling up. God knows who will want to take that business on with all the debt. She will need to find a rich bastard or bitch.'

'Still, we cannot focus on that now. Let's get Miss Simmons in.'

She answered after 10 rings. She must be nervous.'

'Miss Simmons' said O'Rourke. 'Are you available to drop by the police station this afternoon?'

FORTY-ONE

Miss Simmons, thank you for coming in to speak with us again today.'

'Shania wondered if the detectives knew she was chewing the inside of her cheek so hard, she tasted blood.

'No worries.' She trembled.

'We were checking Mr O'Neal's bank records. There are a good few transactions coming out of the business accounts that have been paid into your account.'

'I – I – I don't know.' Shania trembled. 'I – I didn't notice it. M – maybe it was a mistake?'

'Come on now, Miss Simmons.' Marsh leaned towards her. 'You knew about this. What was going on?'

Shania burst into tears.

'We-we were kind of-seeing each other.'

'Marsh raised his eyebrows 'Bit of a conflict of interest, isn't it? Not only your boss but a married man.'

'He – he said he was going to leave Caroline – Mrs O'Neill for me.'

'He said that?' O'Rourke raised his eyebrows. 'Surely you knew Mr O'Neal's reputation? What made you think you were different?'

'He-he told me he cared for me.' Her voice was betraying her.

'How long had you been in a relationship with Mr O'Neal?'

'Like 2 years maybe? On and off'

'On and off?'

'Well like his wife made things hard so quite often we would split but it wasn't long before he was crawling back' Shania moaned.

'That must have made you pretty angry Shania? The fact that Jack kept you on a puppet string for over two years and still did not end things with Caroline? Marsh said sharply.

Shania could tell they were trying to push buttons but it was working. The heat travelled up her neck.

She paused and took a few seconds to answer 'well actually, I kind of liked that I had to fight for him, it turned me on' she shuffled in her seat.

You must have been angry that Mr O'Neal went away with his wife?

Shania stayed silent.

'Did you pick up Mr Walker's hooded top before you left that shop that evening?'

'Tom's hoodie.... no.... I?'

Did you put the hoodie on Shania? I mean it WAS a cold night. Did you leave the shop after the row and then decide to come back for any reason....?'

'No... I did not return to the shop....I... I'

'Maybe you WERE the girl that was finally sick of the whole thing. Maybe YOU lost your temper and decided enough was enough?' Marsh spoke faster now; his voice was rising. O'Rourke was staring straight at Shania.

'Do I need a lawyer?' Shania shouted now, her nerves getting the best of her.

The two detectives sat back and went silent, considering her question. The silence was deafening but Marsh finally decided to speak. 'I would not go leaving the country any time soon'

Shania realised that no amount of fluttering the eyelashes was going to work this time.

Miss Simmons, when was the last time you saw Mr O'Neal?'

'Be – before he went on holiday. It was actually whilst he was away that I came to my senses. I – I had started...'

She faltered.

'Go on.' Said Marsh impatiently.

'I – I had started having feeling for Ben Grey.'

'Your colleague?'

'Yes'.

'Bit closer to your own age I suppose.'

I was going to let Jack – I mean Mr O'Neal know when he came back. I mean I wasn't looking to give up my job or anything...but...I just wanted to pretend it never happened you know?'

'Can you categorically state on record. Miss Simmons...that you did not see Mr O'Neal on the night of his death.

Her heart was now roaring. 'Yes. I'm quite quite sure....'

When the interview was finished, Shania ran so fast out of the station car park it was incredible she was in heels. She stumbled and was violently sick in a bush. Well, wouldn't anyone be if they had just lied to the police....

FORTY-TWO

'Oliver, are you joining us tonight?'

Oliver was ironing a shirt as Thomas walked into the kitchen to grab a beer.

'I have a date Tom so I will let you have the place to yourself' he winked.

'If I had a first date now, I honestly do not think I would know what to do,' said Thomas. 'I have been with Emily so long and I think the rules have changed so much around dating'

'What do you mean?' Oliver said, the confidence just oozing from him.

I swear he does not have one flaw. Not one.

'Well, God knows, do you swipe left, do you swipe right, how do you know you are not meeting a 70-year-old man?'

'Ha-ha you don't Tom, you just go for its man! You definitely think too much' he laughed.

'Like many things in our society these days, it's just so casualised now. So hazy. I met Emily in person, in a bar, had the first date in the same evening, swapped numbers then and there, spoke on the phone, I mean no one talks on the phone anymore.'

'Yeah man is you like 50 or what' Oliver teased. Thomas watched how effortless Oliver was.

Why can't I have this confidence?

'I just mean man that it's all digital communication now, choosing from a pool of people, it's scary. Everyone has your information, no matter how 'private' you set your Facebook. Nothing is sacred. Someone is always watching.

'That's the fun man, live a little eh?' Oliver smiled, tapping Thomas on the shoulder gently.

He grabbed his leather jacket and wallet, a pack of chewing gum and with his perfectly polished shoes, he left and Thomas was alone.

I am glad Emily is joining tonight, it will be nice to have a few drinks and relax properly together.

Emily let herself in as Thomas was preparing some nibbles 'Hey Me, plenty of Doritos and dip, plenty of it' he smiled.

Emily looked a bit nervous and uptight as she clung on to her handbag 'tonight will be the first time seeing everyone. Do you think they will find it strange that I didn't go to the funeral with you? I am still anxious about that.'

'After what happened? No one expected you too darling. Tonight, is not about Jack, it's just a time to relax and have a chat. Check in with everyone'

Emily nodded and her shoulders seemed to drop then, she let her breath out slowly and rose to her feet ready to help with the food.

Gerry knocked at the door next, bringing in several bags with him 'Gerry, anyone would think you thought we would be starving here' Thomas laughed as Gerry came in and shook his hand 'thanks for having me Tom, listen, Denise couldn't make it due to a long shift at the hospital so you have just me I am afraid' Gerry smiled, taking his jacket off. 'Well, you certainly are the Gatsby of our group Thomas' he laughed seeing all the food and drink waiting for them.

Ben and Shania turned up together which made a few eyebrows raise. Ben had brought a pack of beers and Shani, a bottle of wine. 'Here is the master of the minutiae Tom Tom, time to show off your hosting credentials' Ben says, holding out his hand to Thomas. Gerry raised his eyebrows, looking surprised.

Thomas shook it politely, still unable to get used to Ben being 'nice'.

Shania nodded at Emily almost as if to say 'it's okay, I know the truth now about Jack'.

'Have you got any wine glasses Thomas?'

Thomas remembered Oliver had bought some from Wilko.

'Sure.' He led her into the kitchen and pulled two glasses from the shelf.

'Nah babes, only one' she smiled ruefully. 'I'm having this all to myself.' Ben hovered close to her side, cracking open a can.

'Better have one more piss up before I'm on the dole.'

'Oh Ben, not tonight babes. I'm dead depressed as it is.'

He shrugged. 'There's no point having a party is there and putting on all that jolly face bullshit. He looked up as Gerry entered the kitchen to mix a whiskey. 'Is there Gerry? Let's face it, he looked around. 'There's a good chance we are going to be flat on our asses once Caroline sells up.'

'Not necessarily Ben.' said Thomas. 'If we get bought up, even if there's a name change, they won't want the hassle of training new people.' His heart was hammering but his colleagues' eyes were on him and he wanted...needed to reassure them that all was not lost, that Jack's death wouldn't be for nothing. *Unless one of them did it...*

'Well, in terms of myself, it's not something I will be affected by' said Gerry, cradling his whiskey glass, his ring twinkling in the light. 'But it's you lot I feel sorry for. I'm sorry Tom but I don't think it will hurt to get on the websites or down to the Job Centre.'

They all trooped back to the lounge area, past the show cupboard whose door was ajar, everyone had shoved their shoes and boots in. Thomas was grateful. Emily put on a Coldplay CD and Chris Martin's weary voice started from the stereo.'

'Always liked this band.' Ben muttered. 'Never liked admitting it in public though.'

People laughed quietly.

'I always listen to them when I am down.' said Shania, staring into the bottom of her glass thoughtfully. 'My sister runs a tanning salon...guess I could go begging for a job there.'

'Let's sit tight until we know a bit more from Caroline.' Thomas said, slightly impatiently. Why could it be so hard to rally people? 'It was us who made STH and we won an award. The name still carries clout in the city.'

It will never be the same without Jack.' Shania whispered.

'No. But it could be better.' Emily said. 'If not, well there are plenty of opportunities out there. It's a wide world out there'. She was speaking to the group but Thomas felt her mind and heart were singing only to him. 'This could be the opportunity to travel yourself, spread your wings.'

'I consider it bloody ironic I worked for a Travel Agency and the furthest I got was a discount to Shagamu' Shania said bitterly, making everyone laugh.

I remember weaning a weekend away in Paris' Thomas chimed in. 'Jack said I should spend all weekend at the Moulin Rouge...all I wanted to do was to go to the Louvre!' He smiled in spite of himself and his colleagues laughed again.

'Oh Thomas, you are so.... wholesome babes.' Shania smirked. 'You should be in some ruddy museum somewhere, not flogging breaks to old gits with flabby tits!'

'That's what I tell him!' Emily called out. She glanced at Tom and a look of love and of longing seemed to transfer from her to him.

'It's all I've ever wanted to do.' he continued quietly. 'I remember...' he smiled as to himself. 'I was 12...I saved up my pocket money for a National Express coach ticket. I bunked off school, wanted my way to Victoria Coach Station and walked to the National Portrait Gallery. I spent all day just amongst the paintings...I'd seen pictures of them and now...they were all around me. I thought. If I could work here...turn up here every day forever. I would be happy.'

'Guys, remember when Jack made us all work late that hot July weekend? We were boiling and he said 'I'll get those ice cream Sundays in from Bella's? But when they finally turned up, the whole lot had melted through the fucking pots'' Ben smiled 'it was away too hot to work that day. Some of his decisions man....'

Thomas smiled but noticed he had gotten a strange lump in his throat and quenched it with a gulp of beer. His colleagues were looking at him affectionately. His heart suddenly swelled at the sight of them. He loved them. His sanctuary. The life he had built at STH. But after what he had witnessed. His silence in not disclosing information to the police. He didn't deserve the affection of his colleagues. He didn't deserve drinks.

'Excuse me. He spoke. 'You all...make yourself at home.' He went outside and drew in huge gulps of air.

Despite the sombre mood, people started to relax after a few more drinks and showed no signs of wanting to leave. It was like everyone was clinging to each other, as soon as they left Tom's flat, they would disintegrate like a spider's web in the wind.

Everyone started feeling hungry so Emily and Tom busied themselves making sandwiches in the kitchen. His colleagues had gotten bolder and were walking all over the flat commentating on the furniture and giving themselves a tour.

'I really think this could be a great opportunity for a fresh start Tom'. Emily maintained, cutting some thick bread.

'It was really nice you opened up earlier. 'She smiled. 'I had never even heard that story....it moved me.'

Thomas was touched by her emotion. 'Really?'

'Really really.' she paused, walked over and kissed him and reached for her cocktail. 'Let's drink to the future Tom 'she urged. To a new start. I'm behind you all the way.'

His head fell on her shoulder. 'You really think I could do it. Work in a museum.'

'You'd be great. Your passion speaks for itself. You know it.'

Thomas felt the terrible weight on his chest ease slightly.

Gerry accosted him later in the evening still. 'What did you think of Caroline's announcement today? If the offer is there, do you think you would stay on at the agency?'

Thomas considered the question. He was still mulling over his connection with Emily and her urging him to pursue his Art History degree. 'I think there is a lot to think about but that could be an option. Am I ready to let it all go? Do I want to be somewhere where Jack has now gone and a different team? It would be strange'

Gerry nodded 'Yeah, it will be a hard decision but I am sure you will make the right one' he munched on a ham sandwich.

'Nice place you got here by the way.' he smiled.

Thomas was pleased Gerry had come tonight; he did not get out much as his wife Denise was always so busy with her job at the hospital. He seemed to be enjoying the company.

'Where is your bathroom in this place Tom?'

'Just down the hall and to the right? You won't miss it'.

Ben and Shania maintained an easy alliance on the sofa, exchanging comments and nodding their heads knowingly. Shania noticed Thomas watching then and stood up, walking over, she enveloped them with her musky scent of perfume which she had obviously marinaded herself in at the last minute.

'Would you mind if I had a little chat with Emily, please?' Shania purred. 'Go ahead' Thomas replied sceptically, hoping no peace will be broken. He noticed the beer cans starting to mount up so was suddenly happy to oblige whilst he had a quick and sneaky clean up.

Shania twirled her hair around her finger as she followed Emily to the kitchen. Emily looked nervous and paused as she entered. She looked back and let her eyes roam the room for Thomas but he was busy with a bin liner tidying up. Emily knew she needed this chat but at least this way, her mind had a couple more seconds to prepare.

She held her breath as Shania poured herself a wine. 'Emily, I have to be honest...'

She paused and Emily swallowed urging her to continue.

'I wanted to say sorry babe for.... well for Jack and what he did. He had us all fooled but also for ...like... everything really'

Emily let out a deep sigh of relief 'I am sorry how it all played out for you Shania, I would never wish his treatment on anyone.'

'Babes, let's have a shot yeah? Grab the tequila'

They smiled at each other, both feeling a mutual understanding of the other. Emily knocked back her tequila and as it burned the back of her throat could not help but feel she was suddenly part of a hazing ritual but she was happy to bond regardless. If you fall from grace, at least you had grace to begin with.

It was getting quite late, 10:30pm. Thomas was sure Oliver would be home soon. The table, cluttered with cans was beginning to stress him out and his palms were itching. Fetching a bag from the shoe cupboard, he swung his arm, swept the cans into the bag and headed to the kitchen to dispose of the recycling. Hushed voices made him stop in his tracks by the kitchen door. It was Shania and Ben talking in frantic whispers. Or rather Ben seemed to be trying to calm Shania down. She was letting out moans that sounded like an injured animal. Thomas was alarmed at first but reasoned she was probably just drunk; she had quickly accepted a flurry of cocktails after the wine bottle had run dry.

'I c-I can't do this anymore, Ben?'

'Babe...Shan...you're not making any sense. Ben grabbed her wrists but it didn't stop her leaning forwards and planting a kiss straight on his lips. Surely not??!!

Ben pulled back.

'Ben, you are the o-the only one I can turn to!!'

'What do you mean?' Ben hissed. 'You're talking crap. Riddles. Shan, you're a good-looking chick and all but Christ, you are loopy.'

'She wailed. 'D-Don't essay that' she hiccupped. 'I n-need you to listen!!'

'What? That Jack Sprat was the best you ever had?' I don't need to listen to that crap.' Ben spat. 'I can't believe you even went there, that ancient old...

'He is-wasn't ancient.' Shania spat...'He was...mature.'

'Oh really? Mature?!' Ben laughed a mirthless laugh. 'He thought he was Taylor Swift...feeling 22! Well, he felt up 22-year-olds...'

'Don't speak ill of the dead!' she shouted now.'

'I'll speak of him all I want. Don't you stick up for him. He didn't love you, you know that, don't you?'

She burst into sobs. 'You do though, don't you?'

He sneered. 'Love you?'

'My Ben...I need to tell you something.'

He tried to turn away but she grabbed his arm and twisted it like a madwoman. she was no longer looking pretty; her eyes had a wild, manic gleam to them, lipstick like a wild twisted joker...

'What the fuck Shania??!!'

'The murder...the night of the murder...' she gulped. 'I 'I can't keep it in any longer. Must tell someone...anyone...'

'tell someone what??!! Ben now yelled in exasperation, now looking genuinely scared. Shan, you...

Her hands flew up and grabbed his jaw so he was forced to look at her. His face was repulsed.

'Ben. I lied to Marsh and O'Rourke tonight. The night of Jack's murder. I was there.'

FORTY-THREE

'What do you mean you…. You were there? That…. no. You couldn't have been… you…' Ben spluttered, aghast. Beside himself.

'He was alive when I left him Ben I swear on like. My life. He was alive.' She had let go of his face and was now pacing up and down, fingers knotted.

All of a sudden, terror and confusion had sobered them up. Ben could still feel the beer swooshing in his belly but his brain had recircuited. He beckoned for her to follow him out of the back door, glanced around to make sure they were alone.

'What the hell were you doing there? What did you see??!!'

She sniffed. 'I had finally decided to end things with J-Jack…but…'

'Right, okay?'

'But…I wanted to punish him…for what he had done. Stringing me along. I wanted revenge.'

'Why the fuck…Shania, what are you telling me?'

'I went to end it in person, I'd already made up my mind, I think I'd been feeling this way for a while, to be honest. I knew he was no good for me babe, it's just well. When you get a guy like that. Good looking, minted…attracted to you, something inside you flips.

'And what the fuck did he say when you met up and chucked him??'

'I asked that we meet at the shop.'

'Why the hell? Why not down the pub like a normal -whatever?'

'I I had an alternative plan. You know those Dictaphones that got delivered for our hard of seeing customers?'

'Yes? I'm confused.'

'Just let me talk! A few weeks ago, when we had one of our rows, I – I fixed up a hidden security camera – a mini one-in my desk drawer. I put a false back on one of the drawers and I wired it up to my computer. When we arrived at the shop at about 10pm, I also got out a Dictaphone out and pressed play?'

'You were gonna blackmail the guy?'

'I was-going to provoke him into hitting me or ...touching me. So, I could use it as leverage. I I wanted him to give me fuck off money. So, I could start a new life.'

'And what did he say?'

'He was not happy with my decision. He said he wanted us to work it out but I was actually firm and I stuck to my swords'.

'You mean guns, you that've sighed in exasperation, raking his hair with his fingers.

'That too' she said defensively. 'Don't call me that!' The combination of drink and mania were getting to her, she was trying to be articulate but her voice kept quavering and she kept stumbling on her stilettos.

'Anyway, I bottled it...sort of. I just ended up saying...saying that...if he didn't give me what I wanted...he would get his come uppance.' I stormed out and left him at the shop. The next morning, he's bloody dead! If the detectives get a hold of that Dictaphone, my ass will fry. They will put two and two together and make five!!!!'

'Shania. Where the fuck is that fucking Dictaphone?'

'I don't know. Probably scooped up in an evidence room somewhere.'

'Oh hell!! Listen. Shania just keep your trap shut, OK?!@

Shania started crying again and Ben pulled her close to him

'It was awful but it was not your fault. You hear me? It was not your fault.'

Thomas had crept across the kitchen and was listening by the window, still holding the bin bag.

Did Shania just say she was there the night Jack died? How? Why is Ben telling her to be quiet? Could she? Could she have done it?

Footsteps got louder so Thomas quickly moved away from the door. Gerry and Emily were in conversation on the sofa. Thomas' anxiety was burning up from his stomach and he needed everyone to go home.

Ben and Shania emerged from the kitchen 'Hey Tom Tom, I think we are going to get going, this one has had quite a bit to drink and I think it's best we get her back' his arm was around her waist and her makeup looked a bit smeared as if she had been crying.

'Is everything ok? Thomas asked knowing full well it was not. Shania smiled weakly 'y y yes of course Tom. Thank you for tonight, it was great' she sniffed and looked down.

Is she guilty?

Emily and Gerry got up from the sofa too:

'Thomas, I should make a move as the wife should be coming home from her shift, she needs me at the moment smiled Gerry, shaking Thomas' hand.

As the three of them left the flat, Emily went up behind Thomas and wrapped her arms around his waist. Thomas took a deep breath.

'Em, I think Shania could have been involved in Jack's death'

'What? You must be joking?'

Thomas sat back on the sofa but Emily stayed stood still and stared back at him. 'I overheard her talking to Ben in the kitchen and she said she was there that night'

'What are you saying?'

'I don't know what I am saying....'

'Darling, I am worried about you, I know you haven't been yourself and I know you have been massively stressed out but...'

'Em, I heard her! What did she speak to you about anyway?'

'She apologized. For Jack. For everything. I guess for even thinking I would try it on with her man. She was genuine...and less drunk then'

'Do you not think it is a bit suspicious? Why would she go and see him at the office? Especially that late at night?'

'I don't know. I really don't. Darling, I am going to get a taxi home. I need to be up early tomorrow for counselling and I don't want to disturb you. Please get some rest, okay? You need it'

Thomas waited for Emily to get in the taxi safely and then headed to the bedroom and turned on his laptop.

He logged into EarthCam and began searching. He didn't even know what for. EarthCam felt like a sanctuary that used to be a place for him to recharge and forget the things, the world said had to be done. But now. Now, it brought anxiety. He was scared of what he would come across. He still couldn't tear his eyes away.

***

Ben and Shania reached Ben's place and he opened the large door to the foyer of the building. It was dark inside, but as he moved further inwards, the lights automatically came on. That's when he noticed Shania leaning against the dark, concrete wall. The colours were black and silver along the walls and it felt suffocating. 'Let's get you up to the flat and into bed, eh?' Ben said, but Shania was still and staring back at him 'Is it ok to miss him?' she said tearfully.

Ben paused and couldn't find the words to say but he felt the same. He nodded gently.

As they got through the door, Shania grabbed Ben with both hands 'Babes, can you say I was with you if we get questioned again?' she was breathing heavily now.

'But we … we weren't anything…'

'I know but if anything is asked again, we were in bed together yeah?'

'Yes okay' Ben did not know what the label was on their relationship or what was happening but he wanted to protect Shania. Even if it was a lie. He knew all about lies. If Shania. If Thomas, only knew….

FORTY-FOUR

'Mr Hobbes is retired now isn't he, do you think we need to call ahead?' O'Rourke offered.

'I don't think so, let's take a chance and knock.

They turned up at Western parade which overlooked Southsea common, it was a beautiful open space. There were kids playing a ball game and laughing loudly. 'What a nice sight to see for a change' Marsh turned to O'Rourke. 'Instead of stuck on iPad or in front of the box, they are actually out playing'

'You see that sign for Southsea Castle? That was built around the Tudor times during Henry VIII's reign, maybe Mr O'Neal wanted his own six wives but maybe minus the beheadings' O'Rourke remarked.

Gerry answered the door and raised his eyebrows as he saw the two detectives stood in front of him.

'Morning both! What can I do for you?' he said whilst glancing at the ID Marsh was holding up and smiling.

'Good morning, Mr Hobbes, we are sorry to disturb you. May we come in?'

'Of course, please do'

The hallway was bright white, pristine clean and not one sign of a scuff mark anywhere. Gerry led them into a lounge where there was an entire wall full of pictures, memories adorning the walls.

'So, Mr Hobbes, how have you been since Mr O'Neal's passing?' Marsh went straight in and asked.

'It's been a very strange time for all of us, I think. I suppose you could say a bit lost?'

Gerry cupped his hands together, looking at the floor as he spoke.

'We were reading a bit more about the history of the business and we learnt that you used to own half? Is that right?'

'That is right, yes' Gerry nodded. 'We made a good team' he looked up and smiled then.

'What made you give up your share?'

'I wouldn't say 'give up', as that's like saying I didn't fight for it. It was not an easy time but I did what I had to do at the time.' he swallowed hard then 'My wife, Denise…. she…. was unwell'

'So sorry to hear that' O'Rourke added.

'Thank you. I could not give the commitment to the business at the time and it was a real struggle.'

'As your boss, I imagine Mr O'Neal was supportive? How is your wife now?'

'She had her treatment and was able to eventually get through it. It was a dreadfully worrying time for us all. Jack, naturally, had to put the business first….'

'That must have been very upsetting for you?'

'I was not thrilled obviously but business is business, right?'

'We were made aware this week that at one point, Mr O'Neal had actually tried his luck… with your wife Denise. Is there any truth in this that you know of?' Marsh asked.

Gerry laughed loudly 'who told you that?'

'Is there any truth in it?' Marsh repeated

'That is absurd. Of course not. Jack always went for the younger generation when he....'

'He paused then realising his comment.

'Mrs O'Neal was aware of his behaviour, we believe?'

'Anyone with their eyes open was aware of his behaviour' Gerry said then.

'Being both of their friends, I bet that was a difficult situation?'

Gerry got a tissue from the box on the coffee table and gently wiped around his mouth as if biding his time with his answer

'I am 60 years old Detective. It's not my business really' Gerry said sharply shutting the suggestion down.

O'Rourke became interested in something twinkling on Gerry's hand. 'That's an interesting ring, Mr Hobbes.'

'Oh this. Yes. It's my wedding ring. The horse represents Pegasus.'

'How long have you and Mrs Hobbes been married?'

'Thirty years. We married May 1989. Mr O'Neill was best man. He was only a youngster then. Twenty-Two years old. He had just started dating Caroline.

'When did you both decide to go into business and launch your own Travel Company?'

'It was 2011. We both had worked in the industry for a while by then and thought it made sense. We had dreams you know of creating a dynasty. For many years, it was just us, building Safe Travel. Then things got busier. About 2015, we started employing temps. But Jack wanted to build a team from the ground up. It was also clear that he had a flair for the showier side of the business. He persuaded me to pour my life savings into the business but....'

'But what?'

'Denise fell ill. Then business hit a low and we weren't getting the business we needed. Jack had...troubles himself. He gambled away a lot of the money. Splurged on deals that were not good business sense.'

'So, it soon became clear that you were not going to get a return on your investment.' Marsh said.

Gerry was silent.

'You didn't think to take legal action?'

'Jack was a friend.'

'Mr Hobbes. Please don't pretend you were blind to what was going on. Mr O'Neill pissed your money up against the wall. This wasn't just money mismanagement; this guy was taking the bloody mick, wasn't he?!'

'I said there were more pressing matters at hand at that time in my life.' Gerry raised his voice.

There was a silence.

'Anyway, we must thank you for your time and your help. Thank you for your cooperation, Mr Hobbes, we will not take up any more of your time' Marsh replied, nodding to O'Rourke to get moving.

As they returned to the car, O'Rourke turned to Marsh 'I am not sure I believe him' grabbing an apple from his bag. This new healthy regime was leaving him constantly hungry.

'About which part?' replied Marsh.

O'Rourke welcomed a big piece of apple, making a loud crunching sound: 'all of it' he said in between chews.

FORTY-FIVE

Thomas was due to pick up Emily from her counselling session but he had slept in late. He pressed the screen of his phone and noticed the time. 'Shit' he shouted and jumped up immediately feeling light headed.

He threw on a pair of jeans and a T-shirt and frantically searched for his keys. As he rushed towards the kitchen, Oliver was sitting at the table playing a game of cards. 'Good morning, Thomas, come join me, I am playing patience' Oliver grinned.

'That is something I have a lack of this morning mate; I am late picking up Emily from counselling.'

'What time did you get to sleep last night, you look rough' Oliver asked. Thomas did not hear the question; he just noticed the mess that had collated in the kitchen. 'Urgh, look at this place, I cannot leave it like this.' Thomas felt like his eyelids were stapled open, he could not tear them away from the mess

I need to leave. Now.

Suddenly Oliver's voice seemed to get further and further away and it sounded deep and slow like an old record going wrong.

What is happening?

Are those plates stacking up higher and higher? Am I imagining this?

'Oliver, what is happening?'

Oliver appeared to be speaking and laughing but like he could not hear him at all

Have I gone deaf?'

'Oliver helps me please!'

Thomas felt every bone in his body go weak and suddenly he could not see anything. His body crumpled like a puppet that had suddenly been released from its strings. Everything went black.

***

'Thomas! Thomas! Can you hear me?'

Thomas' mind was swirling and he could feel a ringing in his ears. His breath was shallow. He tried to open his eyes but all that greeted him was a bright light. After a while, he began to make out the features of the room. 'Oliver?' he croaked.

'Thomas, you are okay but we think that you fainted darling. I am here. Everything is okay. Can you hear me?' Emily said gently, holding his hand and stroking it gently with her fingers.

'I called the ambulance as I just found you here. You did not turn up to the counselling office so I got a taxi and came looking for you'

'I'm…. I'm…so sorry Me, I I must have overslept and then….' Thomas' eyes rolled back and he still felt unwell.

'Let's get him on to the sofa where he will be more comfortable.' the paramedic said, gently removing the cushion, Emily had placed under his head.

'Are you taking any medication Thomas? Or have you taken any drugs in the last 24 hours?'

'Let's I haven't' Thomas said weakly. 'And no…no medication. Where is Oliver?'

Mr Walker, you have been out for the past 14 minutes, 'You are here alone Mr Walker, your girlfriend found you. I am going to do a couple of tests okay, a neuro test and an egg, I want to listen to your heart rhythm okay? are you able to sit up for me?'

Thomas held out his arm and waited for the cuff on his arm to tighten. 'Everything seems ok, when was the last time you ate something Thomas? The paramedic asked. 'Are you able to stand up for me? I want to check your blood pressure with you standing also please if you can manage?'

'Yesterday...I I don't know what time' Thomas stammered.

'Il put you some toast on, with jam? Emily said 'you need the sugar'

'The good news is there is no sign of a stroke, or postural hypertension. I am just going to go through my presyncope checklist, please relax'

After 15 minutes, the paramedic was writing a few notes and Thomas started to feel better.

'I did get up too quickly this morning. That must be it' he said downplaying his worry.

'Please keep an eye okay and please take at least 30 seconds, I try to sit on the edge of the bed for at least that time before jumping up or I would be on the floor' smiled the paramedic kindly.

As the ambulance crew left, Thomas turned to Emily 'I am so sorry for this morning. I should have been there to pick you up'

'It's really okay, I figured you were catching up on sleep and needed the rest. You just almost gave me a heart attack when I walked in, seeing you on the floor.' she said sympathetically.

'I feel like I need to make a change Me, I am not looking after myself properly as you say. I need to sort myself out don't I'

Emily did not answer, she just put her head on his shoulder allowing him to share his thoughts.

'I think I want to see my mother. Will you come with me but maybe wait outside?'

'Are you sure that's a good idea right now? You have been under a lot of stress and I am not sure....' Emily hesitated

'I have some questions for her,' Thomas said sharply.

'If you think it will help you, then of course, I am all for it'

FORTY-SIX

The Charles Dickens and Nelson neighbourhood was where Thomas' mother was currently staying. The street she lived on appeared so dark and depressing like it had not heard laughter in a long time. Gone, were the shrieks of children playing and skipping ropes turning. Thomas felt incredibly nervous then 'it's been a long time' he said to Emily as they parked up and turned the engine off.

"I am sure Dolores will be happy to see you Tom, you are her baby after all. I'll be right here waiting if you need me' but even Emily sounded unsure.

Thomas walked slowly to the white, rusted front door which looked like it had not been cleaned in a long time

This is a good thing, right? She may be having a good day mentally and be pleased to see me

He hovered by the door looking back at Emily who threw him an encouraging nod. He knocked on the door and waited for a reply. Thomas did not realise that he had started to shiver and the pitch of his heart was rising.

She came to the door and Thomas could not gauge her reaction. Was she furious? Panicked? And hiding it well? She did not smile or frown. She had lost a lot of weight since he last saw her and her hair appeared thinner but maybe that was due to her medication. Her once honey blonde hair was now a shade of mousy grey and her sea blue cardigan was hanging off her frame.

'Hi mum, how are you?'

His mother's eyebrows went up and she crossed her arms. Thomas' stomach sank and he said awkwardly 'May I come in?'

'What are you doing here?' she asked bluntly.

'I really need to speak to you mum. Please?'

She stepped aside and let Thomas come in and immediately he was hit with a dreadful smell of damp. 'Are you keeping ok mum?'

She followed him through to the lounge where the sofa protested gently underneath her.

Neither of them spokes for a while, both waiting for each other to start 'Mum how has your health been recently?' Thomas questioned but Linda just stared back awkwardly.

Eventually she spoke 'So you finally came to see your old' mother eh'

'I miss you.'

'She sniffed 'Really. Yeah. Right.'

'Mum, I need your help.'

She lit a cigarette and sat there, shrouded by smoke. Clutter was all over the table; it was sprinkled with cigarette ash; the remote control was coated in ash. Empty crisp packets and sweet wrappers were all over the floor. The TV was on in the background, showing some headache inducing trash reality show.

'Well, this had better be good. You're making me miss my show.'

'Mum, I have been really suffering recently. It is hard to explain really... I'

'Oh, here we go again, boy. Change the effing record!'

'Mum, I....'

'Thomas, let's be honest. You have always had issues, haven't you boy?'

'I know it was a struggle when I was growing up mum but....'

'A struggle?' Dolores spluttered. 'You were a pathological LIAR. You used to hide my shopping when I came home. Yes. You used to hide food in your room. At first, I thought it was some sort of eating disorder or maybe even a hoarder. Time and time again I'd smell the stench of rotting veg and have to reach under your goddamn bed. But you did it so much Thomas. You did. You did.'

Linda spoke so quickly, Thomas struggled to keep up and was already regretting the visit.

'Yeah well, you were never exactly mother of the year.' he mumbled.

'I did my best, God help me. Do you know what it was like, raising a kid like you??'

'I was a child!' he shouted. I had p-problems.

'You had more than problems, boy. Let's not forget your substance abuse, you dabbled in that one too many times didn't you. The ruddy school didn't know what to do with you, you having those panic attacks, running and hiding in the broom cupboards. I bet half those kids didn't learn what they needed to cos of you fucking things up.

Thomas was shaking his head trying to make sense of what she was saying.

'Even now, look at you. You are staring me down like a predator, you don't ever look away. You are so aggressive; you throw me off balance' she said whilst biting her nails vigorously.

'Mum, please. I was not like this. I am NOT like this. I have never done drugs mum; this is in your head. I did not come here to argue with you...I....' disbelief was in his voice.

She is wrong. Why is she saying this? She is lying

'You came from me Thomas. There is never any remorse for anything you do. Never.' she spoke loudly.

'I - I've tried...'

'You've never tried, boy. You are like your old ma. Both of us. Fucking loony. Lord knows how your bird puts up with you. And you come to ME for help. God help me.' she laughed to herself and turned back to the TV.

Thomas' head began to ache. He couldn't stay in this claustrophobic atmosphere a minute longer. 'I shouldn't have come; this was a mistake' he shouted.

Linda gave him a mocking smile 'something we can agree on'. Go on then, off you bugger, see you in 5 years.'

'I just needed you to love me, Mum. You are right; I am a product of you. Everything I learned, I learned from you. '

'Glad that penny has finally dropped.'

Thomas rushed out of the door, Emily following. He pounded the car with his fists. 'Shouldn't have come back. Should NEVER have done this. She's right, isn't she' a single tear dropped from his eye and splashed the car.'

'She's sick in the head.' Emily said quietly. 'Thomas, whatever happened in your childhood. She could have got help for you but she didn't. And I bet that haunts her'.

'I need to get better Me; I can't go on like this. I don't know what's real and what's not, sometimes!!' Emily held him as he cried.

FORTY-SEVEN

Denise was getting nightmares again. She had always struggled with her mental health. She had heard the detectives questioning Gerry. She had gone to the toilet to be violently sick.

Her therapist had told her to keep a journal, so this is what she would do.

'No one knew about this diary. Not even Gerry.

She had been a religious girl once. She was terrified of God judging her for what she had done. Once in a mad fit of thought, she thought about going to confession.

But this diary would do for now.

She would pour her heart out.

Then she would telephone Caroline. At the right time.

FORTY-EIGHT

Thomas opened his eyes and noticed the beautiful sunrise igniting the colours of Emily's bedroom. He could not remember falling asleep but he was so exhausted, Emily had insisted he stay with her so she could make sure he was looked after. He did not deny her this request. He turned to Emily who was also awake and he felt his eyes smile as he looked at her, the many hues brightening up the smooth skin on her face.

'It's early' she whispered. 'Let's go back to sleep' but Thomas did not want to sleep. His brain felt electrified with anticipation. Her scent sent him into a heavy trance and he pulled her close to him, his arms wrapped around her back. As their bodies touched, it was like a hand sinking into a silk glove. The perfect fit. Thomas and Emily locked eyes and he knew no matter what was going on in his life, he felt safe here. In this space. In this bubble. The facade they show the world melting away.

Emily kissed him hard as their hearts beat faster together, it was intoxicating. Emily wore a dusky pink lace nightie and it was so soft over her pale skin. Her deep, chestnut hair tumbled down her back. She no longer hesitated when they became intimate and Thomas no longer had to fight to hold back. He always wanted her to feel safe and assured and he never wanted the moments to end. In that moment, they became one. One mind. One purpose.

Emily led with her head on his chest and they led together in peaceful comfort 'Good morning' she giggled cheekily. 'Good morning angel' he said staring at her heart melting dimples.

'I need to shower for work' she smiled. Thomas gave her a teasing look 'just five more minutes?'

Thomas heated some croissants and reached into the fridge for the strawberry jam as he waited for the coffee to brew.

I do not need anyone else. As long as I have Emily. I have more than most.

Thomas' phone began to ring and it brought him back down to reality.

'Thomas? Detective Marsh here. Are we free to take a look around your flat this afternoon? We have a search warrant?'

'Um…er …. sure'.

'Thank you. See you at about 3pm.'

'Who was on the phone?' Emily asked, walking into the kitchen.

'The detective. They want to come to my flat today to take a look round.'

'Just protocol, right?'

'Yeah…. I think so.'

'It will be fine darling.'

Thomas texted Oliver.

'Oli. Detectives are coming over. 3pm'

FORTY-NINE

'I am not sure what to expect from today's visit?' said Marsh as they approached the door.

'Do you think we will find something meaningful?' asked 'O'Rourke.

Marsh hooked his sunglasses on the breast pocket of his shirt as they waited for Thomas to come to the door. He ran his stray hazel eyes over the space as the door finally opened.

'How are you, Thomas?' O'Rourke asked softly.

'Not bad' he muttered.

'We have requested this visit to have a look around your flat. This is standard procedure.'

'I understand.'

Thomas stood back, feeling apprehensive as the detectives brushed past him.

The detectives began pulling open drawers. They reached the shoe cupboard. Marsh reached in and began pulling out trainers and... he stopped. He stared. His face remained impassive but there was a definite twitch of his jaw and his eyes widened ever so slightly. He slowly reached further in and pulled out.... A plastic bag containing.... his hoodie ....and a bloodied hammer.

As the detective held up the weapon, gloves concealing his hands, Thomas' eyes shifted and he collapsed in the narrow hallway. He began to weep as O'Rourke held the door open and for an instant, he looked like he considered running. *Just run. As fast as your legs can carry you.*

Marsh spoke in the same flat tone: 'Thomas Walker, I am arresting you on the murder of Mr Jack O'Neal. You do not have to say anything. But it may harm your defence if you do not mention when questioned something which you later rely on in court. Anything you do say may be given in evidence'

The words were in the distance almost like he had gone deaf and a dull throb filled his head. No. Not now. It cannot be. Could it??!

This cannot be happening.......

FIFTY

'Mr. Walker. I need you to understand that this is not looking good. We need to understand why the murder weapon would be in your cupboard?'

Thomas who had been sat staring into space was shocked back into the moment with a jolt of electricity. Panic coursed through him, making him desperate, maddened.

'You need to listen! You both need to listen to me right now, OK? I- we had a gathering at the flat and everyone was there: Me, Emily, Gerry, Shania, Ben......

'So let me get this straight. One of your friends or colleagues or whoever they are to you, somehow, came to the party with a hammer covered in blood and decided to hide it when you were busy making ham triangles and getting the jam tarts ready?' Marsh said, raising his eyebrows. 'Forgive me, Mr. Walker if I find that a trifle hard to swallow.'

'Well, they must have not only brought the goddamn thing but yes, when I was you know, performing the usual party hospitality, they must have taken the opportunity to stash it!' Thomas fought back tears. 'Everyone came flooding into the flat with coats, bags. It wouldn't have been hard to do. Oh goddammit, why?? Why would one of them do this to me, why?'

'Well, it is certain beyond a shadow of a doubt that STH was housing a murderer for quite a while.' the detective continued. 'Everything points to the attack being premeditated. This wasn't a random opportunistic act.'

'Well of course it wasn't! Thomas yelled. 'You think some prick is walking around with a hammer in their bag for kicks?'

'Mr Walker. Let me finish my point. Not only is the murderer of Mr O'Neil an employee of his, but on the compass of suspects, I must iterate to you that the needle is continually swinging towards you.'

'Why would I kill Jaa-Mr O'Neill?' Thomas leant back in his chair and let a tear clinging to his eyelid, roll back into his iris. 'What motive do I have, detective?'

'You see how this looks don't you?' O'Rourke added. 'Do you know how many years you are looking at for murder?'

'I HAVE NOT MURDERED ANYONE!!!!!!!'

'Why would one of your colleagues want to do this to you then?'

At this comment Thomas let the tears roll.

'That is the question I have. Why would they indeed. I always thought I was well liked. Respected. This is why I liked going to work. Seeing these people every day. They got on my nerves sure but having that routine, seeing them every day made life...easier. But now I know you can't trust anyone. Whether or not my colleague just wanted to frame me because they were...desperate. Or they wanted revenge on me for God knows what.'

'Can you think of anything at all that might have provoked one of your colleagues to do this to you then?'

'No' Thomas whispered. 'Maybe they were jealous.'

'Have you ever seen behaviour by your colleagues that would have you think they were capable of this?'

Thomas shook his head.

'Well then' Marsh rubbed his eyes. 'I want to believe you Mr Walker, I do. But the fact remains that there has been so substantial evidence that places other STH on a higher platform on the suspect's scale. This hammer really is damning. We of course will send the item for DNA tests but...'

'But what?'

'Whilst we are waiting for the test results and gathering more information, will accompany us to the station. You will be taken into custody and your solicitor will secure a hearing with you as soon as possible to see if you can be granted bail but being honest Mr Walker, with your history, this will not hold in your favour. Mr Walker, I must stress that a confession will help reduce your sentence but at this moment in time...you are looking at 20 years in prison.

Now was the time to be honest...

'Detective. I have an alibi! Yelled Thomas. My flatmate Oliver Creswell was with me on Sunday night of the murder. And I – I. I SAW THE MURDER!! I SAW THE MURDER LIVE ON EARTHCAM!!!!!!!!!!!!

FIFTY-ONE

The interview room at the police station was cold and dark. All that could be heard was the hum of the cassette recording.

Marsh and O'Rourke had been lost for words for a few seconds. They had then put Thomas in handcuffs and bundled him into the police car. Now they sat in the interview room, still reeling from Thomas's outburst that he had witnessed the murder.

'I need you to repeat that please.' Marsh said slowly and clearly.'

Thomas began shaking. 'I – I was too scared to ss- say.'

'What is this EarthCam? Marsh leaned forward. 'I need you to tell us everything Thomas. And by that, I mean everything. So, you say you witnessed the murder? I need you to take me through your every action that Sunday.

Thomas took a deep breath and told them everything. Once he started, he found he, could not stop. The words were tumbling out of his mouth like water.

'Why in God's name did you not tell us this?' raged Marsh. 'Did you know you could have jeopardised the course of justice?!'

'Not to mention your story will be hard to corroborate,' said O'Rourke. 'We will need to check your computer to see and we will need to speak with Oli- '

'You can speak with him now!' Thomas raged. 'I I can I call him?'

'You may step outside and make your one call. What are your housemates' full name?'

'Oliver- Oliver??' My mind...I can't think!!!

Thomas was becoming hysterical.

'Right OK call him. Tell him we need him here urgently.' Said O'Rourke.

They put Thomas into a witness room whilst he awaited Oliver.

Oliver showed up 15 minutes later...

'Calm down T-bag, it's all good. We know you haven't done anything' Oliver said confidently, playing with his plastic cup. Once again, Oliver oozed confidence.

'They were asking about Emily' Thomas said frantically, getting up from his seat and holding his head in his hands.

'What if they think Emily did it? She gets attacked and within a couple of days, Jack is dead. I mean it does not look good, does it?'

'You know you heard that conversation between Shania and Ben. I think it's time you try and turn the attention away from you and Emily.'

Thomas stopped now. 'I don't remember telling you that?'

Oh mate, you really are out of it aren't you? of course you told me'

Thomas started getting more frustrated now, his hands in the air 'I am losing it I swear' he said pacing the floor.

'I think you forget you haven't done anything wrong. YOU haven't killed anyone Thomas?'

'But I watched a murder and did nothing about it. Does that come under perverting the course of justice or whatever?'

'Keep your voice down T-bag and no. If you knew the killer and the victim at that point then, yes? Maybe'

'Well, this killer was wearing my hoodie which means I bloody do know them!'

'And where is that hoodie now?' Oliver said exasperated.

'I don't fucking know, on Mars?' Thomas' eyes wild, raising his voice. 'Oliver helps me man please!'

'You need to start turning the heat on the others. Everyone has a motive it seems but you are innocent and we assume Emily is too, right?'

'I actually don't know as I was in the flat alone remember! You got back from the cinema at that weird time. How do I know YOU didn't do this?'

'Don't start turning the tables on me T-man I am here to help you. What if you did it?'

'YOU AREN'T HELPING ME!!! NO ONE IS!!! I CAN'T TRUST ANYONE!!! NOT EVEN MYSELF' Thomas screamed at the top of his lungs. 'I CAN'T COPE ANYMORE'

Thomas sat on the floor then, the cold relieving the sweat that had congregated throughout his body. He was hyperventilating and needed to breathe. The detectives ran in with a brown paper bag realising the commotion.

***

'Thomas, its detective Marsh, you are okay, just breathe for me Thomas.'

'Oliver.... where is ...... '

'Thomas, it's just us you hear me? No one is here. Oliver is not here' it's just us.'

***

Thomas looked up, shaking still 'don't patronise me. Where is my friend? What have you done with Oliver? I poured the water for him. Did you see him leave? I think I upset him...I'

'Thomas, there is nobody here. '

With that, Thomas broke down and started to cry. 'God, I need help…I think I am going mad!!'

Marsh paused then, clasping his hands together on the table, 'Thomas according to our records, you live alone. You do not have a flat mate at your address.'

'He was here just now!!!' We were talking.'

'Mr Walker. We have been watching you for the last 20 minutes. You were sat in silence for 15 of them and then suddenly you became really animated and started having a conversation and gesturing wildly.

'Stop feeding me bullshit Detective. What you trying to frame me or something??'

Thomas fired out another text to Oliver…

Hey man, I came back to the flat and the place is empty of your things? Please let me know everything is, ok? Why did you leave the police station? I'm worried! Please call me.'

Thomas stared intently as the message was sending but it did not want to go through. Thomas checked the outbox and stopped breathing. 99+ messages, storage was getting low. There was a chunk of messages that had not been sent. As his thumb scrolled upwards and upwards, there were masses of unsent messages. All to Oliver. Oliver. Oliver. Oliver. The name swam around his eyes like a whirlpool. Thomas realised; Oliver never got a single one of these. A deep painful gasp of breath made him realise he hadn't breathed in over a minute.

He caught a glimpse of himself in the mirror and heart hammering went and stood up close to it. The lines on his face were deeper than ever before, crow's feet making him look 40 years old, dark rims around his eyes, chapped lips, stubble. The person staring back at him wasn't him, it was the face of a madman. Then he looked to the side of him and saw Oliver sat on his bed smiling. 'Jesus Christ man you gave me a fright! Where the hell have you been'

'Oliver kept grinning. 'Don't you understand T-Bag? I've never left you. I'll never leave you again…'

'Stop pricking around, be SERIOUS! Thomas whipped round. No one was sitting there. There was only the echo of his voice.

The penny dropped.

'You will understand. Why I am who I am.'

All of a sudden, as if a box had opened in his mind...a host of memories came flying free...

Thomas and Oliver Walker.

Two identical twins.... sleeping next to each other in a cot.... he could reach out and touch Oliver's hair....

A walk on the beach, skimming pebbles...

'His hand in another little boy's hand....

'The white-hot stench of the flames as the house fire ranged.

'His sobbing mother carrying him to safety...'

'Him shrieking with fear as she tried to go back in for Oliver....'

'Don't leave me mummy!'

'But don't let Oli die!'

The fire has started so innocently. An iron left unattended whilst a single mother struggled with two screaming babies. Dolores had run upstairs. Oliver was still asleep in his basket but Thomas had been in the middle of being changed. She's managed to get Thomas out but collapsed in smoke inhalation trying to reach Oliver.

Oliver had left the word in body last night. But he had lived on. All these years. Speaking with Thomas…being with him…. the twin who never was…. the twin who should have lived…. the twin living through Thomas…….

Thomas smiled slowly and began to chuckle to himself. His shoulders shook, his mouth opened wide, he threw his head back, his arms in the air and began to laugh maniacally….

He allowed himself to be dragged to the cells by Marsh and O'Rourke, his maniacal laughter a horrid echo down the corridors….

***

The dawn brought the breakfast news and crispy and soggy newspapers were peddled to supermarkets, newsagents and front doors. The headlines ranged from the Daily Mail:

DELINQUENT OF SINGLE MOTHER CHARGED WITH MURDER to The Star:

HAMMERHEAD FOUND IN PORTSMOUTH: NOT THE SHARK KIND!

A more moderate paper carried the following headline:

ARREST MADE IN O'NEIL MURDER CASE. COLLEAGUE CHARGED.

The journalist had sourced a photograph of a wan looking man in his late twenties. There had been no opportunity of getting a snapshot of the suspect as he had been taken straight into custody. However, journalists had wasted no time in scouring social media for the most appropriate picture:

It is a murder that has shocked the country. When Jack O'Neill's body was found outside the building of Safe Travel Holidays in Southsea, Portsmouth, it had been assumed it was a mugging gone wrong. O'Neill 52, had built the business from the ground up and handpicked a small pool of colleagues. His loyalties however were in vain as it was revealed yesterday the chief suspect in what is now a murder case, is one of his colleagues.

The suspect is Thomas Walker of Mafeking Terrace, Hayling Island. Walker, 28 had been an employee of the travel agent for nearly two years. On Wednesday, police visited his home for questioning and during a routine search, found the murder weapon in a cupboard in Walker's flat.

The weapon it can now be revealed is a blood-stained hammer that delivered a fateful blow to Mr O'Neill's head.

Seamus O'Rourke, one of the detectives heading the case, made a statement yesterday to say this find is 'significant.'

'Mr Walker has been a prominent suspect from the start of our investigation' he said. 'We now have hopes we can get this to court and can secure a conviction which will be of some comfort to his grieving family.'

The paper can now reveal that Walker's upbringing has been far from ideal. Raised by a single mother, Walker, we can now reveal, has been plagued with mental health issues since childhood, recently diagnosed with a form of schizophrenia. Early thoughts suggest that Walker had been hearing voices urging him to commit the murder although why exactly this is remains unclear. Sources close to the case speculate Walker had designs on O'Neill and the business, projecting an unhinged persona that was the trauma of his childhood, manifested. Walker was also an avid use of the internet and the Google app 'Earth-Cam. Sources close to the suspect say he regularly retreated into a virtual world and preferred to love there rather than in reality. He even claims to have witnessed Mr O'Neill's murder live on EarthCam, although this is being treated as highly unreliable.

Walker has entered a plea of not guilty. The trial is scheduled to begin in 8 weeks' time.

Good morning, Britain had managed to persuade Gerry to appear on a virtual panel where he was joined by a popular psychologist and a social media vlogger and 'mouthpiece' ironically heaping criticism of social media and the negative implications of living in a virtual world. Gerry looked solemn and said he would never have suspected Thomas but 'you can never know who you can trust' and 'I hope that justice will prevail.' '

FIFTY-TWO

Later that morning, Thomas was led in handcuffs to the medical wing of the prison.

O'Rourke accompanied him.

'Your girlfriend has put in a visitor request.' He explained. 'But first, I want to refer you to the prison doctor.'

'Why are you being kind?' muttered Thomas dully. 'I'm your new prime suspect.'

'You are a human being who quite possibly is in need of help, whatever you have done.' O'Rourke said simply.

All this time. He was there. He was talking to me. I was so sure….

'Can you hear people talking? Do you think it's about me? Are they laughing?

He was still reeling from the shock of coming to terms with the fact that Oliver, his dead twin, had manifested in his head. So, it was true. He was officially crazy. He probably did kill Jack. He had clearly been imagining EarthCam too. It had clearly been him hitting Jack over the head with a hammer.

He deserved to rot in hell.

'Mr Walker? Thomas Walker, please come on through'

Thomas nodded in agreement and the Doctor led them to his room, O 'Rourke following.

Dr Miller looked like he was in his mid-fifties. He had a warm yet professional face. He gestured for O'Rourke to sit Thomas down. Thomas, who was connected to 'O'Rourke with handcuffs, had no choice to obey.

'Mr Walker. I understand you have been having hallucinations.'

'I have been seeing someone. Someone who I believed to be real. Someone in my mind...I guess.'

'How long has this been happening?' the doctor said gently.

'A while... '

'Who is this person, for example, is it someone that has passed in your life?'

'No... he is...he was.... a brother. Oliver'

'How did you lose your brother?'

'In – in a house fire when I was a child. Oliver was my twin brother. My mother saved me...she tried to save him too...but.... she couldn't. I'm the one who shouldn't have lived.'

'You believe that?' said Dr Miller. 'You feel you don't deserve to live?'

Thomas shrugged. 'There's nothing to live for anymore. I don't deserve life.'

Is there a history of mental illness in your family Thomas?'

Thomas pauses 'Yes, my mother. She has suffered for many years. Does this mean I... could...?'

'Not necessarily, but it may mean you are more susceptible to mental illness. Have you ever tried any counselling? I think possibly speaking to one of our team here, could be very beneficial for you and also some medication whilst you are...housed in custody.

Thomas started to cry as this all became overwhelming. 'I do not know who I am anymore' he sobbed

Doctor Miller sat patiently 'You clearly have a lot of unresolved trauma. Trauma that manifested due to the events in your past. But I can help you.'

He addressed the detective. 'Detective. Can I request that Mr Walker be given his own cell for his safety?'

'That can be arranged' agreed O'Rourke.

'So, I was a twin. I repressed the memory. Oh Lord, what else have I repressed?'

Dr Miller stood up. 'I would like you to sit in my library for a while. I need to sort a few things out. I would like you to sit in private. You can have a look at the books and magazines to occupy yourself. This does mean I will need to lock the door to the library.

'I understand' Thomas muttered.

'O'Rourke said he would be back in a couple of hours.

Thomas had a look around the room. It was a small library with mostly books on psychology and sociology. He settled on the sofa with a couple of books, noticing a dusty old pile of newspapers on the coffee table.

One of the papers sat open on the mid page and that's when he saw the article:

'In loving memory of well-loved Pompey Parish councillor ADDINGTON Stanley (Stan) aged 93 years, passed peacefully on a memorial bench at the local cemetery whilst visiting dear late wife Edna Addington. The bench was built for Mr Addington's wife after she passed eight years ago and it is believed that Mr Addington went to the bench daily to sit and talk to Edna. Mr Addington was a loving husband, Father to Paul and Daniel and Brother to Tony. The funeral service is private but donations are welcome and may be sent to Albert Marsh Funeral Directors. Deeply missed, loved forever.

Oh no, Stanley died

That is when Thomas noticed the date: Monday 12th June 2017

What? How is this possible? Have I been speaking to a ghost?

Thomas dropped the paper from his hands. He felt faint, almost like the carpet had been whipped out from underneath him and his brain stuttered for a moment. Thomas looked around. He felt like the leading man in a play, a dramatic play. He just needed the curtains behind him and the stage lights heating up his face.

***

Thomas walked out two hours later with a prescription for medication, some books he'd been allowed to back to his cell and handcuffed to 'O'Rourke who was leading him to his cell where he would remain until the hearing.

He had confessed everything. How he had repressed memories of his dead childhood twin Oliver, how the grief of losing a son had drove his mother mad. How they had spent his whole childhood not understanding each other. How this manifested in his OCD. How he projected his loneliness onto others. So much was slowly, very slowly starting to make sense. He was going to get help. If he was to spend the rest of his life behind bars, well at least he could find some answers.

***

He spent a lonely evening in his cell, only being able to read for a short while before the instructions for lights out.

He tossed and turned on the hard bed having odd dreams about Oliver, his mother.

Emily's application for a visit had been accepted. She came to see him after lunch. Thomas waited in the visitor room with a bright orange jacket. She gave a strangled cry when she saw him.

'Thomas!!!! I will get you out Thomas!!!!' I promise Tom!!!'

She moaned in frustration when she tried to touch him and was forbidden to by the guard.

They sat down, both trembling and took each other's hands. Thomas felt he had so much to ask her.

'Em...how long have I been like this?!'

'Tom...you...you haven't been yourself in a while I'll admit that. But I didn't know it...it went this far!!!'

'Emily, can you do something for me please. Can you contact my mother, Dolores?'

'Who- of course Thomas.'

'tell her to come and visit me. We haven't spoken in a while but...I I need her.'

She nodded. 'I will go see her. Tom, so are you they going to charge you?'

'They have sufficient evidence according to them. '

'Thomas. I love you.'

'I love you too.'

FIFTY-THREE

'Wow what a ruddy turn up for the books.' Said Marsh.

'Indeed.' Said O'Rourke. 'The murder weapon, the murder outfit and the murderer in one go. A trifecta.'

'Do I detect sarcasm from you?'

O'Rourke shrugged 'It All seems so...convenient.'

'I agree it has fallen into our laps a bit. There's still plenty of lines of enquiry to follow up. We need to arrange to get hold of Walker's computer to check recent activity.'

'I will arrange that with forensics' said O'Rourke.

'I'd also like to quiz Walker on EarthCam a bit more.'

'In what way?'

'Well, if Walker really is telling the truth and he witnessed rather than committed the murder, I wonder if we can get a history of EarthCam for that night.'

Marsh seemed lost in thought. 'It seems a bit pie in the sky but I'll allow you to pursue it.'

'Thank you, sir.'

'Now, another line of enquiry to follow up. I tell you what. I tell you what, O'Neill and his women.'

'Yeah-who is it this time?'

'I'm still plundering all the transactions that have been going out of Safe Travel Holiday main account. There was a Standing Order going out to yet another bint. A woman by the name of A Grey.

'O'Rourke raised his eyebrows and looked at the board at the picture of Ben's face.'

'Exactly. There may be no connection but I need to track her down.'

'What else has been coming from the accounts?'

Marsh signed. 'Loads. O'Neill wasn't spending much money on marketing. It was all restaurants, wining and dining, expensive suits, car rentals. No wonder the business was going up the creek.'

'Crikey.'

'Which leads us back to Hobbes. I cannot see how he can sit on his laurels whilst not demanding a single penny back. Why was he being so lenient with Jack… and don't give me that bull about them being friends. Friendship only goes so far when money is involved.'

'How about phone records?'

'We've got some transcripts of texts between him and Miss Simmons. She's certainly not in the clear yet. Very salacious. The team had a WhatsApp group but that's mostly banal crap…memes etc. Now, there were a few texts between Mr Hobbes and Mrs O'Neill.

'Oh really?'

'Yeah. Strange texts. I think they were talking about customers. This leads me to think that Hobbes has been more involved with the business in some secret way or another. The texts reference people called Mr Runner, Mr Twain and Mr White. I can't see any records of dealings with any people of this name. We will look into that but for now, there's a few other priorities.'

'Very good. So, what's next.'

Marsh smirked. 'Get me a doughnut. And then I want you to look into A Grey'.

FIFTY-FOUR

Another few days later and Thomas had yet to hear about Dolores. However, he did get another visitor. Shania.

Thomas felt an odd sense of fear and relief when he saw her coming towards him to sit facing him.

She could be the reason why I am sitting here.

The usual waft of her perfume making its way to him. She slid her handbag from her shoulder and sat down. It was only then that she turned to him and gave him a watery smile. Her eyes were full of tears.

'Oh Tom! I wish I could hug you right now!'

'Thomas felt weak but at her words he felt a glimmer of hope. 'You mean...you don't believe I'm guilty.'

She glanced around, reached over and squeezed his hand.

'You are a lot of things Tom but you aren't a killer.

Nah there is no way Shania is Jack's is a killer …. But Thomas, she WAS there.

Thomas was surprised to find that he had missed Shania too. It made him realise how attached you could get to colleagues, to people who you saw more than your family. Yet...you could not know them at all.

'Shania. I don't even know what's true anymore. I'm being seen by a doctor. They think I have borderline psychosis...I….'

She waited.

'I have been hallucinating the personality of my dead twin brother. My dead twin brother who died in a fire when I was a kid.'

'Oh Tom!' Shania clapped a hand to her mouth.

'Now I know why mum is so screwed up. She – she had to decide who to save. Me or O-Oliver. She chose me first. Then the fire escalated and she could not go back into the house to reach Oliver. He – he died. We – we were 3 years old. I think – I think I've repressed the memory for so long'.

Be careful what you say now. Do NOT give too much away

'Oh shit, what did they have to say?' she tapped her long talons on the table.

Thomas fidgeted in his seat and thought he would test the waters. 'They spoke to me about EarthCam because I was keeping an eye on the shop that night, remember?'

Shania looked uncomfortable 'oh…. yes, I remember you was doing that so did they ask if you saw anything?'

'Yeah…of course. I said I saw a figure …wearing my hoodie…. hit Jack over the head with an instrument.

Her lower lip trembled.

'Shan…. there's no easy way to say this…I'm just going to come out with it…. 'I overheard you and Ben that night of the gathering. You were there? At the scene of the murder?' Thomas steadied himself, trying not to let his voice tremble.

'I erm…. I … didn't know you heard that. You know I was very drunk that evening, I actually can't really remember much of what I ….'

'Shania, please talk to me?'

She sighed then 'He was alive when I left him. I swear on my like...life Tom. Like if you find me to be lying, I would shave my hair off and never wear nail extensions again to prove it to you'

Thomas couldn't help a smile then; she did have a sense of humour sometimes and somehow, he believed her.

She looked down then and sniffed, Thomas was trying to work out if there was going to be crocodile tears or genuine and he was surprised to see hurt in her eyes.

'Tom...I have a confession.'

She told him about arranging to meet Jack at the office and her blackmailing plan with the hidden camera in her desk and the Dictaphone.

"What were you thinking Shania?' asked Thomas sadly.

'I don't know.' She wiped her eyes.

'But that doesn't make you the killer Shania. The killer appeared after you left.

'Yes, but I was the reason he was there in the first place.' Her face crumpled. 'He was an asshole but he did not deserve that. 'OH my God! How many secrets have we all been keeping?'

'This is the point. And then the hammer and my hoodie are planted at mine. It's beyond all reasonable doubt that the killer was ....one of us. And if we are believing each other now that we each didn't do it.... he chose his words carefully. 'Then...then...it would have to be...Gerry...or Ben...'

'What about Emily?' asked Shania defensively.

'It would not be my girlfriend.'

'What makes you think it would be my boyfriend?'

'I don't know dammit! But can't you see how it looks to Marsh and O'Rourke? We all have motive! But only one of us did it.'

'Well, as the diagnosed loony tune, you would have more motive.' Shania said coldly.

'How could you – 'he was about to shout but stopped himself.'

'Sorry' they said in unison.

One of us is guilty

'Shania. Can I ask your help?'

'She wiped away a tear. 'Of course.'

'Can you...can you also do some digging around...if you know what I mean?'

An unspoken agreement passed between them 'I understand.'

A bell signalled the end of the visiting time.

'I'll come back she muttered and hurried out without another word.

FIFTY-FIVE

It was Friday when he got the confirmation that Emily had spoken to Dolores and she was coming to visit him.

Thomas was looking into the face of his mother.

'Mum'. He croaked.

'T- 'She tried to say his name but words failed her

Instead, she just just looked at him her mouth trembling. 'You…. look awful.'

'I know.'

'Have – you been eating?' She swallowed, her body trembling.

'If I'm honest, no, not much.

'Well, at least you are honest she croaked.

'Mum, we need to talk. This can't go on. I need to…. understand.'

She didn't say anything but continued to look at him, eyes slightly watery.

'Mum, you understand what I'm saying don't you…'

'Yes, she whispered.

He gestured. 'Please. Mum – just sit down.'

She dropped her handbag on the floor and started ringing her hands.

Their eyes met.

'Mum, for Gods' sake.'

At the desperation in his voice, she dropped into the seat.

'How come it took so long?' he demanded.

'Emily called me the other day and…. I was…. I was trying to build up the – the courage to see you. What's gone on Thomas? Why have they bagged you up?'

Her face crumpled up.

'They think I killed my boss.' He said shortly. 'To be honest, I don't really blame them given my track record.'

'Please don't tell me you did it!'

'And if I did, would that make a difference?'

'Oh, don't start going on about our relationship!

Our relationship is shot to hell mum! Dammit! Why am I like this…why??? There's so much going on in my life and I can't…I can't tell you…and it just kills me, Mum! It's been you and me all these years. We should be close; nothing should be able to drive a wedge between us but…we live in the same city and we never see each other!'

'Well, you don't make much effort.' she croaked, jabbing a finger at him.

He swiped it away.

'No, I don't Mum…because you don't. You are my parent! For Gods' sake, I know I'm an adult now but you never ask how I am, you never call except to berate me and you never even wanted me around as a kid. I want you to care mum. Care to call me to check I've washed my socks. Or or…that I'm eating properly. Mum, I need to get this off my chest, you were a lousy parent!

'I did my best alright? Your father buggered off and I was left with a child who never slept. God help me Thomas you were always in and out of my room, always saying you were ill, always monsters int the cupboard. I tried to serve you dinners but you refused them. I didn't know what to do with you boy, and I was alone...all alone! A tear trickled down her face. An' I weren't well, was I? I was in so...so much PAIN!!!'She was suddenly racked with sobs.

'Mum, I know! I know! I remember now. Mum, I remember Oliver! 'Thomas was sobbing himself. 'It must have been awful for you. Raising me all alone.'

'Yes, and you are a ruddy chip off the old block, aren't you? You must know son, you weren't all there, you weren't right in the bleeding head. But neither was I!!

Thomas felt shaken by her words. He knew a part of her was right. They were parallels of each other. Two damaged souls whose lives had gone horribly wrong.

'Mum, I need to understand what's wrong with me. Once I know what's wrong with me. I can fix it.' he whispered. 'I'm going to tell you things you won't like but I need you to listen Mum. I love you and I need you...to listen.'

She remained silent.

'I have been hallucinating for many years. I am obsessed with order and control. I have become embroiled in something. I was so alone; the internet became my only consolation. And because I was on their such as lot of the goddamn time, I was always viewing life through a lens, never engaging in it. Never present in mind. And through this, I have become embroiled in a situation that I don't understand, I don't want to be a part of but now I have no choice. I was witness to a murder, mum. My boss. But the police suspect me. Someone has tried to frame me. I don't know what is going to happen to me but I am frightened. My friends are frightened. I frighten myself...'

'The doctors must have said something mum'. He took her by the shoulders. 'Mum please...'

She was shaking now and stood up...'T-The docs said you had inherited some genetic psychological disease. T-They said it was hereditary. Thomas...you...got it from me. You are right lad; it is my fault. I live with that burden day in day out and I try and block out the feelings know, if I can eat, drink, smoke enough it numbs the reality that I cursed you with this illness.'

'But if you had just been honest'. He pounded the table. 'I would have been aware of my condition.'

'I'd hoped. If I ignored it, you would...get out...from under my care. You would... flourish without me...I would flourish without you.' Her tears were rolling down her cheeks now.

'No Mum, not anymore. We need to help each other. Face up to any feelings we have. No more running. Not anymore Mum. I'm tired.'

They reached across the table and grabbed each other's hands.

'We have wasted so many years.'

Thomas was fighting back more tears. 'We will never get them back. I feel like I'm...wasting my life.'

'You are a young lad. You are my boy; you can claw some time back. It's too late for me but not for you.'

'Oh son, how can I help. Please tell me.'

'I need for us to be able to talk with each other. If I have kids one day, I want them to come sees you. Make my upbringing not be in vain.'

She nodded, crying. 'I'm just a simple woman, what do I know about the world, really? I helped bugger up your upbringing. I've been hiding from you as much as you have hidden from me.'

'Let's change this. Let me have hope.'

'Mum. I miss you. I want you in my life.'

'I miss you too my love.'

They held each other's hands and cried together. The guard didn't intervene.

'I believe you are innocent my darling,' said Dolores. She patted his hand. 'And I haven't fought for you for many years but dammit I'm fighting for my boy now. I am getting you out of here.'

FIFTY-SIX

For his safety, Thomas was in a cell on his won which he appreciated.

The bell had just gone to signal bed time, so he was all prepared to try and get a night's sleep. A visit from O'Rourke surprised him.

; You are excused from sleep for a bit.' said O'Rourke. 'I .... need your help.'

Thomas sat up with an interested expression.

'I want you to tell me more about EarthCam.' Said O'Rourke,

Startled, Thomas nevertheless obeyed. He told of his hobby, how much he loved going on EarthCam, how it was an escape from the real world. O'Rourke listened intently.

'So, if I am to believe you' that you were indeed the witness to this murder and you have been framed. I must Say it will be a tall order, Thomas. You have no one to vouch for you being at home and the murder weapon was found at your flat. Bout- can you – do you know if you can re watch Old EarthCam footage.'

'I I don't know.' Thomas admitted.

'If I took you to a computer tomorrow, can you see if you can?'

'Yes. Thank you.' Said Thomas. For some reason he trusted O'Rourke.

'Right then. Well, I will let you get some sleep. The was all from me.' O'Rourke got up.

Despite everything, Thomas felt he slept a bit easier that night.

FIFTY-SEVEN

When Shania kept thinking about Ben and how in the last few months, he seemed to treat work more of a burden than a blessing. He seemed especially angry or so she had noticed anyway, since Gerry said he was leaving. Maybe he expected a promotion? Not to get fired obviously would have been in his plan. Of course, he would not be happy with Jack after getting fired, but Shania could not help but question everyone right now. *Who would want Jack dead?*

All of us. All of us have a reason.

Shania walked to the kitchen, she poured herself a glass of wine and made her way to the bedroom. She sat down on the fluffy cushions looking across to the night table where a picture of her and the team sat; her and Jack snuggled together, Thomas next to Gerry on the other side and Ben on the end of the table. They all looked really happy and she felt a lump rise in her throat.

Damn girl, you had more curves in this picture. I need to eat some more carbs for sure.

She got her phone out and sent Ben a text about meeting at his, to which he of course replied straight away

He is so easy, it's kind of annoying. Jack was always a challenge to me.

She checked her hair and makeup in the mirror and with a spritz of her perfume, she was on her way.

Ben opened the door and immediately, Shania could smell cigarette smoke. 'I thought you were sticking to the vape?' she asked suspiciously.

Ben looked at her and rolled his eyes 'I don't smoke...smoke normally...but it's been a stressful time hasn't it.' He held the door open for her but quickly turned his back and began heading to the kitchen.

Shania raised her hands and called after him 'Oh sure because smoking casually will not lead to smoking more and more. If you want to delude yourself, be my guest.' She followed him into the kitchen, wrinkling her nose at the stale smoke and general state of the place.

'Hey, what's up with you?' Ben questioned then. 'Wine?'

He looked like he had put on a lot of weight around his middle and he looked so much older than what he was. His hair almost looked streaked grey in the light. He did not look like a criminal but looks could be deceiving.

Shania put her handbag on the counter and poised on one of the bar chairs Ben had picked up on E-Bay. 'Yeah, sure. Whatever. I'll have a Rose if you've got it.'

'Picked one up especially babe.' he smiled a half-arsed smile, plucking it from the fridge. Shania could immediately see it was the cheapest brand about. She felt a flash of irritation but then a pang of guilt. Ben was out of work after all. He poured it and she accepted it graciously. His stomach bulged as he sat down too and cracked open a can.

Ben glanced up; his expression serious 'Can't believe Walker has been arrested! Can you believe it was him who carried it out? Who would have thought it??!!

'We don't know that yet.' Shania said sharply.

'What's not to know. Babe, the weapon was found in his house!'

'Or someone planted it there.'

Don't talk crap babe.' Ben had his back to her.

Shania decided not to hold back about Thomas.

'I went to visit him today.'

'You what?! Are you insane?' he whipped around. 'What good did that do?'

'Well, he was honest and said that he heard our conversation at the gathering at his house.'

'What? Are you fucking joking? We do not need more people knowing this?' Ben shouted.

'I just explained it to him. I think he's got many of his own problems but he seemed to be cool with what I said and it's the truth anyway. I have been sitting on this guilt' she cried.

'That's true, I am hoping he keeps it to himself through' Ben replied. 'His ass is on the line now. Looney tune though he is- did you read the papers about him? He will want to throw the shit and smear everyone else.'

'Come off its Ben. If he does then we all do. We area all guilty in the eyes of Marsh and O'Rourke.'

'Why does everyone bum then? And for the record, no that's not true. Thomas went up the guilty hierarchy when the bloody weapon was found at his house and the fact, he's an eye!'

'Don't call him that!'

'Why?' Ben sneered. 'Oh, don't tell me you are falling in love with Walker now? First O'Neill, then me, now Walker. Who's next> Hobbes?'

'Oh, screw you, Ben!' Shania shouted.

'OK forget I said anything! You know you can trust me right, babe? I didn't kill Jack. '

Ben smiled at her and went to the kitchen. Shania desperately wanted to believe him. Why was she having doubts?

I'm going to your bedroom for a bit.' She spoke.

'Whatever he called.

As Shania entered the bedroom to turn on the computer, she was greeted with a stench of incense sticks which she assumed Ben used to drown the smell of the smoke with.

'Jesus', she held her nose and felt her heart begin to race as she scanned the room with her eyes.

'Stop being stupid Shania, you aren't going to find anything' she whispered to herself.

As suspected, it was your average guy's room with too many computer games, dirty socks scattered across the floor and a ton of 'Men's protein' magazines which Shania grimaced at. She disliked the whole 'Manosphere' scene.

She pressed the on button on the computer and waited for the start-up message but the computer was already loaded. She went on to Google Chrome search to begin but did not even know what to type in.

'Jack O'Neal death latest?'

That's when she noticed a big pile of newspaper clippings and print outs under the desk.

Frowning, she grabbed the series of papers, she noticed they were all articles on Jack and the business. 'Jack O'Neal owner of STH wins award', Jack O'Neal welcomes his 1000th customer', Jack O'Neal scoops up 3 Awards at Holiday Maker of the year', 'STH wins Gold Medal at British Travel Awards', STH owner champion conservation' 'local businessman voted boss of the year.'

'Ben, what is all this?'

'What's that?' he shouted from the kitchen.

'All these papers and prints?'

Ben rushed in then, looking slightly panicked

'Oh…. erm, was just…. I wanted to see if there would be any clues in the news of the killer. I know I've watched too much tv yadda yadda yadda….'

'Oh. OK. 'She said quietly.'

'I'll be in, in a minute.'

As Shania looked at the dates on the papers, she realised that every single one, was way before the murder, in fact, some were from years back. What was Ben really looking for?

***

They googled for some up to date news about the O'Neal murder case but so far, nothing else had been made public. They searched Jack's social media profiles and scrolled through Facebook. Something caught Shania's eye. Jack had tagged himself in the town of Yeovil, in November. Shania pointed this out to Ben.

'I can't remember Jack going to Yeovil in November.'

Ben looked startled. 'Oh. Um yes. He went to check out some premises. Was thinking about expanding Safe Travel.'

'To Yeovil? It seemed really odd. Shania's heart sank. She betted yet another notch on Jack's bedpost. But something made her take a mental note of the date and the pub he tagged himself in. She was going to do a bit of independent investigating herself……

FIFTY-EIGHT

Why did Ben have newspaper clippings from so far back? Was he just that fascinated with Jack's life? At the end of the day, he was a 50 something player who aside from the business, didn't really have much to show in life apart from his string of women. Maybe Ben was just looking out for me? Shania thought. Something does not add up though.

Ben had given her a spare key to his flat. He had texted her to say he'd gone out for the evening Shania could not help herself. She felt compelled to look further around the flat? But what for? She did not know but something did not add up. Would Ben want to hurt Jack?

As Shania went back into the bedroom, the floor felt cold and gritty and she wished she hadn't kicked her heels off. Who knew what is clinging to her bare feet? She noticed Ben had opened the window behind the sagging curtains. The feeble brightness lit up the filthy window still and behind the curtain was a pile of pornographic magazines. Shania rolled her eyes 'am I dating a 16-year-old?' she whispered to herself.

She looked across to the cheap looking wardrobe, the door had seen better days and had several holes dented on it. Perhaps his punching bag?

As she opened the door, she was greeted with the smell of stale smoke; parting the shirts and jumpers. At the back of the wardrobe, she noticed a brown backpack. The backpack that Ben wore to work.

Guilt gnawed at her, he was her boyfriend, what was she thinking. And yet... hands trembling, she went for the zip and emptied it. It did not seem to have anything important in; two packets of cigarettes, tissues, a betting slip, a bus card, until she opened the front compartment.

A Nokia 3310. The new version. What was he doing with a second phone? Especially when he always had to have the latest iPhone.

Shania tried to turn the phone on but it was dead. She spent the next few minutes looking for a cable but gave up. Her eye fell on Ben's MacBook. Heart hammering and leaving the door ajar for sounds of Ben returning early, she logged in and brought up Facebook. She typed in 'Benjamin Grey' into the search bar. Of course, he was already her friend. Shania was not silly; she knew that Ben had fancied her for a long time.

She started sifting through old photo albums but could not find anything of significance. Most were of Ben hammered with a drink in his hand. She thought she would try 'photos of Ben' which of course is his tagged list.

Up came some slightly embarrassing pictures from someone called Agnes Grey. Ben never discussed his family so Shania couldn't be sure which family member this was. Whenever Shania brought up family in the past, Ben would close up. It was clear that it was not up for discussion.

As she swiped through the pictures, she noticed one photo in particular. This Agnes was next to Ben on the beach. He was in a baby sun hat with dinosaurs on. He had sand all around his mouth whilst holding what looks like a jam sandwich. Agnes had her arms around him and they were both smiling for the camera. That's when she noticed the tagline 'my little boy'.

Shania hesitated for a moment. It's amazing how much information you could get online about someone these days.

There are more questions than there are answers when it comes to social media and developments of intimate relationships. Everyone is desperate to develop a coherent identity but nobody knows if people are necessarily engaging in real self-presentation. 'I cannot be sure who this woman is' Shania said to herself now conscious of the time and Ben returning.

She decided she was willing to take the risk. She needed to be sure who was dating and why he was investigating her ex before the murder.

Even now, without Ben providing any detail, she was determined and able to piece together the jigsaw of the information available on his family. Scary really. She clicked on Agnes' profile, she found a location, an age, an email address and even a workplace for her. Journalists do not need to work hard for their information anymore.

Something else caught her eye. Yeovil.

Ben had been cagey when saying about Jack being in Yeovil. Was this a co incidence? She had to know.

She clicked send message and her thumb hovered for a while

'Hi Agnes, I am unsure if I even have the right person but I am Ben's girlfriend. I was hoping we could talk? Privately if possible. Please do not mention anything to anyone

Shania x'

'I cannot believe Thomas is all over the papers' spluttered Ben

'There is no way he killed Jack' said Shania sharply. I went to visit him and to be honest, I did not think he would see me but he did. He is adamant that someone planted the hammer in the shoe cupboard and it would have been at the party'

'Well, no offense but haven't you read the articles and heard the latest? Thomas has not been well…. mentally. How do we know HE didn't put the damn thing in the shoe cupboard?' Ben spat.

'He has been struggling yes but he would not do THAT' Shania argued as her pocket vibrated. She got out her phone and noticed an email come through from Agnes Grey. Her hear began hammering.

And she quickly turned her screen off.

'You are always sticking up for him,' Ben said bitterly pacing up and down the room. 'Maybe it was Emily because she got sick of his bullshit?'

'I thought you had sorted this vendetta with Thomas Ben? It's like you have gone to square one again?'

'It's not that but I do not like that he is trying to point the finger….and I am feeling stressed about the job situation…. Why do you keep checking your phone?'

Shania scanned her phone quickly and all she saw was

'Please do not tell Ben, yes, I will meet….'

'It's nothing, I was waiting to hear from …my dad. He needed me to do a food shop. Ben…I – I'm going to be away this weekend.'

'You are not going to see Walker again, are you?'

'No. No.' I just need to…clear my head. Crazy week you know.'

On the way home, she stopped at Portsmouth and Southsea train station and bought a train ticket to Yeovil. Her money was dwindling. She's had to go on the dole soon if Caroline didn't find a buyer for Safe Travel. God, what a joke of a name. She felt her life had never been in more danger.

'Thomas could have done it. Or Gerry. Or…or my boyfriend….' The train to Yeovil was thankfully quiet, giving Shania plenty of time to think and plan.

People had always thought she was a bimbo. A good for nothing Barbie doll. She was sick of that image. She was going to do something useful.

Agnes had refused to give her address but had said a coffee house where they could meet. Shania EarthCam med it. It looked suitable. She had turned off her mobile phone so it wouldn't pick up where she was. The last thing she wanted was to signal she was in Yeovil.

***

Shania walked into the coffee house and noticed Agnes almost instantly. She looked different to her pictures but then didn't everybody these days? With filters, apps to change your entire look, you could never be sure what to expect. She approached her tentatively adjusting her shoulder bag and took a deep breath 'Agnes?'

The woman looked up and smiled. 'Shania'. She stood up and gave her a brief hug. She was an attractive woman, late forties with curly brown hair and her eyes as she pulled back, Shania registered with a start, were the exact colour and shape of Ben's. She had an air of glamour about her and smelled like Coco Chanel. *Good taste* Shania thought to herself.

Agnes motioned for Shania to take a seat and Shania obediently sat in the adjacent wicker chair. It was a quaint yet cosmopolitan 'trendy' place. Picking up the menu, there was a choice of light lunches and deals when twinned with cocktails.

'I think we are going to need some of those.' Agnes smiled rather sadly, getting out of purse. 'This is my treat, I insist.'

'Oh, you really don't have to' Shania felt flustered.

'No, no I want to...please ...have anything.'

Shania felt self-conscious. She never frequented places like this, she didn't have the money. She and friends would happily sit and order pitchers at the local Wetherspoons. Wanting to look sophisticated, she settled on the prawn sandwich with a pitcher of Woo Woo. Agnes summoned the waiter to place the order. Then she sat back, relaxed and looked sadly at Shania.

'It seems we have a lot to talk about' Agnes says. 'How long have you... been with my son?'

'It's actually quite new...we are quite new but obviously I have worked with him for a long while now.' Shania added.

'And where do you work again?'

'Safe Travel Holidays. In the city centre.'

Agnes smiled. 'Excuse me for being nosy. I have to content myself with observing my son's life from a panoramic view. Does he like his job?

'I- I think so. In fact, I know so. He was the best sales person in the team until... until another colleague came along.'

'Really?'

'Yeah, kind of got his back up a bit.'

Agnes smiled. 'Boys.'

'Yeah. Boys.' Shania noted sadly. 'Do you know what though. Our other colleague, he's a real good sort, really decent. He and Ben probably have more in common than they think.'

'I have not heard anything from Benjamin since. Well, it's been a few years now.' Agnes looked down, 'I want to know that he is, ok? I was surprised when I received the message from you if I'm being really honest.

'I thought you might be. I am sorry for that. I have been so worried about him Agnes. I thought maybe if I spoke to you and his dad, perhaps you could advise? But then you say you haven't seen him in a few years! God I am sorry. How like...stupid of me'

'It's okay Shania.' Agnes said kindly, putting her hand on top of Shania's. 'I have not seen my Benjamin, no, but I also have had nothing to do with his dad' she sipped her peach schnapps, the aroma lingering. Shania had a feeling a story was coming and she waited tentatively.

'I was just out of university when I met Ben's father. I had been studying Hotel Management and he Travel and Tourism. He told me his name was John Neilson. He was young and had dreams of launching a travel company. At the time, he was so charming and sweet. I was eighteen with rose tinted glasses on.

Anyway, we had a couple of one-night stands, you know how it is.' She looked down, clearly embarrassed.

'We've all been there' Shania laughed nervously. Agnes didn't return the laugh.

257

'Anyway…a few months later, of course I found out I was pregnant. I will always remember that completely paradoxical feeling of excitement and terror. I took him out for a walk, I told him and…. he laughed in my face. He thought I was joking; can you believe it?! And when he saw I had a straight face, well, that's when his whole demeanour changed. He ranted at me for 5 straight minutes, asking how I could have been so damn stupid…even though it takes two to tango. He did not even offer to discuss options with me or come to the doctor. He had already moved on with another woman or so he said!'

'What do you mean?' Shania asked.

Their conversation was paused whilst the waiter brought over their pitchers and lunch. Agnes thanked the waiter politely and continued with her story.

'He was already WITH another woman. It was not a case of moving on after me…oh no no, Agnes's voice grew steely and bitter. He had cheated on her with me and had obviously decided that the side salad did not match the main meal. It was not until he launched his travel company with a friend that I found out his real name…. '

'So, it wasn't John?' Shania leant forward. Who was she kidding? She knew who this mysterious man was.

'No. His name was Jack O'Neal….my Benjamin is…WAS his son' she said sharply. 'And he was your boss? I am guessing?' she added. 'This must be a terrible time for you. I'm sorry'

Shania decided to not mention that she too had been a notch on Jack's bedpost. That information was not needed and she wanted to learn more.

'I did not and still do not believe in abortion. I knew I had to raise him, with or without Jack…without a father. It was such a difficult time. My parents had obviously had designs on me marrying a wealthy bachelor…a ring on the finger before a bun in the oven…but what could I do? The deed was done. My parents grudgingly accepted the situation and to be fair they tried their best but…' she took a bite of her sandwich, lost in thought.

'It must have been very difficult for you.' Shania prompted.

It was in all senses...emotionally, mentally, financially. Ben struggled massively without a father figure. It was heart-breaking when the kids would make cards in Primary School for Fathers' Day and he would come home crying because he didn't have a daddy. He saw all his classmates with their dad on sports day, swinging them round. He was envious. I don't blame him. I was envious.'

'Did you ever meet anyone else?'

'There were few short-term relationships but once the reality hit of dating twenty something with a kid...no. Men my age, they wanted to whisk me off to Venice or Paris and what mother could do that without taking boxes of Pampers and formula...it certainly killed the romance.' She smiled.

'I was naive to think that there would not come a day when he would want to know who his father was. Now someone has taken it upon themselves to take his father away for good'.

Shania's heart was in her mouth.

'He he has never spoken about it much with me.' She mumbled.

'So does Benjamin know that you know about Jack?'

'No' she looked down. 'I found you off of my own back.... did Ben...ever go looking for Jack?'

'Well, it got to the point when he was 13, in secondary school. Puberty was starting to kick in and suddenly I was the cause of all his problems. This is when things got.... darker and our relationship really started to deteriorate. He started back chatting me, saying it was my fault that his dad wanted nothing to do with him. I was a shit mother. I tried compensating. I bought him a games console, tried to do 'boy' things with him that he liked to enjoy. One day, after a particularly bad row. He...he.' She rubbed her cheek. 'He just started smashing up the living room. Punched the pictures to shards of glass, up ended the furniture. I think even he realised what he was turning into. He fled the house and was gone all night. I was frantic. It turned out he'd crashed at a mate's and I got the call at 1am when they wandered in to his mate's house and his mate's parents had been having kittens. I then sat him down and told him, I begged him to believe me. I showed him a picture of Jack...I explained I had begged him to be part of our lives but he hadn't wanted to know. It kind of placated the situation for a bit. At least Benjamin had a face and a name for his inventory. For a while even his marks picked up a bit...but' Her voice trailed off and she took a large gulp of her cocktail.

Shania's head was swimming. There was so much to take in.

'So, Ben...has been aware that Jack's his father...for a while.'

'Yes. Shania...what is the real reason you contacted me?'

Shania took a moment to answer. Answering would mean looking Agnes in the eye and she was frightened. Frightened of verbalising what she had most been fearing.

'Agnes. Thomas Walker has been arrested for the murder of Jack. But I went to visit him in prison. He is adamant he didn't do it. And I – I believe him.'

'There's something I haven't yet told you. I – got back in touch with Jack. Before he died. I found him after he won that travel award thing.'

'What did you say to him?'

'I – I began blackmailing him. I said I wanted revenge for the way he treated me. How he had never paid a penny towards me. I – I lied and said I had gone to a local paper and was going to expose the story. How this oily greasy womaniser had left me high and dry. He panicked; said he would pay me hush money. I started getting a handsome monthly amount in my account. He had to take the money from Safe Travel Accounts so his wife wouldn't find out. You know the ironic thing is?' She laughed then. 'A horrible laugh.' He knew I had a kid of course. He didn't know that Ben was his kid! Isn't that just a hoot?!'

Shania was shaking. 'So...so Jack knew he had a kid with you...but didn't know it was Ben...and Ben...knew about Jack?? Oh My God. Who am I going out with??!!

'Shania.... please don't tell me what I think you are....'

'I think' Shania cut her off. 'That I do not know my boyfriend at all. I think.... I think I am dating Jack's' murderer....'

FIFTY-NINE

The next morning, O'Rourke took Thomas into a witness room.

'Can you see if you can get on EarthCam for me again?'

Thomas logged into EarthCam. He showed O'Rourke the app.

'Fascinating stuff' said O'Rourke, 'Can you show me Safe Travel Holiday office?'

Thomas obeyed.

He tried to replay back the footage from that fateful Sunday evening.

'The footage would only go back 12 hours.'

Thomas sat back in his chair, rage boiling inside of him.

'This is my fault. I fucked up. I should have brought the computer to you when I Had the chance.'

'You should have done.' O'Rourke said quietly. 'But there's no point crying over spilt milk.

'Do you think I did it, O'Rourke>'

O'Rourke looked at him evenly. I cannot confirm that off the record to you, Mr Walker. But I will say, despite all evidence pointing to the contrary, I found your story very compelling. So, if EarthCam is not an option, I have found information from Safe Travel through Instagram, Twitter, Facebook, there is no stone I haven't turned.

Thomas thought about mentioning the Dictaphone but there was no point in getting Shania in shit. Unless she was the one …no…she was helping him…it wouldn't be proper to grass at this point….

'Thomas' said O'Rourke. 'Did Mr Grey ever mention anything about his family?'

'He never talked much about his mum. He never knew his dad said Thomas. I know his mum is alive but they are no longer in touch.'

'Interesting.' O'Rourke made a note.

'I might need to come back to you about EarthCam another time Mr Walker.'

'Yes, certainly.' Thomas muttered.

He had a feeling O'Rourke was cooking up a plan.

SIXTY

Shania didn't know how she made it home. Terror coursed through her but... she had to know.

Upon arriving back at Portsmouth and Southsea, she headed straight for Ben's flat. Could she trust he wouldn't hurt her? If what she suspected was true?

Ben let her in.

'God, you look pale 'he moaned. 'How was your weekend?'

She entered without smiling.

'I know Ben.' She said quietly.

'Know what? Stop talking in Riddles Shania.'

'I know...that ...Jack was your father. '

Ben leaned against the wall, breathing hard.'

'How the fuck did you ...'

'I went through your things. I tracked down your mother.'

'What the fuck...you scheming...'

'What's more,' said Shania. 'I think it was you who went to confront him that night. If you love me Ben, like you say you do, you will be honest with me...did you kill Jack?'

Tears were streaming down Ben; s face. When he spoke, it was barely a whisper. 'Yes.'

Terror coursed through Shania. So, it was true. It was all true.

'And you are sitting here right now whilst Tom is rotting away in the slammer' she whispered. 'How could you?'

'Oh, Walker is just collateral damage!' ben spat in fury. 'He's a pawn!'

'You can't let him go down!' Shania screamed!!!

Wait a minute!' Ben started walking towards her and she shrank back moaning. This isn't another O'Neill situation you are pulling on me is it. There's no fucking Dictaphone on you is there?'

'No, she sobbed.' I'm not here because I hate you!'

'Of course, you hate me!! He shrieked 'They all hate me!! But Jack – dad was meant to love me!!! I deserve his business. I'm the rightful owner.'

'Ben. You need to do the right thing and confess.'

'No way. Just desserts have been done. He rejected me. He got what he deserved. Deserting my mother. He was a parasite!!'

'I will also be confessing!' sobbed Shania. 'I'm going to tell Marsh and O'Rourke about the Dictaphone.

'NOOO!! Shouted ben 'You'll go down for blackmail. You will go down in my place.'

'Well, if in go down, I'll have Thomas for company and you can live your life in peace and security, knowing that we are serving time for your deeds.'

'NO SHANIA. I LOVE YOU!!! I NEED YOU!!DON'T LEAVE ME!!!

Ben threw his arms around her legs. He was squeezing so hard it hurt.

'You will lose everything 'he moaned.

'Well at least I'll finally gain some integrity by telling the truth.' Shania said and suddenly saying it out louse made it so much kore clear for her. 'I'm going to do the right thing. Oh, I won't grass on you. I will just tell my truth. The choice will be yours whether you do the same.'

She removed the sobbing Ben's arms from her legs. She was fully preparing to be chased but he did not have the strength anymore. He just kept sobbing hysterically as she let herself out of the door.

SIXTY-ONE

'I'm here to see Marsh and O'Rourke'. Shania said, arriving at the station the next morning.

They were both in the breakout room and came out immediately.

'Miss Simmons, do you have some new information for us?'

'Yes, I do.' Said Shania shakily. 'I have quite a bit actually...

***

'Well, we are rounding them up like flies!' said Marsh.'

'What will she be charged with?'

'Perverting the course of justice. Blackmail. Not murder though. She wasn't the murderer.'

'I don't think so either.'

'I also don't think it was Thomas Walker.'

'Who do you think it is out of the remaining ones then?' asked Marsh.

Before O'Rourke could answer, the phone rang.

'Mr Ben Grey is here to see you both.'

SIXTY-TWO

Ben sat in the waiting room of the police station. Ben thought it was all over. Thomas had been arrested so what more was there to worry about?

The detective had called this morning informing some new evidence had come to light and they needed his assistance with the enquiry. Ben had caught the next bus to the police station and was ushered into the waiting area where he sat clutching a plastic cup of the free coffee from the vending machine.

So why did he feel so nervous?

'Mr Grey?' O'Rourke came into the lobby. 'Follow me, please.'

Feeling queasy, Ben followed him into a claustrophobic interview room. A plastic table with a recorder was waiting. One chair facing two.

He sat in the chair and Marsh and O'Rourke did the same, Ben could not read their expressions. Marsh switched on the recorder and gave the date and time of the start of the interview.

'How long did you know Jack O'Neal?' Marsh started.

Ben paused and his shoulders squared up and he felt defensive.

'How long is a piece of string? It was quite a while'.

'Can you be more specific?'

'Well, at least three years I would say, you asked me this in a previous interview? I am sure of it?'

'Is that all? Three years?' Marsh questioned.

Ben shrugged not really understanding what Marsh was getting at as he stared at him a bit too long without blinking.

'Has it been three years since your first meeting or three years since you found out he was your father?' Marsh said sharply.

Ben sat stunned. *How does he know?*

'What?'

'Jack O'Neal is your father isn't he Ben?'

'I... well....'

'He is your father and you took the job at Safe Travel knowing this didn't you?'

She wouldn't have told? She wouldn't.

Ben shakes his head pretending this was a bad dream.

'You had been watching him for a long time, hadn't you Ben? Obsessing in fact. It may have been three years at Safe Travel Holidays, but your infatuation was a lot longer, wasn't it?' Marsh pushed.

Ben began to cry. He refused to believe that Shania had thrown him under a bus.

'You took the job there after months and months of stalking your father didn't you. Mr O'Neal being the man he was, got to you didn't its Ben? It must have been hard? All those women? He was so busy with his lifestyle, that he did not want to acknowledge his son did he Ben?' Marsh said confidently now.

'Do you want to know what I think?'

Ben felt the hairs on his neck rise.

'I think, you took the job wanting to know your father. I think you tried your hardest to get close to him. To build that bond. You were the number one colleague before Mr Walker, weren't you? Only that pissed you off when Walker came in. It took the spotlight from you I imagine?'

Ben was crying now and shaking his head

'You went there that night didn't you Ben. You were fed up as O'Neal had fired you and you wanted your own back.' Marsh pushed.

'Do you want to know how fucking hard it was. Every single day. Knowing what I knew.'

Marsh sat back in his chair satisfied.

'We noticed regular amounts of money going to a Mrs A Grey. A NatWest account. From the Safe Travel Holiday account. We did some research, called the Bank. Didn't take us long to put two and two together. She apparently has been blackmailing him for a little while.

'I did not know that.' Gulped Ben.

'I tried to tell him. I wanted him to acknowledge me. Just to fucking care even for five minutes. I wanted him to admit he knew about me. I wanted him to say I am sorry Ben. I am sorry I left and completely ignored the fact that you are my son. His words where he did not have any spawn.'

'That must have been very difficult Mr Grey'

Ben continued, 'Thomas joined the company and ruined all of my plans. I was the golden boy. But. As soon as he joined, he would steal my dad's affection just by breathing. I wanted him to see the man I had become without him. I wanted him to see I was a hard worker and I was worthy of being there. All he cared about was where or when his next 'lay' was coming from.

My dad always had ulterior motives, I mean in hindsight, he had set his eyes on Emily...Thomas' bird. Who would not like Emily....?'

The detectives urged him to continue, nodding slowly.

'I liked Emily...for a long time. I felt like Thomas had come in, not only to steal my job and my dad's affections but also the girl I cared about.

Ben paused realising that he may be admitting more than he should here.

'I met Emily a while ago. She was working in the local and I got chatting to her. This was way before Thomas was on the scene. We chatted and I was convinced that she had finally noticed me....'

'What happened next?' O'Rourke said

'Same thing that always happens. I was rejected.' Ben bit his lip so hard; he could taste the metallic blood.

'I must have misread the situation. I waited for her to finish her shift so I could surprise her with some tickets to a band that was playing that night. Only she was not interested. I really thought she wanted me but once again, I was nothing to her. The way I am nothing to my dad.'

'What did you do when she rejected you?'

'Well, I was annoyed but that's another story. Having to watch her with Thomas after that was hard. What did he have that I didn't?'

'I take it Mr Walker knows about your little history with his girlfriend?' Marsh said

'Actually no, he doesn't or if he does, he has not mentioned it.'

'Surely, Emily would have recognised you though? When your lot have all been together?' O'Rourke added.

'Ah that's the sad thing see. I make such little impression on people; I do not think she has even looked at me twice. She forgot who I was. I am impossible to love. To be wanted'

Ben looked down into his lap now.

'When word got around that dad had tried it on with Emily at Gerry's leaving do…. I snapped. I was so angry. He needed punishing. Thomas for coming in and taking everything and my dad for just being…. him. Thomas deserved what he got. It's not like he was doing anything with his life anyway'

'Mr Grey are you admitting to the murder of your father Mr Jack O'Neal and also for setting up Mr Thomas Walker? Please clarify for the tape'

Ben screwed up his face.

I – I knew he was coming back from Devon with his wife. I – I stole the spare key from Safe Travel Holidays safe once when I was being Jack's dogbody. I was always nipping in. He never checked the tapes. The night he returned to Portsmouth, I – I gave him an anonymous call at his home. Saying someone was breaking in to the office. It was 2am but he came anyway. I knew he's come. Didn't even call the cops. Thomas – I mean Mr Walker's hoodie was draped over the chair. I – I put it on to camouflage myself. He got there, surprised there was no break in. Instead, he found - me. I had it all there. Newspaper clippings. I'd done my research. My colleague Gerry Hobbes - you've questioned him, told me all I needed to know. He – he knew I was going to meet Mr O'Neal –

Marsh looked up sharply. 'Mr Hobbes knew you were going to go to the office to set up Mr O'Neal.'

'Y – yes. I confided in him a lot. He was always there for me.'

'Anyway, usual story. Dad told me he wasn't interested. He never wanted kids. How dare I come round sniffing for a job when I knew damn well who he was. How dare I hoodwink him. I followed my dad out of the shop that night. We had a heated conversation and I just lost it.'

'Where did you get the hammer?'

'It was – it was in Mr O'Neil's office. He once tried fixing a broken shelf. I remember it being in there. Something made me crack. I GRABBED it, AND IT WAS ONE REJECTION TOO MANY. I – I followed Dad out of the back of the shop, back towards the front. I began chasing him. I hit him. Hard.'

Ben sobbed now, punching the table hysterically as he said the words 'Yes, I fucking killed him. It was me! It was ME. I hit him in anger but I didn't expect him to…. it's not what what what…. I wanted.'

'You are saying it was manslaughter?'

Ben screamed. I JUST WANTED SOMEONE TO LOVE ME. I WANTED MY DAD TO LOVE ME.'

Marsh and O'Rourke sat in stunned silence.

'C – Can I make a call to….my mother please?'

'You may make one call.' Said 'O'Rourke and motioned for the officer to take Ben Grey, to the cells for the manslaughter of Mr Jack O'Neil….

TWO WEEKS LATER

'I suspect you are feeling the walls close in on you son? What I am struggling to understand is, you almost got away with it. You WANTED Mr Walker to get the blame. The problem for you Mr Grey is thanks to the Dictaphone, which we recovered on information from Miss Simmons, plus your love for Miss Simmons which meant you could not bear to see her go down, led you to the one decent thing you have done in this whole sorry state of affairs and turned yourself in.

Ben looked around the courtroom. There is probably not a single person in this place that thinks he's innocent now or will fight his corner. He did not deserve it anyway.

They say time heals all wounds but I never did move past Jack being my father. That wound is forever. Scarred within me. I am a murderer and I murdered my own father.

Ben recalled the whole argument in his mind as its being described, the sweat was pouring down his back. He felt like he was in a greenhouse, trapped in the thermal heat and he just wanted to smash the glass into a million shares. He did not care if those shards stabbed him at this point. This was hell.

They fucking know what it's about. I have explained it a thousand times

'I I I was telling my dad…. I was telling Jaa, er Mr O'Neal that he is my father'

'And for the court, please can you explain what Mr O'Neal had replied?'

'He did not believe me….'

'What were his words? Do you remember?'

Ben felt a sticky feeling on his thumb and realised he had ripped the skin off with his anxiety. Blood was trickling around the nail bed.

'He. asked about my mother and I explained who she was and when it would have happened. He. did not want to know…he…'

Ben swallowed back the tears and he could feel himself choking up. He looked up to the small windows right near the ceiling. A golden beam of light was sneaking in through the pane. He could forgo seeing the daylight. That feeling of the fresh, warm morning sun on his face. He could suffer nothing but bleak walls for company but to not see Shania again? He could not live without her.

Ben could not stop the tears now 'He denied knowing my mother and when I eventually got it out of him, he still did not believe I could be his....'

'Please go on.' the judge nodded.

'He called her a slut. He laughed and said anyone could be my father as she was the town .... the town bikes.' Ben looked down, wiping his nose on his sleeve.

'I told him he was an asshole and I could not believe he was not listening to me. He wound me up. He sniggered. I explained to him that I had got the job at Safe Travel to get closer to him. I wanted to know my dad....my.... I just wanted him to acknowledge me. To love me.' Ben sobbed again. This was all just too much.

'So, then you hit him, you punched him in the face' the prosecutor questioned.

'You can see on the tape I did so I don't know why you are asking that....'

'Answer the question please?'

'Yes, I punched him' Ben concluded.

'You now storm out of the shop but not before grabbing your Colleague's hooded jumper. There is still no weapon in your hand at this point. There leaves Mr O'Neal turning left out of the shop. Please explain what happens next for us?'

I put the hoodie on and I left the shop. I went to walk away. I really did. I had every intention of walking away....'

'But you didn't, did you son. You let Mr O'Neal get the better of you?'

'Yes… I did. Jack walked out of the shop and locked up. I held back near the bins which is where I found the old hammer. I …. I just lost it. I walked up behind him.'

'Yes?'

'I paused for a split second but it was like…like my body just took over. I was so angry. So so angry' Ben pleaded. 'I said 'for me….and for my mum…. DAD and I did it.'

'And you planted the hoodie and hammer in Walker's flat, framing him?'

'Yes.'

Ben was shaking now. He looked across to his mother Agnes who was sitting within the crowd. He could spot her a mile off. Tears streaming down her cheeks whilst hidden behind big, black glasses. Shania directly behind her with a solemn look on her face and next to her, was Thomas.

'What did you do afterwards? Please talk us through your movements?'

'I I I was shocked at myself and what I had done. I could not think. I panicked. The blood was pouring out of his head. I then noticed that the hoodie I was wearing was splattered too. I panicked and …I just ran.'

Everyone in the courtroom listened to Ben's every word. He felt paralysed stood there.

Mr Grey. I refuse your plea to bail, owing to the fact that there is no confidence that you will show up on the day your trial starts. You will remain in custody with no option for bail. Take him down.

Ben howled as he was pulled down the dock almost as to the depths of hell.

'MUUUM!!!!' He screamed.

'BEEEEEN !!!!!!' shrieked Agnes, howling in grief.

SIXTY-TWO

Denise sat trembling by the phone. Her diary clasped to her chest. She had poured her whole heart out in this journal. She couldn't keep her secret in any longer. She had to come clean. To her best friend. Even if she lost everything.

Her hands shaking violently Denise dialled Caroline's number.'

'Hello Denise?' Caroline's cool tone came through.

'Caz, yes, c – can you meet me today? In – in the mall? I have – something to talk to you about.'

***

Caroline was late as usual, but Denise did not mind. Lord knows she had had enough to deal with these last few months.

Had decided she was going to confide in her friend her low mood, of feeling hopeless, of waking up sweat drenched in the night. Her appetite was shot to hell; she'd tried to eat a tuna sandwich at lunch and had to run to the bathroom. Of course, there was no way she could tell her friend the whole truth....

She scanned the mall's open plan square and Caroline came into view, solemn faced and tense looking. She spotted Denise and hurried towards her. Dez, you sounded terrible on the phone! What's going on?' Caroline looked at her, eyes full of concern. 'Wait one minute...' She took advantage of there not being a queue and ordered a flat white, bringing it to the table with a wad of napkins. She handed the napkins to Denise who accepted and dabbed at her eyes.

'We have been friends for a long time'. Caroline said slowly. 'You know you can tell me anything.'

'I am feeling so low Caz, I....can't eat.... I'm struggling to sleep...I feel so...'

'Hey back up Denizen.' Caroline rummaged in her handbag for a tissue.' When did this all? come on?'

'A- a couple of months ago.' Denise took up the tissues and dabbed her eyes.

'I'm tired in several senses I suppose. I am around death all day...every day.'

Caroline frowned. 'But you have been in this job for a number of years now. What's changed?'

'Maybe I've just h-had enough. Being around death all day. It-it desensitises you...numbs you.'

'Have you spoken to a higher-up? I know the ways of the corporate world. They have to offer you support.'

'No-no, you know me. I'm stoic. I don't like a fuss.'

'Well sometimes a fuss is necessary. You can't be the strong one all the time.' Caroline took a sip of her coffee but kept her eyes fixed on Denise.

'I can't talk to Gerry right now, I feel a million miles away from him, even if we are led next to each other in bed you know? Oh God Caz, I bet you would give anything to be next to Jack. I am such a selfish cow. Please ignore me, I am not thinking straight'.

Caroline made a funny expression that Denise couldn't fathom. She turned away for a second and made a kind of grimace. It only lasted a split second and then she was back facing Denise.

'Yes, of course things have been...difficult for me. But I don't have the Monopoly on sadness Denise. Life must go on.'

Denise nodded, reassured that Caroline had relaxed back into her calm expression.

'You know sometimes, if I could, I would escape to a new life somewhere, a fresh start. But I always think I have unfinished business right where I am.'

Denise sniffed. 'You are so much more practical than I am, Caz. Always level-headed. Rational.'

She reached over and tugged at the lapels of her friend's coat and saw Caroline's eyes widen in alarm. But she held on as if for dear life. 'Caroline. II have been keeping such a lot in. It's weighing on my mind....'

'Good God, Denise.' Caroline looked around in alarm to check no one was watching. 'What is this madness?? What is on your mind?'

'I think I'm going m-mad. I must talk to someone...anyone.'

We are getting you home.' Denise felt Caroline's arms under her shoulders, hoisting her up. She put an arm around her friend's shoulders and allowed herself to be led across the plaza to the parking lot...

***

Once home, she led down on the couch, tears trickling down her cheeks as Caroline made drinks in the kitchen. She came in with two mugs of tea. Denise left her diary propped up on the table. Her heart hammered just to look at it.

'You say you need to talk to someone' Caroline repeated, sitting on the couch next to her. 'So, is it Gerry...have you had an affair?'

'No. No, no affair.' Denise whispered.

'OK...so it's work?'

Denise was silent. 'In – in a way...yes.' She groped for her mug and took a sip. The tea tasted ghastly.

'Have you ever loved someone so much...you would do anything to protect them?'

Caroline didn't answer but continued to stare. Again, her expression was unfathomable.

'I have had to cover up...for a colleague.'

Caroline frowned. 'Malpractice you mean?'

'Yes' Denise swallowed. The lump in her throat was expanding and her heart was surely going to burst out of her chest.

'You'll hate me.' She murmured. 'I'm an awful person.'

'Denise, you are scaring me now. Look, whatever it is, surely coming clean is the best thing? I mean...is this something that could cost you your job?'

'Oh yes.'

And worse. Oh My God. lied on Jack's autopsy. It wasn't a hammer blow that killed him. It was...'

Her head was now spinning like a whirlpool. The last thing she remembered before she passed out was Caroline reaching out for something across the table

SIXTY-THREE

Gerry threw his keys on the side and switched the oven on ready to make dinner. The house was quiet apart from the grandfather clock ticking away. An heirloom from Gerry's father. 'Denise?' he shouted up the stairs. 'Denny?'

Gerry climbed the steps pressing his hands on the aertex walls and he muttered to himself 'Wallpaper would be more up to date; this will be a pain to get off eh Den? Are you awake?'

The stairs creaked from beneath him and he froze on the step midway, he swore he felt a hand on his shoulder. A puff of breath on the back of his neck. 'Jack? You are spooking me out now' Gerry sniggered to himself as his body demanded him to move quicker.

He pushed the door of the bedroom gently and scanned the room where he could see the bedside light on and she led on the grand two-poster bed. She must be asleep. Her work uniform led on the stool of the dressing table untouched from this morning. Didn't her shift start at nine? Gerry looked across to the exquisitely upholstered bow-backed chair, the washing still piled up from earlier.

He was about to turn around quietly and leave her to rest for a bit longer when his heart jumped. Her iPhone lay on the floor beneath the chair? An odd location? Had it fallen off the seat? That's when he saw it. He looked closer at her. There were bottles of pill packets scattered around her. He ran over to the bed and felt her wrist, her body was not yet cold.

'Denise!!!! Denise!!!!!' he yelled but she was not answering. 'Oh my god!!!! Denise wake up! Please'. Her hair tumbled over her face and as Gerry swept it back, he gasped at the paleness of her face. The coldness of her skin. Her eyes used to glisten and sparkle but it's like the light had gone out. All this time, she had spent working on corpses and now…. Gerry grabbed his phone from his pocket and dialled 999.

***

He sat quietly on the edge of the bed, staring at the silver framed photograph on the dressing table. Denise was smiling at him, in a long white wedding gown and a delicate veil over her face. Standing next to her, on the front porch of the church, her father in a navy-blue suit, matching waistcoat and dusky pink tie, smiling so proudly. Her wedding flowers were made out of foam, as she disagreed with 'destroying beautiful plants' for one day. They now sat proudly on display on the dresser. Across from the picture, was her pile of classic books 'Charlotte Bronte, Hans Christian Anderson, Jane Austen… and on top, her paddle hairbrush. He rubbed the bristles with his fingers.

Denny always took such care of her hair. He used to watch her brush it before applying her face cream and getting into bed. What will he do without these routines? She always had such beautiful hair; it was one of the first things he noticed about her when they first met. Their first date at the local funfair, both of them clutching candyfloss, her hair whipped back on the waltzes, mouth wide in laughter.

When he had first started building a business with Jack, she was always there to welcome him home or would wake him up in the morning with hot chocolate and they would read the papers together and do the crossword. She loved her words and was always writing, dreaming, and planning. Now that mouth had been stuffed with pills, pills that dissolved into her blood, putting a stop to her thudding heart, the hair would fall out and she would be like one of the corpses she used to examine on a cold, hard slab. What had he done? This was all his fault; he had done this. His face screwed up in a miserable howl...Denise…. he wailed….

I'm sorry. I couldn't help it. Falling in love with someone else. Falling in love with….'

'Mr Kennedy, I am so sorry for your loss. Is there anyone we can call for you?' the voice sounded so far away as Gerry looked around. The police had arrived and were taking photos of the bedroom but he could not bring himself to move.

Mr Kennedy, did you know your wife was taking medication? ...Mr Kennedy?' The gentle female officer had knelt down in front of him.

Gerry was staring out the window now 'How did I not notice? How did I not see this coming?' he croaked.

The trees swayed against the black, murky sky. 'I should be putting dinner on…. I….'

'Mr Kennedy, let's call a family member for you or a friend you trust?

Gerry lifted his head to the ceiling and raked a hand through his hair.

'I want to call Caroline…. Caroline O'Neal'.

SIXTY-FOUR

Marsh and O'Rourke sat together in the local after work, both with a celebratory pint.

'I can't help but feel sorry for that Ben kid' O'Rourke shook his head whilst staring at the cheese and onion Walkers crisps in the middle of the table. Marsh had not opened them yet and O'Rourke could not help but stare, his mouth watering.

'The guy was not right in the head.' Marsh looked back at him in disgust. 'He's a murderer'.

'He wanted to know his dad. He wanted to be loved and respected. He got a job there to get to know him. I can understand that' O'Rourke said, taking a sip of his beer.

'Then why not tell O'Neal sooner. Get him 'happy drunk' as the kids say these days and come clean?'

'But he did come clean. That night in the shop, Grey told O'Neal and he laughed in his face.'

'It's not an excuse to take someone's life....'

'I know. God, I know.... sorry. You know me. I try to see both sides. I just struggle to believe....'

'The case is closed O'Rourke. We did it mate! Now drink up and let's get another, eh?'

They both stared at the menu intently and were spoilt for choice 'there is really nothing better than pub grub is there? Burger, chunky chips and a beer' Marsh grinned.

'Actually, I am looking at the super cheesy lasagne with EXTRA cheese. It's deserved right?' O'Rourke did not wait for the response. He put the order in with the waiter along with his 'diet' coke and waited for the waiter to walk away before he pressed further. Something was making him scratch his head... not in the literal sense but he needed to discuss it. He needed to tick all the boxes in his mind.

'Did anyone see the body before the funeral? Did anyone...request?'

'Absolutely fucking not. The guy was not in .... After the bash to the head, there was nothing to see. Of course, the morgue arranged for photographs to be shown to Mrs O'Neal.'

'Yeah, my wife was asking about it and I had to explain to her that these things are not like what we see on Netflix shows or films. They place the photos face down and then the person identifying takes his or her time to turn them over and usually if a gruesome photograph can be avoided, like in this case then it will.' O'Rourke said, tipping the now empty bag of crisps in his mouth, trying to lap up every crumb.

'She had to identify...what she could and was given grief counselling. I think they showed her his back as that had a distinctive tattoo on the shoulder blade. That was enough for her. She knew it was him. You remember reading the autopsy report?'

'I do.'

'I don't know. O'Rourke said. I still get a nigglonmg feeling. That we have missed something.'

'That's common O 'Rourke. Relax, we got a full confession. Grey will go on trial and likely will get 10 years. Let's order food. I'm starving.'

As Marsh put a request in, O'Rourke got a chill at the back of his neck 'wait that sounds like.... fucking hell. The wife just walked in' O'Rourke cursed and put his head down clearly not wanting to be seen. He peeked around again and noticed

Marsh's wife behind her. 'For fuck's sake man, you traitor! You invited the diet police?' O'Rourke hissed under his breath/

'I promise I had no idea they were coming here... I thought they were at their Weight Watchers meeting?' Marsh insisted laughing and then shouting 'Hi ladies' nice and loud much to O'Rourke's anger.

As the two ladies walked over, O'Rourke was urgently looking for a tic tac in his pocket to hide the cheese smell then it dawned on him that a super cheesy lasagne was heading his way any time now. Fuck.

'What have you been eating darling; I can smell it from here?' Pandora questioned. Pandora - O'Rourke's wife. Currently having a semi midlife crisis over her weight and aging skin. She meant well, but was overbearing at the best of times. 'I had a crisp from Marsh's bag darling...better call the police...oh wait ha ha'

'Here are your meals gentleman, quarter pounder burger with chips and the chef's special three cheese lasagne with EXTRA cheese. Can I get you any salt or sauces?'

O'Rourke was motioning to the waiter to shut up with his hand but it was too late.

'Ah I am very sorry but this cannot be my husband's dinner, he is on a very low carb, practically plant-based diet I am afraid' Pandora spoke loud enough for the whole pub to hear.

'I am heading back to the office, see you at home' O'Rourke got up from his chair and walked. Marsh quickly paid the waiter who had given the meals to the ladies, kissed his wife breezily and went after his colleague.

'Domino's delivery then?' he grinned as they walked to the car.

Back in the breakout room, they tucked into a supreme cheese pizza.

'Feel like a game of chess.' Marsh asked.

'Why not?'

They played silently each deep in thought.

Paws moved. Bishops moved. Knights moved. O'Rourke was starting to see Marsh's point of view as looking at life on a chessboard. He went to move his queen...

His queen

The flash of inspiration hit him so hard. he lost breath!'

'Holy Shit! You look white as a sheet!!!' yelled Marsh.

'Marsh! Quick! I need to see the autopsy report, RIGHT AWAY!!!'

'What now?! What's going on?'

'Marsh. I think there is about to be a serious miscarriage of justice!

O'Rourke rushed to the computer. 'Death by hammer blow to the head. This report didn't look right...not detailed enough. In their rush they hadn't picked it up.'

'I have some contacts at the hospital. I think this is a rogue document!'

Marsh's eyes widened.' I need to know exactly what you are insinuating!'

His eyes only widened further as O'Rourke described his suspicions.

'If you are right O'Rourke, this turns the case right on its head.'

'Please let me follow up on this, Marsh. Trust me! I will treat you to an all you can eat Chinese if you let me take the lead on this!'

OK' said Marsh. 'I trust you.'

'Grey did not mention anything about strangling. He admits to hitting him, watching in shock for a few moments and whipping the hoodie off before doing a runner. How can this be right? O'Rourke said, not realising he was raising his voice.

O'Rourke scanned the page, his eyes wild. 'Reading this, there was irreversible damage within just one minute to O'Neal's brain.

Petechial haemorrhages, conjunctival surfaces of eyes and skin of face etcetera, etcetera. JESUS CHRIST!'

'But but ...the pictures. What happened to the fact that his skull was so caved in, they had to identify by the tattoo?' O'Rourke said, beginning to sweat.

'Someone was covering up.... hang on, there is more pictures in the attachment'

'Look at this picture. Yes, the blow to the head can be seen here but look at his neck. The large handprint marks....'

O'Rourke took the picture and had to sit down 'and the size of those hands.... That is not a woman's hands that's for sure and look at that imprint? Is that a wedding ring? A Celtic ring. FUCK'

'How did we miss this? There is only one suspect left who fits this? Thomas, Shania, Emily, Ben... none of them are married. Oh, Christ do you remember your inappropriate comment about a night of passion with the scratches on his wrists/arms - fixing his wife's car my arse. More like the markings over a man desperately trying to fight for his life. How are we so blind?

'I don't think Mrs. Hobbes killed herself after all. Marsh concluded.

'Neither do I' agreed O'Rourke.

'This is a cover up gone massively wrong....

***

A few calls to the hospital and the expert technician sent over the records again for O'Neill.

So, is Mr Walker a free man now?' asked Marsh.

'Well, he is for now. But...I'm sorry to say a complicated spanner in the works has just landed on our doorstep.'

'That doesn't sound good. Hit me.'

'Well, it appears we have a confession...but not a murder weapon.'

'What!! So, the hammer wasn't used??'

'Oh, the hammer was used alright. But get this, our forensic team have been re-examining the photos of the body. Something didn't add up. They called upon the hospital to provide the autopsy report.'

'Can you remember what it said?'

'The official cause of death was trauma to the head caused by Mr Grey with the hammer blow. But – BUT. Get this. It wasn't the full story. There were further injuries. Injuries to Mr O'Neal's neck...'

'So, Mr Grey, hit him with a hammer and then proceeded to choke O'Neal. Well that ups his charge from manslaughter to murder.'

'No, Mr Grey definitely fled the scene after hitting O'Neal with the hammer. The neck injury came later. After the hammer attack. The neck trauma was done separately.'

'Oh, my lord...have we fucked up??!!'

'I don't know. But SOMETHING DOESN'T ADD UP. A missing move on the chessboard. A missing piece of the puzzle.'

'Who signed the autopsy report...who ruddy signed it. We need to speak with them PRONTO'.

'That's the other snag. The person who performed the autopsy is dead themselves. Last week.'

'The name....... give me the name!!!'

O'Rourke pursed his lips. 'Mrs Hobbes.'

***

SIXTY-FIVE

'I thought we'd come face to face. Thomas said.

'I hear they are letting you out.' Ben mumbled. 'Following my confession.'

'They are.'

'Look Beni just need to ask. Why? Why did you do it firstly?' And secondly, I know we have never seen eye to eye...but why did you want to frame me for murder?'

I panicked. It – It was never meant to be this way.'

'Would you have been prepared to see me go down.'

Ben nodded.

'Wow'

They both looked at the prison wall.

'You and I have more in common than we think said Thomas. Shit relationships with our parents. We should have gone out drinking more.'

He thought he saw a really small smile play on Bends face.'

'Please forgive me.' He whispered.

'Ben, I forgive you, OK? Lord knows I didn't help matters by not going to the; police sooner Wirth EarthCam. I'm still gonna pay the price for that for withholding information. Shania held back info. I'll bet Gerry has his skeletons. I think we all contributed a bit towards this case.'

'Shania is the 1st person to ever really care about me.'

'Thomas said. 'I know and I think you care for her too.'

'I do. Part of the reason I couldn't let her take the fall. Do you think she will wait for me?'

I don't know Ben. I can't say. You have got to serve your time and go from there.'

'Do me a favour Thomas.'

'What's that?'

'Travel. Live your life. Don't fuck it up any more than you already have.'

'Thanks. I will.'

Silence again.

'You know, something is still irking me, Ben.' So, I was just you who masterminded this whole thing?'

'Yes' Ben looked down.

'I'm not sure I believe you.'

'Believe what you want.'

Thomas turned to face him. When I get out, I am going to help you, Ben. I don't know how or why but I will find a way, understand?'

Tears pooled in Ben's eyes. 'You can do fuck all...buy. I appreciate the sentiment.'

They stood for another hour, in silence, just staring into the sunset until they were called in by the prison guards.

SIXTY-SIX

I cannot believe what I had to do today. My Gerry was a wreck. The police had paid him a visit at the house and were suspecting all the STH colleagues. They definitely suspect Gerry because somehow, they got the information about Jack trying his luck with me.

They also found out about Jack rinsing Gerry for the business putting him in the firing line with a motive for the murder. When he came home that night, he assumed I was asleep but I saw him hurry into the bathroom and whip off his shirt. He tried to put it to the bottom of the washing pile but as soon as he went downstairs for his 'nightcap' I went to the bathroom and saw the blood-soaked stains. He kept it to himself for days but then after I carried out the autopsy report, he was demanding to know the ins and outs. The report was clear that strangulation is what killed Jack, not the blow to the head. Not only that, but a Celtic ring was pictured imprinted around the neck. He did not even have to admit it then, I saw the look on his face. My husband was guilty of murder. Then the information just came spilling out

I could not let him go down. I couldn't. Not my Gerry. I did what I had to do and I changed the report. I did not really feel bad at the time as Ben had hit Jack which could have easily killed him. I know Gerry said he had been grooming Ben for a long time. Winding him up. Putting little pieces of information into his head to keep that bomb ticking. He knew it was only a matter of time before that bomb went off. He kept saying Jack needed to be taught a lesson and Ben was the one to do it. He clearly did not believe that himself because he followed Ben there that night. He said he couldn't trust him to carry out the work. 'You can take the horse to water but you can't make it drink' were his words. He knew Ben was too weak. He sat and hid...behind the bins behind the shop. Jack had finished locking up and was accosted by Ben. Ben confronted him about Jack being his father. He was shouting and screaming at him. He struck him. The strike was meant to have killed him. But Ben couldn't see it through. Gerry was listening, fuming as the lad panicked and ran off. Gerry confirmed in his head what he had suspected; Ben didn't have the bottle. He went to the front where Jack was lying injured. Jack knew he was there. He knew what Gerry was about to do. His comeuppance had finally come. He held his hands out to stop him but Gerry clamped his fingers around Jack's throat and held... and held them there. So hard that an imprint of his ring scarred the throat. He didn't bother to move the body, with the blow to the head from Ben and the strangulation, people would assume he had been attacked by a mugger and died trying to defend himself. Moving the body would have made the situation more suspicious. Now, poor innocent Thomas has been arrested and he does not deserve it. What have I done?

SIXTY-SEVEN

Thomas' shoulders felt lighter than they had in a long time. The sun was shining, warming his skin as he walked towards Safe Travel Holidays. They had changed the decor outside, a royal blue which was actually very tasteful with a sunset style gradient of colour on the side of the building.

Very inviting Thomas thought to himself.

After Ben's shocking manslaughter confession, Thomas had been released. The papers were now chock full of the latest gossip...O'Neal's secret love child.

Thomas had started his new medication a week earlier and he felt level headed and in control. He was not sure if that was partly a placebo effect but regardless, he was in a better place mentally thanks to the psychiatrist and support from his mum and Emily.

'You must be Mr Walker!' a charming, slightly older lady stepped out of STH. 'I am Cindy Baker, the new manager of Safe Travel Holidays. You are quite the legend of these parts I hear' her smile was kind and genuine as she opened the door to Thomas. She was in a navy suit; it was smart with pinstripes. Ashy blonde hair cut into a wavy bob.

He could not believe his eyes as he walked in the door. The office was completely different, the desks were placed opposite each other rather than dotted around the room. The young team were smiling and busy on phone calls. Thomas' heart ached for a second, remembering the better times with his team. He tried to work out which was his desk but Cindy had already made her way out the back for the last of his things. 'I am so sorry I couldn't keep you on with us Thomas, as you can see, the team is a pretty full house' she smiled with a pang of guilt on her face.

'To be honest Cindy, you have done me a massive favour, I needed that push to actually go out and 'follow my dreams' Thomas rolled his eyes at his cheesy comment but he meant it.

'Where are you off to?' she smiled.

'Well, my girlfriend and I are going to do a bit of traveling for a month or so as she has taken a career break and then I plan to come back and try some work in an Art History Museum'

'Well, that sounds fantastic' said Cindy kindly.

Thomas smiled and meant it. It's been a while. It's a good feeling. 'Then it will be a case of finding us a house. It's time to move on with things. I have dragged my feet for a long time now and I need to close the door on what no longer leads anywhere you know?'

'Hey Cindy, we have a couple in this afternoon, looking for a break to the Great Barrier Reef in Oz for a month? What do you think I should suggest?'

Cindy smiled at Thomas 'Got anything for us? For old times' sake?' she nudged.

Thomas took a deep breath and grinned 'Heart Reef is the place to go for romance. You can take a flight out to marvel at the pure turquoise waters but you can see the composition of coral which has naturally shaped itself into a heart. It's somewhere I would love to see with Emily one day'

``It's a shame you are leaving really, I know you would have been an asset to the team?' beamed Cindy.

'It really means a lot to me Cindy but I think keeping my baggage of the past, will stop Emily and I moving forward. I may be making a mistake but it's time I risk it. We have waited long enough.' Thomas smiled.

'I get it. Well, you have a fab time. I'm sure you are looking forward to a new beginning. Live while you are young, that's what I say.'

'Too true. 'Thomas knew all about that.

'I'm thinking about changing the name' she said wistfully. 'New Beginnings Travel Agents.'

'That's a great name.' Thomas said warmly.

'Yes, draw a line under that terrible incident. I've got such exciting plans for this place. It has always been my dream to own a travel agent. I'm glad I get to keep Shania. She's a right smart cookie. I'm making her head supervisor.'

'She deserves it.' Thomas smiled and he meant it.

Before he left, he made a beeline for Shania's desk and hugged her. 'Thanks Shania. I'll miss you.'

'Miss you too, Tom Tom. Keep in touch on the gram?'

'Absolutely' he smiled. 'I'm sorry about Ben.'

'Me too.' She said sadly.

He hugged her again and then for the final time, walked out of Safe Travel Holidays.

But he didn't walk far. And before long, Shania came out to join him.

'You got the message from O'Rourke, right?'

'Yes, I did. She said gravely.'

'He didn't say too much'

'Nor to me.'

'Our charges will be reduced if we cooperate with him.'

'So, what does he want us to do?'

'You need to come with me. Have you cleared your lunch with Cindy?'

'Of course. So where are we going?'

Thomas smiled 'Have you ever used EarthCam before?'

'What that weird evince you were always on?'

He laughed. 'Yeah, the device that always scored me top marks for sales.'

'Bighead!'

Thomas explained how it all worked.

'This all sounds very interesting...but how does this help Marsh and O'Rourke?

They are forbidden to divulge anything. But from what I can gather on the grapevine...they seem to think there was another murderer. Ben hit Jack but did not deal the fatal blow...'

'Who do they think did it?' gasped Shania.

'Do the math.' Thomas whispered. 'You are in the clear. I'm in the clear.' Ben, they suspect was in on it but was...let's say a pawn...'

'You are not saying they suspect Gerry? Oh no!'

'Look I don't know. But we need to get to the station asap.'

***

Marsh and O'Rourke under a recording were finally able to divulge the top-secret information to Thomas and Shania who sat with their mouths agape.

'So, as you can see, we need your help.' Said Marsh. 'Mr Walker, are you able to set us up with an EarthCam account? Now we are going to be very interested in a particular plane that will be leaving Heathrow and landing in Lisbon. And we need to capture some information.'

'And as you are so good with cameras' said O'Rourke. I have to make a few calls over Skype to some contacts in Portugal. I speak a little Portuguese but I need someone to navigate Google translate and translate some documents that will be set over.

'Got it,' said Thomas.

Miss Simmons, can you help with setting up some secret bugging equipment around these addresses?

'E.E.A. sure.'

'Well, our traps are laid.' Said Marsh. 'All we can hope for now is a check mate....'

SIXTY-EIGHT

They wouldn't get the big news until next week.

Thomas sat down with his caramel latte and lemon cake. Following her prison visit, his mother and he had continued delicate contact. Thomas had initiated another face to face meet at a coffee shop in Gunwharf Quays.

She felt a genuine warmth when she came through the door. She looked younger. Happier. Hopeful.

'I hoped that my one visit to you in the prison wasn't a fluke.' She smiled.

He smiled back/ 'Not at all. It's good to see you.'

Dolores smiled weakly. 'I got myself a little job, a local café. Thomas, I am getting help. Finally. I'm sorting myself out and well….'

'Is this a fresh start?' asked Thomas smiling.

'Yes, it is. We have wasted so much time. I have wasted so much time. No longer.'

After some small talk, Thomas said 'so I was wondering if you would consider coming with me to one of my counselling sessions'

Dolores hesitated and sat back in her seat.

'I have been enjoying talking things out with someone, you know, everything that has happened. Ben, the trial, moving on from Safe Travel, Jack…. It's all been so much to deal with.

Dolores did not say anything then but she held out her hand and took Thomas' within hers. A nod between them. Subtle. But enough.

'So, tell me more about your planned trip?' she smiled.

'You tell me more about this job first mum'

They smiled together.

SIXTY-NINE

'Thomas it's great to see you again, how are you since our last session?'

Thomas smiled as he walked into the calming, pastel blue therapists' room. A picture hung on the wall in front of him 'function with dysfunction'

The room itself was soothing with nature sounds playing gently in the background. It was plain and relaxing, simple yet inviting.

He sat down on the sofa as Mia handed him a glass of water. The boxes of tissues sat next to him as usual; on the little round table. Thomas felt he would not be needing them tonight.

'How have the breathing techniques been working for you? Are you sleeping better?

'In for four, out for seven' Thomas smiled.

'How is Dolores? Did she find the session together helpful?'

'She did'

And how do you feel about her opening up, about the past? Her taking responsibility for her mental health?'

Thomas took a deep breath 'it feels like there is still a lot to be discussed but it's got off to a great start'

'That's brilliant news' smiled Mia, making notes on her pad.

'Tell me, how are you feeling about the travel plans with Emily?' she asked.

'I think it's what we both need and we are looking forward to it'

'And is Emily still seeing her therapist too?' Mia added.

'She is. She has also signed up to some anxiety management courses and she joined a group for victims of abuse. She's met some new friends there too.'

This is all very positive news. Now, I have to ask... has Oliver made an appearance since....'

'No, he has not.'

'I am guessing the medication is working well for you then?' Mia smiled.

'Yes, I should have started it sooner'

***

Thomas left feeling happy. His mood lifted even further when he saw Emily waiting for him with a big bunch of flowers.'

'I'm proud of you she whispered.'

'I'm proud of you too.'

'Looking forward to starting your new job?'

'I am but I'm looking forward to travelling first.'

'Me No, you go.'

'I just need final confirmation from Marsh and O'Rourke that A SUCCESSFUL ARREST HAS BEEN MADE. I 'LL BE ABLE TO TERLL YOU MORE TOMORORW.'

'I can live with that she smiled.'

'Has Oliver visited you?'

'No.'

'Shall we go and visit his grave sometime.'

'I'm not quite ready just yet, but yes, I'd like to.'

'Well, I'm always here for you Tom. Always.'

'I know.'

They linked arms and walked slowly back home along the seafront.

SEVENTY

The airplane sat on the brightly lit tarmac waiting to depart. The airplane felt like home. Like when you take a wonderful nap mid-afternoon on a Sunday after a roast dinner. It was easy to relax. The engines roared and everyone sat back in their seats with ease. Looking out the window, a storm was coming. The sort that would bring the soul cleansing rain and it was much needed. The heaviness was coming to a peak and it would soon be time to rest and reset after the canopy of clouds parted.

Caroline tightened her seatbelt of seat D27 and shut her eyes, what a stressful time it has been. She was not at the finish line yet but the hard work has got her here. They say a phoenix rises from the ashes and Caroline believed this was where she was supposed to be.

As the plane began its smooth ride, the air stewardess brought over a bottle of their finest champagne, courtesy of seat D26.

'I cannot believe what a useful pawn Ben was on the chessboard, should have known that he would fuck things up though, poor kid.' whispered Gerry.

'That's his problem now....' Caroline sighed 'if he got everything right in the first place, he would not be in the situation he is in now'

'Just cannot believe we got away with it all.

'It was useful in the end though?' Caroline smirked

'I mean, thank goodness I followed him and strangled him to finish him off. It did not take long to smother him. My ring took some damage.' He smirked.

'You can buy us both new rings once we are in Portugal.' She smirked.

'Indeed.'

'Did it feel good? I never asked' Caroline, a slight smile nudging the corners of her mouth.

Gerry did not answer, his eyes were fixed on her and he just gazed for a while before answering 'it's the strangest thing but it was a relief'.

'A man that does not falter in a crisis, I like it' she winked.

'Do you miss Denise?' she added.

'I do… so much. The secret must have been too much for her to bear. I should never have got her to hide any paperwork or put her under such pressure…' Gerry's eyes glazed over then and put his head down and Caroline almost felt guilty. She had made Denise' death look like a suicide by overdose and no one had questioned otherwise. She threw the packs and pots of pills everywhere after Denise had well and truly passed out. Her cocktail of pills would certainly have done the trick. She could not risk Denise's guilt ….

'For her to take her own life, I'll never forgive myself for that…. I know Denise would never have wanted me to go to prison so the least I can do is stay out of it right?'

Silence fell between them for a bit when Gerry finally got up to use the toilet. He smiled and gave a tiny nod as he walked past a trolley cart full of chocolate and goodies.

'I will have a croissant and a pot of jam please' Caroline smiled. 'The diet is on a break for a while…. holiday mode'

Caroline held the tablets in her hand tightly, she read the box. 'Adults take two tablets…. Maybe 4 …or 5 then' she whispered to herself. With one eye on the toilet, Caroline grabbed the knife from the croissant and began crushing the tablets. If anyone was to notice, they would just think 'oh she is a nervous flyer' or 'maybe she has a headache'.

Gerry takes a while to come back because there is a queue for the toilet, giving Caroline plenty of time to crush the box of pills.

Talking about Ben being a pawn on the chessboard she smirked in her head. A pawn is the chess piece that falls first, then the bishop and Knight are still about to protect the King. But the queen is the most powerful piece on the board...

She opens her purse to reveal a stiff new passport, the likeness of the fake photo is uncanny. Her new name. Amelia Earnshaw (after Amelia Earhart who disappeared whilst flying over the ocean never to be seen again. Earnshaw well just because Wuthering Heights is one of her favourites and she has been in some sick relationships.

She had thought Jack was her soulmate but he had screwed her over one too many times. She turned a blind eye to all his affairs for so long until one day she snapped. The plan had taken years. Saving up money in a secret account, regular visits to her sister in Portugal had given her the opportunity to research properties in remote villages outside of Lisbon, she had signed up for Portuguese classes online and was now at B2 Level so she could work out there. She had thought Gerry was the answer and when he had told of his and Jack's history, the two of them had come up with the perfect plan. Made even better once that idiot kid Ben had confided in Gerry, saying he had bashed the bastard's head if. It was all so convenient. But Gerry had started to grate on her, he and Jack were as bad as each other. And he's at least 10 years older. Amelia doesn't want to be wiping asses and going on mystery coach trips with an old man...this is the chance of a new life and one that must be taken alone. Besides, it's all karma, right? Ben will be out and the true murderer of Jack meets his rightful sticky end....

She was so pleased she had outwitted those chumps Marsh and O'Rourke too.

Gerry returned to the seat and took up his glass.

'Alegria a beer' she smiled.

He smiled curiously as he sipped his drink. 'What's that mean?'

'Portuguese for 'Cheers!'

Ah he smiled and took another large gulp.

Caroline turned away and a smile curved her lips as she raised the glass to herself. 'Cheers!!'

EPILOGUE – THE AIRPORT
Humberto Delgado Airport, Lisbon, Portugal

The Portuguese sun was scorching and the aircon at the airport was a welcoming relief. Marsh and O'Rourke sat at table, accompanied by two Portuguese police.

So, are you sitting quietly' said Marsh? 'Then I will begin to relay you with this sorry tale.'

So, O'Neill and Hobbes went into business together. As a 23-year-old fresh graduate, O'Neill seemed to have it all, good looks, women, one woman in particular, Caroline. His head is turned by a young woman by the name of Agnes Grey. She's gets pregnant by him. She comes to him begging him to acknowledge his child but he turns her away emotionally and financially. Agnes Grey raises her son Benjamin in poverty.

Benjamin grows up and becomes curious about his dad. In a fit of frustration, Agnes confesses one day that his biological father is Jack O'Neill. Ben concocts a plan, to move to Portsmouth, hunt down Jack, get to know him and then confess his parentage, hoping Jack will have grown to love and admire him.

Meanwhile Jack has double crossed his business partner Gerry Hobbes by screwing a load of money of Gerry stays on grudgingly. But he didn't stay out of a friendship. He has been seething for many years, plotting revenge. One of the ways he took revenge was seducing Caroline, Jack's wife. He saw this as part 1 of the ultimate revenge. The second part was to take back what he was owed from the business and escape with Caroline to Portugal.

To add more fire to the mix, Jack had hired Simmons after flirting with each other online and who was convinced would leave his wife for her.

Grey trolled O'Neill by catfishing him to gather information on him. Once Jack clearly showed no interest in children and when he fired Grey from Safe Travel, this was the last straw. Grey made it his plan to confess to O'Neill once and for all.

An opportunity for all parties happened when Jack decided to take his wife away for the weekend.

Mrs O'Neill and Mr Hobbes plotted. They had decided that Ben would be the pawn and carry out the murder. Ben had already confided in Gerry that O'Neill was his father.

Little did they know that Simmons was plotting something also. She too had had enough of O'Neill's games. She thought she's taken advantage of the whole Me Too campaign and blackmail him into giving her a chunk of money. She messaged him on her own burner phone saying to meet her at the office once he and Mrs O'Neill were back from Devon. This would have been about 10pm. O'Neill gets to the office. Miss Simmons is already waiting in the office, having stolen the spare key from O'Neill's office. They talk. She says she wants to cut ties with the relationship but doesn't want to leave empty handed. She wants to be paid for all her time wasted on him. Unbe known to O'Neill, she left a Dictaphone running and has also wired a small camera to record from a little extra compartment in her office drawers. This is why this was never found in the initial search of the office. Simmons deserves more credit than we gave her. You know Dictaphones so blind and partially sighted people can use them to record information? They had some as part of their Equality and Diversity Campaign. Anyway...anyway...so Simmons, presses record and orchestrates a conversation with O'Neill making it sound like he was touching her against her will and saying she will go to the police and drag his name through the mud. With O'Neill's womanising ways, that will be a stain on the business and his character. Now O'Neill is knee deep in debt, he's got no way of paying Miss Simmons. He tries to keep her sweet but she won't have it. She whispers to him that if he doesn't cough up, she's going to a well-respected female journalist who always loves a good Me-Too story. She whispers it so it wouldn't be picked up by the Dictaphone. Sad old game it was. She storms out of the shop at about 11pm, intending to pick up the Dictaphone and camera the next day. O'Neill stays in the shop, clearly plotting what to do. The Dictaphone and camera keep running. We can hear him shouting and swearing. He's clearly trying to figure out a get out plan. And then...around midnight, in walks Mr Grey.

Mr Hobbes has wound Mr Grey up to an extent that Mr Grey could be capable of killing. As Kellie Hawke, Bane continues to catfish O'Neill. O'Neill replies that he is in his shop. This gives Grey an incentive to stop by the shop and finally confess. He lets Mr Hobbes know he is doing this. Unbe known to him, Hobbes follows him and waits by the bins at the back. We found his footprints.

At this point though, Grey has no intention of harming O'Neill. He is hoping for a warm welcome as O'Neill's son and a future in the dynasty of the business.

However, Hobbes is banking on a different outcome….

O'Neill is shocked to see Grey of course. He drops the clanger by saying he is his son. He confesses the whole story, how Agnes let slip who his father is, he sought out Mr O'Neill and made sure O'Neill gave him a job…he catfished O'Neill as Kellie Hawks to find information on him. Mr Grey breaks down in tears. He says he always wanted a relationship with his father. He and Jack can get to know each other, they can be something to each other. The past doesn't matter etc etc. And O'Neill goes ape shit. Absolutely apeshit. We hear him tipping over the shelves, bookcases. He screams how dare Ben make a fool of him like this? Why does everyone come around him wanting to screw him for everything he has? He's obviously still smarting from Miss Simmons. He tells Mr Grey that he is as good as useless, just like his dead-beat mother. He will amount to nothing… he is nothing to him. At this point, Ben flies into hysterics. He screams at Mr O'Neill that he ruined his life. He grew up in poverty. O'Neill screams at him to get out. They tussle.

Mr Grey finds a hammer that was left behind by mistake by one of the recent renovators of the office.

O'Neill runs out of the door first. We think he wanted to barricade Mr Grey in before calling the police but Grey burst out just as Mr O'Neill turns his head. He is hit hard on the temple and falls to his knees. Mr O'Neill is then punched by Mr Grey and holds up his hands to defend himself. Mr Grey then hits him again on the other side of the temple, knocking Mr O'Neill out. This is when Mr Grey bottles it. The enormity of what he has done sinks into him. In panic, he flees the scene, leaving Mr O'Neill for dead.

But this is not the end of the story. O'Neill is still alive for now. Hobbes has been watching and listening by standing on the large bin down the back of the alley. He is frustrated as Mr Grey is meant to be contacting him once he is done with the job but it's clear he's it's up. Hobbes now has to finish the job. He emerges from the alley and strangles Mr O'Neill, leaving an imprint of a ring on O'Neill's neck. He then re arranges the body to look like a mugging gone wrong, forgetting crucially to remove O'Neill's wallet. Amateur.

So now the plan has been pickled and Gerry now has tracings of him on O'Neill. He needs to make sure that the autopsy does not reflect the full extent of injuries. Lucky for him, his wife Mrs Hobbes works at the hospital. He breaks down and confesses all to her. Only he re frames it a bit. He frames it that Mr Grey wanted to kill O'Neill all along and he is taking the fall for the kid. He needs his loving wife's help so his ass doesn't fry. She is to tamper with the autopsy report to reflect cause of death as only the hammer blow and not the ring wound from the strangulation. , Mrs Hobbes is terrified of losing her husband so goes along with the plan. So, by the time we get the autopsy, it has been doctored, excuse the pun, by the hospital.

Unbeknown to Simmons, Hobbes and Grey, Walker has witnessed the attack on EarthCam. However, he only sees the first hammer attack and not the strangulation.

So, picture this, we have Mr Grey, too terrified to confess to the killing, unknown to him that it wasn't actually him that dealt the final blow. Miss Simmons who knows she didn't deal the final blow but is terrified she will be in the frame by orchestrating an altercation and thinking she will be implicated. Walker who is terrified to come forward because of Grey grabbing his hoodie and thinking he will be framed.

It all sounds like the perfect crime doesn't. Three little pawns on the board, doing the work of the knight, Gerry for his queen, Caroline.

However, the plot thickens further. You see, Mrs O'Neill had her own plan on the side. She never intended to share the goods with Mr Hobbes. Mr Hobbes was just a useful idiot to carry out her plan and Grey was an even more useful idiot. Mrs O'Neill had been planning for years to get rid of Mr O'Neill. She was planning to get a bit chunk of life insurance and get all the goods from the business and start a new life teaching English in Portugal. Sad old game she didn't factor on O'Neill having jack shit- he's knee deep in debt for living the high life. Kept it from her very well.

Anyway, back to 50 shades of Grey. So, he's now saddled with the murder weapon A. And Walker's hoodie. He just panicked when he grabbed the hoodie but he's a desperate man now and is thinking he can palm it off on to someone. Anyone. Walker and he have always had a fractured relationship. Mrs O'Neill decides to sell up the business and reverse Ben's sacking. She knows she needs to keep him close for now. Mr Hobbes and her of course know about the tampered autopsy although Mrs Hobbes doesn't know that Mrs O'Neill knows.

Mrs O'Neill calls the staff and explains that whilst she is selling up, their jobs will be safe. Walker suggests a gathering at his flat. Grey sees an opportunity. Arriving at the gathering, he puts back Walker's hoodie and stashes the hammer in the shoe closet. Done and dusted you would think. But then the girl he has fallen in love with, Simmons deals a devastating blow. She confesses to Grey that she was there at the office to set up O'Neill. This is a spanner in the works framing Walker. If the person he loves gets embroiled it will be all his fault.

Meanwhile Mrs Hobbes' depression and anxiety is getting worse and worse. She is terrified that she will be found out about the tampered autopsy and her ass is gonna fry. She also has become scared of her husband; she didn't know he would be capable of such a thing even though Mr Hobbes says O'Neill deserved it. Desperate, she pours her heart out in her journal.

She makes the mistake of confiding in Mrs O'Neill who finding out that Mrs Hobbes is coming close to cracking, cannot have the plan fuck up now. She laces Mrs Hobbes drink with pills and Mrs Hobbes' death is registered as suicide. Even Mr Hobbes thinks this is what actually happened. Still, this now clears the pathway for him and Mrs O'Neill once the life insurance and business money come through.

The plot thickens. Of course, in another routine search, we find the hammer and hoodie in Walker's apartment and he is now suspect numeri uno. BUT – Keep up – Walker was suffering from psychosis due to a childhood trauma. Whilst he is in custody, he confesses to witnessing the murder on EarthCam.

Simmons, who has grown closer friendship wise to Walker was devastated at his arrest and still wracked with guilt. She has also become suspicious of Grey and decides to research stuff on him. She tracks down Agnes Grey who confesses to Shania that O'Neill was Ben's father. Simmons still can't prove beyond doubt it was Grey but decides she cannot see Walker go down. She will confess and hand in the Dictaphone and mini camera. So, then she is arrested and becomes the prime suspect.

This is the final catalyst for Ben to have a breakdown. He arrives sobbing at the station confessing all. It seems like we have our man and he is put in a cell awaiting trial. Goodbye the end you say.

Well, we must admit, we thought we had our man. Walker and Simmons were released but even they were having doubts now about Grey. I must admit I wasn't. I thought it was cut and ride and the trial were just procedure. Grey had said he was guilty after all.

But O'Rourke had his doubts and I must commend him. He felt something was missing and due to a very well-played game of chess, worked out we hadn't nailed our queen. He went over to Mr Hobbes' house to comfort him and was surprised to hear that Mr Hobbes had booked a flight to Lisbon. Something about this felt odd to O'Rourke. He remembered Mrs O'Neill banging on about Portugal. He asked if he could take another look around Mrs Hobbes' room and lo and behold – found her diary. Detailing about the false autopsy.

Alarm bells were now ringing. O'Rourke had a contact at the hospital through some charity work he had completed there. He called in a favour and the original autopsy was retrieved, showing the true cause of death – strangulation and a photo of a bruise and an imprint of a ring of a Celtic design on O'Neill's neck. The exact shape of wedding ring on Mr Hobbes' finger.

Next, O'Rourke posed as a prospective student and tracked down the teacher at the language school where Mrs O'Neill had been attending learning Portuguese. She was an extremely almost too enthusiastic student.

Next, with the help of Walker, O 'Rourke was able to retrieve a historic record of EarthCam and what do you know? Keep the camera rolling and what do you see: Hobbes coming out from the alley and finishing O'Neill off.

We looked into his phone records. He had clearly used a burner phone sometimes but there were messages to Mrs O'Neill on his phone. On the surface they seemed business like but they were coded. They used code names for all the people they were talking about: Walker was Mr Runner, Mr Grey was Mr White, Miss Simmons was Miss Twain. No points for originality on their part.

Anyway, we found out they were both on this British Airways flight heading to Lisbon. O'Rourke, being the popular devil he is, had spent the summer in Portugal om a GAP Year and had made some connections again. His friends helped translate some important documents to get the help of you lot here to the airport right now!'

Marsh took a deep breath.

'Wow that is some story.' Inspector Martinez said impressed.'

'I hope you both get er...what you call it in England... a pay rise, yes?' laughed Inspector Jimenez.

'Well, I think we couldn't have done it without each other.' O'Rourke smiled at Marsh.

'Indeed. A bit of compassion. A bit of logic. The Sarge was bloody right, damn him,' said Marsh.

Well said O'Rourke. 'I shouldn't say this but I'm Irish, I like a drink and officially we won't be on duty until the plane touches down in 1 hour...I say we get a round in.'

To his surprise everyone roared in approval.

The waiter brought over a tray of beers.

'It has been a twisted case.' Said Marsh.

'Full of twists and turns and lies.' Said O'Rourke.'

'Still' said Marsh. 'It's all about technology...and it's all about the chessboard. Such is life. The pawns. The knights. The Kings. And the Queens. And it's our job to work out who we all are.'

They all roared their approval.

'Well, only one word left to say.' Grinned 'O'Rourke.

They all clinked their bottles together.

Alegria a beer'

CHEERS!!!!

THE END

****

Acknowledgements

The idea for 'Earthcam' came to me about 02:30 in the morning after being told our flights were cancelled for our dream trip to New York. Depressed and disappointed, I thought to myself 'I wonder what 'Times Square' is up to right now. Upon searching Google, it came up with a live camera feed where I could see New York in live time. It looked like a ghost town, with just a couple of people crossing the road. This is when I thought to myself: Imagine witnessing a murder live online and feeling completely helpless of what to do yet unable to even look away to get help. I ended up setting the novel in Portsmouth rather than NY as I wanted it to feel claustrophobic for the reader.

A special Thank you to my sister Anna-Marie and my editor Siobhan for all your support, guidance and honest approach.

A thank you also to my best friend Claire who sat through the different plots, the tears and tantrums and everything in between.

Lightning Source UK Ltd.
Milton Keynes UK
UKHW022003290622
405159UK00008B/75